# THE GENERAL'S DESIRE

**San Diego Soci**

Tess !

Seasons ...

Published: 2017

Published by Seasons Press LLC

ISBN: 978-0-9994319-1-7

Copyright © 2017, Tess Summers

Edited by Amy Briggs

Cover by OliviaProDesigns

This book is available in print at most online retailers.

This is a work of fiction. The characters, incidents and dialogues in this book are of the author's imagination and are not to be construed as real. Any resemblance to actual events or persons, living or dead, is completely coincidental.

This book is for mature readers. It contains sexually explicit scenes and graphic language that may be considered offensive by some.

All sexually active characters in this work are eighteen years of age or older.

# The General's Desire

*Falling in lust is easy but falling in love is more than they ever imagined.*

Brenna Roberts hasn't had the best luck with men—from her deceased philandering husband to most recently being stood up for a date and having it announced in the gossip section of the newspaper. She's beginning to doubt that good guys still exist. Then she meets decorated Marine General Ron Thompson. Stoic, handsome, and all alpha... he's literally her hero when he saves her from a bad situation.

Decorated Marine General Ron Thompson isn't looking for love. Lust maybe, but not love. As a military star on the rise, he'd rather keep his head down and his focus on the prize—promotion. But when the widow of professional baseball player Danny Roberts sits down at his table at the Sterling wedding reception, everything changes. Lucky for him, he's always been the type to go big or go home, and he's going big when it comes to her.

But she's not sure she's cut out to be with a military man for anything more than just a fling. The sex may be amazing, but the long periods apart and his inability to discuss his work might be too much for her to handle. Except he keeps saving the day, making it impossible for her to stay away.

*The General's Desire* is a feel-good romance featuring main characters in their forties with open-door scenes and romantic touches that will melt your Kindle and your heart.

This is Book 2 in the San Diego Social Scene series. Each book is a stand-alone with an HEA and no cheating.

# Free Book!

## Do you like free books? Get your BONUS Tess Summers book!

BookHip.com/SNGBXD Sign up here to receive my newsletter, and get San Diego PD SWAT Captain Craig Baxter's love story, exclusively for newsletter subscribers. You'll receive regular updates and be the first to know about my works-in-progress.

# Table of Contents

# The General's Desire

## Prologue

*Brenna*

"No, he did not! You're kidding! Brenna, please tell me you are kidding," Cassie Sullivan yelled through the patio door before flopping on a blue, outdoor lounger at her older sister's San Diego beach house. The weather was unseasonably warm for the fifteenth of December.

Brenna Roberts walked onto her patio carrying two glasses of white wine and handed one to her younger sister.

"Nope. I'm not kidding. Stood the fuck up. No call, no text, no email, no nothing. I sat there like a fool for over an hour."

"Oh God, how embarrassing! I'm so sorry." Cassie took a sip before setting the glass down on a side table. "Do you think the restaurant staff knew you were stood up?"

Grimacing but still managing to chuckle, Brenna replied, "They wouldn't seat me *until all parties had arrived*. When no one else arrived, they kind of had an idea."

"Ouch." Cassie wrinkled her pug nose and hugged an orange throw pillow. "And you still haven't heard from him?"

Brenna shook her head and sat down in an oversized chair that was the same cornflower blue as the lounger. "Not a peep. He didn't return my call or my text."

"Maybe he forgot? Or switched up the location?"

Brenna scoffed. "Then why hasn't he responded to me?"

Her sister sighed. "Well, did you at least tell him off?"

"What would be the point? Standing someone up says a lot. I think it's a pretty big *fuck you*. I'd just be wasting my breath. Me telling him off would probably only help him justify what he did."

Cassie took another drink of wine, seeming to be lost in thought as she absorbed what her older sister said.

"Screw being the better person. I'd drop a carton of eggs on that asshole's fancy sports car, and maybe slash a tire or two. Don't you think you deserve better than being stood up, without even an apology or explanation?"

"Oh sister, I *know* I deserve better than that. I just wish he would have done it on the first date, instead of the fifth."

As if still not wanting to accept someone had stood her big sister up, Cassie suggested, "What if he's been kidnapped?"

Brenna narrowed her eyes at Cassie. "Really? Come on. Pretty sure *kidnapped rich bond trader* would at least make the local news. We would have heard about it by now. You think the media wouldn't be all over Ray-*mond* Reitmeier's abduction story? He's a pretty big deal, just ask him." She overemphasized the second syllable in Ray's name to mock his pretention.

Cassie gave an obligatory giggle at her sister's attempt at a joke while she sat with her nose in her phone, then made a face. "Uh, you said people at the restaurant knew you were stood up?"

Brenna dragged out her next words with a raised eyebrow. "Yeeeaah. Why?"

Cassie flashed the phone screen at Brenna. In the *Out and About* section of the local paper was a picture of Brenna from about a year ago with the headline *Would You Stand Her Up?*

"Apparently their sources say you were pretty distraught at being stood up."

"I even gave the bartender an amazing tip," Brenna said in mock indignation. Being in the *Out and About* section wasn't new to her, so she wasn't that upset.

Cassie started to read the photo caption aloud. *"Brenna Roberts, the stunning widow of Padres second baseman, Danny Roberts—"*

Brenna interrupted her. "Do you mind? I lived through it; I don't need to hear about it, too."

Cassie kept reading, only silently.

"God those people are like vultures," she said, throwing her phone onto the matching lounger next to her.

She sprang to her feet and paced back and forth on the patio, then stopped and glared at Brenna, who hadn't moved from her spot on the oversized chair. "Why are you so calm about all this?"

"Sweetie, how many times were Danny and I in that rag? There's no point getting upset about anything in there. You're just wasting your energy."

"Oh, I know. Nobody believes anything they print anyway. I'm talking about the dickhead who stood you up. I mean, who does that? How fucking hard is it to text a simple, 'hey can't make it,' instead of just leaving you hanging for the bottom-dwellers to feed on. God I wish you were still writing. I'd love to see you kill that dick off in your next screenplay." Cassie narrowed her eyes and pointed a finger at her sister. "You'd still be able to do that, right? You haven't gone soft, have you?"

Brenna gave a sly smile and curled her legs under her before taking a drink. Holding the wine glass with both hands, she left it at her lips and murmured, "Let's just say I can picture a good-looking bond trader meeting an untimely—and painful—demise."

Cassie always said her big sister was passive-aggressive when it came to her writing, especially when some of her characters ended up dying on the big screen. Brenna preferred to think of it as cathartic. If people thought they recognized themselves or others in her characters, well, she couldn't help that. After all, her characters were fictional, and like the copyright in all her books said: any resemblance to persons, living or dead, was purely coincidental.

"Bren, when the fuck are you going to start writing again?"

# Chapter One

*Brenna*

Unable to sleep, she lay in bed looking at the black, scoop-neck cocktail dress hanging on her closet door. She was attending her first social function as a single woman since her husband, Danny, died almost three years ago, and she was nervous. She wasn't sure how she'd be received tomorrow night, but hoped it wasn't sympathetically. She hated that look she got from people once they found out she was a widow—the sad head tilt with the downturned mouth, usually as they reached out to touch her somehow.

Her real estate agent, Ava Ericson, was co-hosting a black and white New Year's Eve ball with Travis Sterling, one of the city's most eligible bachelors, although since he was co-hosting the party with a pregnant Ava, Brenna doubted he was very eligible anymore. She liked Ava and had planned on asking Ray to be her date when she RSVP'd for two. After he stood her up, Brenna phoned to let Ava know she wasn't able to make it after all, but somehow ended up agreeing to attend by herself before she hung up.

Brenna hadn't been entirely honest with her sister a few weeks ago when they sat on her patio, and she told her about Ray. Truth was, her feelings were a lot more hurt than she'd let on that he had stood her up without so much as a text or call. He had been really determined in the beginning to get her to go out with him, and she'd found him handsome and charming. She quickly realized he was more into the chase than anything. Brenna knew once they slept together, the hunt would be over and he'd move on, so she never let it get that far. Even though she knew he was not long-term material, there was a little bit of ego that made her believe once he'd gotten to know her better, he'd be interested in more than just sleeping with her. The way he had dismissed her without a second thought bruised her pride. Her ego might have been hoping he'd call and apologize, maybe grovel a little, but it didn't happen.

She looked at the floor-length dress and smiled. After finally gaining back most of the weight she had lost after Danny's accident, Brenna had enjoyed dress and shoe shopping, and for the first time in a long time, looked forward to going out.

\*\*\*\*

The doorbell rang at Brenna's house at ten-thirty in the morning on New Year's Eve. Her Labrador mix, Zona, bound to the door, barking to alert her in case she had missed the bell.

Brenna heard Cassie call out, "Hey bitch!" and then the door close. Her sister was kneeling down and roughly rubbing Zona behind her black ears when Brenna appeared in the doorway of the kitchen, wiping her hands on a dish towel.

"You're early. You're never early. What's up with that?"

"I don't have any food at my place." Cassie grinned as she stood and walked past Brenna toward the fridge.

"Gee, help yourself," Brenna muttered and followed her sister into the bright, modern kitchen overlooking the ocean.

With a bowl of cereal, Cassie sat down at the kitchen island and watched Brenna cut sugar cookie dough into football shapes on the grey, granite countertop.

"What's with the cookies?"

"I'm taking them to Tucson with me tomorrow. Danielle and I are going to a party to watch football. I figured I'd try to get in touch with my domestic side and bring something that isn't store-bought."

"Is anyone yummy you know playing tomorrow?"

Brenna laughed. "No, it's college games on New Year's Day. Besides, I only know baseball players, not football players."

"Still haven't heard from assface?"

"No, and honestly, I don't expect to. At this point, what could he possibly say? He's way too proud to admit he did anything wrong. Even if he did, it would be half-assed in a take-it-or-leave-it kind of way." Brenna sat quietly for a minute then shrugged. "He can fuck off. I swore after Danny I would never let a man treat me poorly again. The only reason I put up with it from Danny for so long was because he was such a great dad."

"Hey, about my beautiful niece. Why did Danielle only stay a week for the holidays? Is she mad at you, or is she dating someone?"

Brenna frowned. "She said she had to work. I don't think she's mad at me. She asked me to come visit her. She hasn't said anything about dating anyone. I guess I'll find out tomorrow."

In between bites of cereal, Cassie asked, "So, are you coming home tonight, or do I get to sleep in your comfy guest bed?"

"No, I'm staying at the hotel tonight and going straight to the airport from there at noon."

"You're lucky I'm a loser, and the best New Year's Eve plans I had were no comparison to being here on the beach with Zona and the fireworks." Cassie smirked.

"I really appreciate you doing this for me last minute. Zona is such a baby when it comes to fireworks. Luke was going to stay, but then his department decided everyone needed to be on call tonight. I'm only gone for a few days. You don't have to stay past tonight. I think he is still planning on covering the other nights. We'll ask him when he gets here."

Cassie pointed her spoon at Brenna and waved it in circles at her. "Yeah, I need to know a little bit more about this Luke guy before I run the risk of bumping into him alone."

Brenna snorted. "Sweetie, once you meet him, you're going to look for ways to run into him alone. He's delicious."

Her little sister pursed her lips, unconvinced. "Well, if he's so *delicious*," she made air quotes as she said the word delicious, "why haven't *you* jumped him? I mean, he's Mr. Altruistic and everything. He's right up your alley."

"Um, because he's way too young for me. If I were even ten years younger, maybe. But since I'm not even close to thirty-four anymore, ain't happenin'. *You*, on the other hand, are thirty—"

Cassie interrupted. "You look like you're in your thirties; does that count?"

Brenna gave a fake smile. "Aw, aren't you sweet." Then dropped the smile. "I'm still not paying you."

"God you're such a cheap ass," Cassie said, sliding off her barstool to pour more cereal and spilling a little on purpose for Zona, who had been patiently waiting for her to drop something. "I don't know why I even agreed to help you out!"

Brenna smirked. "Because you love me, and because I live on the beach."

Cassie poured more milk into her bowl while pretending to consider what her sister just said. "Oh yeah. Not to mention your hot tub and stocked fridge."

"Ya know, I have a hard time believing the pharmaceutical business is doing so badly that you can't afford food."

"Oh, business is booming! I just got a bonus big enough to pay my car off." Cassie grinned as she hopped back on her seat and shoved another spoonful in her mouth.

"So why don't you have any food at your place?"

Cassie jerked her head back like the answer was obvious. "I'm too lazy to go to the grocery store. Besides, I like mooching off my sister, the rich widow."

Brenna put a pan of cookies in the oven. "For the record," she said as she closed the oven door, "I'm not rich because I'm Danny's widow. His money is in a trust for our daughter. I'm rich because I've written a damn fine screenplay or two in my day, thank you very much."

Cassie rolled her eyes. "Yeah, yeah. I always forget about what a bigshot you are until I see one of your movies pop up on TV and think, 'Hey! That came from my sister's imagination!'" In a gentler voice, she asked, "When am I going to see something new from you?"

Brenna glanced away. "I don't know, Cass. It's...complicated."

"Well, hurry up, would ya? I want to see assface get schmucked!" Cassie grinned and drank her milk from the bowl before continuing. "Oh, and I want to go with you to the premiere. When you and Danny's picture would show up in magazines, I'd tell people, 'that's my sister!' For some reason nobody ever believed me, even though I look just like you, only with darker hair. If I were your date on the red carpet it would give me some serious street cred."

"Street cred for what exactly?"

"I don't know, just because!" Cassie laughed. "One can never have too much street cred."

"Sorry to be the bearer of bad news, but I don't think I'm going to be helping your *street cred* any time soon."

Cassie started to protest as she slid off the stool, but then seemed to elect against it.

"Did you decide on a dress for tonight?" The younger girl changed the subject while rinsing her dishes in the sink.

"I did. I couldn't figure out which shoes I like better though, so I bought them both to have more time to decide."

"Well it is your lucky day because I am an aficionada of footwear. Let's see whatcha got."

Upstairs in Brenna's room, Cassie went through Brenna's huge closet. Taking garments with their hangers, and holding them up to her body in the mirror, she came upon her sister's wedding dress.

Tracing over the satin fabric, Cassie sighed. "Do you miss him?"

Brenna was tugging the black dress down from her hips when she stepped out from the dressing area of the closet and noticed Cassie touching her wedding dress.

"Every day."

Cassie cocked her head. "Even after everything he did?"

"Even after. Just because I didn't want to be married to him anymore didn't mean I stopped loving him. We were madly in love once, and we have a great kid. I wouldn't trade that for anything."

"Am I going to go to hell for being glad he died before your divorce was final?"

Brenna pulled her hair up off her neck and turned around for Cassie to zip her dress. "Probably," she said over her shoulder with a smirk. "But everything of his is going to Danielle anyway, and that's where he would have wanted it."

She turned back around, and Cassie let out a whistle. "Wow! You look freakin' hot!"

They came out of the dressing area so Brenna could do a runway walk in two different pairs of shoes. As Brenna paraded up and down her bedroom in mismatched heel heights, Cassie glanced out the window where something had caught her attention. Brenna stood on her tiptoes to see what her sister was gawking at but couldn't get a good look.

"*Who* the hell is that?"

Brenna limped over and slid the curtain back to see Luke Rivas had pulled into her driveway in his black topless Jeep with no doors. He was in a well-worn pair of Levis, a tight gray t-shirt that clung delectably to his muscular chest and arms, and aviator sunglasses on his tanned face. His short black hair only slightly messy from the wind blowing on the ride over. In the passenger seat was his Golden Retriever, Rex.

"That's Luke and Rex."

"*That's* Luke?! Good Lord, he looks like sex on a stick! Shit, here I am in my freaking yoga pants and messy hair bun. Thanks a lot for the heads up."

Brenna grinned and smacked her sister's butt. "Told ya. Your yoga pants make your ass look great, and you're freaking adorable in your messy bun, so go be your charming self and answer the door. Watch out for Zona though. If she knows Rex is here, she will beat you to the door, even if it means knocking you over. She loves seeing her boyfriend."

Zona had been one of Luke's foster dogs before Brenna adopted her and had grown attached to Luke's furry boy while living with him.

Cassie walked toward the bedroom door, shaking her head. "Aw, Zona, too? Doesn't anybody play hard to get anymore?"

Brenna laughed then called out just as her sister reached the doorway. "Wait, which shoe?"

Turning to look for less than two seconds, Cassie replied, "Open-toed, definitely." She was out the door and bounding down the stairs when the doorbell rang.

After Danny died, Brenna had more money than she could spend, and did a lot of pruning in her life. She got rid of the monstrosity of a house in Rancho Santa Fe her husband had insisted on, along with all the expensive cars and furnishings that went with it. She also sold the condo and cars in Phoenix they had for when he was at spring training, along with the place in Miami Brenna hadn't even known about—his love nest she assumed. She set aside Danny's portion of the proceeds in trust for Danielle, gave some of it away to causes she supported, and was still left with more money than she would need in four lifetimes.

She also cut out fake friends and people only interested in being associated with her so they could drop her name. She didn't have the energy for it anymore. That left her with a small, select group of people she now socialized with because she wanted to, not because she had to. Her little sister was one of those people—blunt, honest, and with the biggest heart of anyone Brenna knew. She loved hanging out with her.

Her daughter, Danielle, was also someone she devoted her time to. Danielle was a freshman at the University of Arizona, her dad's alma mater. Danny had been a stand-out second baseman for the Bat Cats and was drafted in the second round his junior year. Unlike many of his peers, he quickly rose up from playing AAA baseball and made it to the big leagues. He was a rookie playing for the Padres when Brenna met him almost twenty years ago.

Brenna decided to buy a place in Tucson so she would have somewhere to stay when she visited Danielle. Cassie and Luke were splitting dog-watching duties while she went house hunting at the end of January, which was why Brenna had invited them both over that day. She thought it would be easier to have the two of them in front of her with a calendar as they divvied up the days. Not to mention she had wanted to introduce them to each other in a not-so-obvious way. Judging by the way the two kept shyly smiling at each other, her instincts had been right about the two.

So much for her sister playing hard to get.

At least Brenna's instincts still worked when it came to other people. She was, however, not so confident in her abilities when it came to her own love life.

# Chapter Two

*Brenna*

She had finally gotten used to being on her own, but still couldn't help feeling sad thinking about the previous New Year's Eve parties with Danny as she got ready for the ball. They really had made the perfect pair, at least to anyone on the outside looking in. *Ken and Barbie Baseball* was what the *Out and About* section called them whenever they were photographed together in public. He'd had dark brown hair, green eyes, and was athletic, handsome, and cocky. She was blonde and always immaculately coiffed. She looked damn good, thanks to a personal trainer who kicked her ass almost daily, and a plastic surgeon who lifted her boobs, hid her Caesarean scar, and injected her with Botox on a regular basis. Being married to a professional baseball player for all those years, she had to look the part of a player's wife and compete with the diamond dolls—a fancy way of saying groupie sluts.

Sadly, she hadn't competed successfully. His last mistress had made sure Brenna knew about her; which backfired, since Danny dumped the girl because of it. The prospect of him losing half of everything in a divorce trumped whatever the other woman had been doing for him in the sack. Unfortunately for him, Brenna had had enough of looking the other way when it came to her husband's transgressions and filed for divorce. She'd almost relented when Danny laid on the charm; he had always been so good at that. But she had allowed herself to see a life without wondering and worrying about what her husband was up to, or who he was with, and she'd liked it. Still not enough to start writing again, but at least the possibility felt like it was there. It was a start.

Brenna put her earrings in and smoothed her dress as she checked out her reflection in the mirror. Turning to check her backside, she took a deep breath. *Here goes nothing.*

\*\*\*\*

*Ron*

As he drove to The Plaza, Major General Ron Thompson wondered what the hell he was doing going to this party tonight. Ava had invited him, so he felt obligated to go. He had been the first person she told about her pregnancy, because they'd talked about dating before she found out. He had a sneaking suspicion she and her baby's father, Travis Sterling, were going to announce their engagement tonight. He was happy for her; she was a charming and beautiful young woman who deserved someone she could settle down and have a family with. Ron quickly realized after learning about her pregnancy he would have been all wrong for her in the long run.

He had to admit though, he was horny as hell. He'd just gotten back from two months in the Middle East, but it'd been almost a year since he'd been with a woman. His job, and frankly, his standards kept him from dating much. He'd love a beautiful lady he could have an intelligent conversation with at dinner, then take home and fuck senseless, but they seemed to be in short supply these days. Or maybe he was just too picky.

But having high expectations was his nature. It had served him well with the Marine Corps and wasn't something he could just turn on and off. Which was probably a good thing since he was responsible for a lot of Marines' lives.

God, he hoped there was decent alcohol at the open bar tonight. Knowing Sterling, it would all be top shelf. There'd be no complaints from him about that, but he probably wasn't going to be staying long anyway.

As soon as he walked through the doors, Ava, in her pink Cinderella gown with her adorable pregnant belly, grabbed his hand and pulled him over to meet her friend Tracey. He knew Ava was trying to offer him a consolation prize since she didn't go out with him. Her friend was cute, but a little young, and not really his type. He could tell he wasn't her type either, and they each went to their respective tables after only a few minutes of chitchat. Travis and Ava made the announcement the party was their wedding reception; they'd gotten married earlier that day. Ron watched the two of them together, obviously happy and in love, and he felt something he couldn't quite name.

*Regret? Jealousy?*

He'd been married to his career so long, he wondered if finding Mrs. Right just wasn't in the cards for him. Maybe he fucked up and missed his chance when he was with Sarah. Maybe he should have gone after her when she'd left. He thought he was doing what was best for her. He couldn't give her what she was looking for, so he let her go. But if he were honest with himself, he did miss her. He hadn't found anyone else who even sparked his interest.

Ron looked around his table at everyone dressed in black or white, not a splash of color to be seen. At least people followed directions—it was a Black and White Ball, after all. His own white tuxedo jacket offset his black bow tie and pants. The girl who sold it to him said he looked like Humphrey Bogart in *Casablanca*.

He wasn't so sure that was a compliment.

Now if only he could find his Lauren Bacall.

People were offering the usual polite hellos and brief introductions around the table, when the most beautiful woman he had ever laid eyes on looked at the names on the place cards, then smiled as she took her seat. She introduced herself as Brenna Roberts. He felt his breath catch in his chest when she charmingly glanced down after he caught her eye, her long blonde hair fell forward around her face.

Mrs. Sewell, the older woman sitting next to her, put her hand sympathetically over Brenna's and said, "I'm so sorry about Danny." The gorgeous woman tucked her hair behind her ear with a meager smile and replied she was doing all right.

*Danny Roberts? As in,* the *Danny Roberts, second baseman for the San Diego Padres?*

Ron knew Danny had been killed in a car crash a few years ago; it was all the news talked about for a week. Sizing his widow up, he had no trouble believing she had been a professional ball player's wife. She was damn-near flawless, even if some of her parts were probably not authentic. No woman her age had real boobs that perky, but he was perfectly fine with how high hers sat.

Genuine was overrated.

Her skin was like porcelain, and her lips... man, her lips. An image of them wrapped around his dick flashed in his head, and he suddenly applauded his decision to attend Ava and Travis's party after all.

*Thank you, whoever made the seating chart, for putting her at my table.*

He asked everyone at the table if he could get them anything from the bar, and when Mrs. Sewell looked like she was going to offer yet more sympathy to Brenna, the beautiful woman jumped up and said she'd go with him. Ron admired the view as she walked in front of him in a long black gown that hugged her curves perfectly while showing off her shoulders. He wasn't the only one who noticed her.

They'd just gotten their drinks when she gave him a flirtatious smile. "So, is there a Mrs. Thompson?"

He grinned back. "Why? Who wants to know?"

He got distracted momentarily when she sucked her drink through a straw, but managed to catch her teasing reply. "At least every woman at our table. I'm sure they all have a sister, daughter, or granddaughter they're dying to fix you up with."

He raised an eyebrow. "*Every* woman at our table?"

She blushed as she smiled at him but didn't look away.

He didn't take his eyes away from hers when he lowered his voice and said, "There's no Mrs. Thompson—present or past. And there's only one woman I'm interested in being fixed up with."

She did look down this time but kept smiling. "Oh? Anyone I know?"

He was about to respond when he saw her eyes narrow and a scowl form on her lips. Ron glanced over to where she was looking and noticed a dark-haired man with a salt-and-pepper beard and wire-rimmed glasses in a black tailored suit accompanied by a chubby, yet attractive, woman in a white gown that was probably a size too small. Her chunky white jewelry matched her dress perfectly, and her brunette hair with blonde highlights was in a styled updo. She lightly held onto the arm the man offered and could have blinded someone with the huge diamond on her left ring finger. The pair looked like they were comfortably bored with each other's company.

"That son-of-a-bitch," he heard Brenna mutter as she shook her head.

*Goddammit.*

He'd hoped since she was here alone, she was available. It appeared that might not be the case.

*Don't jump to any conclusions. Let this one play out.*

Leaning against the bar, he asked, "Friends of yours?" as he gestured to the couple with his glass before taking a sip.

She stood there looking at the bearded man, almost dumbfounded, and didn't seem to register Ron was speaking to her, and instead appeared to be contemplating her next move. Finally, she looked at him and offered a forced smile. "If you'll excuse me, I see someone I need to say hello to."

He watched her make her way to the couple. She definitely had a nice ass.

*Fuck, I hope she's not the crazy kind.*

Wait, maybe he did. That might be fun to watch, too.

Turned out, the look of panic on the man's face as he saw Brenna approach was entertainment enough. She stood talking to the couple, reaching over to stroke the man's arm on occasion, and Ron watched him jump and wince as if in actual pain when she did. Meanwhile the woman who Ron assumed was the bearded man's wife, shot her husband the dirtiest of looks as Brenna spoke. Finally, Brenna offered the lady her hand to shake, then patted the man on the cheek. She turned around with a satisfied, smug expression on her face and headed back to where Ron was standing.

Grinning, he was not prepared for what she said next.

"Ron, it was lovely meeting you. I'm afraid I have to be going," she declared as she set her drink on the bar.

He caught her wrist with his free hand when she turned to leave. With her head cocked, she looked up at him, then down at her wrist in his grip, then back at his face.

Ron took his time letting go of her, before he picked up her drink and tried to hand it back to her.

"I'm not sure what that was all about, but I was looking forward to dancing with you tonight, so I'm afraid I'm going to have to insist you stay."

He didn't take his eyes off hers.

Fuck, she was gorgeous. He hoped she didn't leave because he didn't want to make an ass of himself when he followed her out the door like a puppy dog.

But he would.

She stared at him, sizing him up. He could almost see the wheels turning in her head, wondering who the hell he thought he was.

*General Ron Thompson, at your service, darlin'... Your full service.*

"Well, *that*," she gestured to where she'd just been talking to the couple, "was discovering the guy who I'd been dating for the last month is actually married, and has been for twenty-two years."

"Oh, man." He looked over at the pair who were trying to have a discreet argument. At least they didn't seem bored with each other anymore.

"Yeah, so I really don't think I'd be very good company tonight," she stated like her mind was already made up to leave. She was obviously unimpressed with him.

Ron stood up taller.

"Why don't you let me be the judge of that? Tell you what—stay until after dinner, dance a little. See if your mood changes. What's the harm in that? Besides, it will hurt Travis and Ava's feelings if you leave before then." He nudged the drink he was still holding at her.

She frowned, but reluctantly accepted it. "What if I'm still not having a good time?"

He winked and touched his glass against hers. "You will be."

# Chapter Three

*Brenna*

She studied him carefully through narrowed eyes.

*Okay, Ron, I'll give you that you are good looking with the best damn smile I have ever seen, even if your nose is a little crooked. And your southern drawl is sexy as fuck. Not to mention you look pretty freakin' hot in your tux. But still! Not tonight—can you not understand I'm not in the mood?*

She'd just found out a guy she'd dated, albeit briefly, was here with *his wife,* and Brenna had been nothing more than a potential piece of ass to him. She wasn't exactly in a flirtatious frame of mind anymore.

Ron seemed cocky enough to believe he could win her over. She chuckled at the thought. He had no idea who he was dealing with. Neither he, nor anyone else for that matter, was going to put her in a better mood.

Unless his name was Jack. As in Daniels.

In fact, Ron's self-assured attitude made her want to be flippant and sarcastic and knock him down a peg or two. Did he really imagine he even had a shot with her *tonight?*

Yet he did have a point. It would be bad form to leave before dinner was even served. Plus, she didn't want Ray to think he had chased her off. That would just make it look like he had hurt her. Her pride wasn't about to let that happen.

Since Ron's ego seemed to think she would be easy to win over, she wasn't going to worry about being polite. Or charming for that matter. And she sure as hell wasn't going to flirt with him, regardless of how attractive she found him.

Brenna drained her drink and gestured to the bartender for another before turning her attention back to Ron.

"Forty-four, female, San Diego."

"What?" Ron asked. He seemed confused.

"Oh, I just figured those were going to be your next questions. You know, *Age, Sex, Location*?" She'd visited enough chatrooms to know the drill. He, however, obviously had not because the joke was lost on him, and he looked at her like maybe she was crazy.

"Never mind," she said as she rolled her eyes.

The expression on his face suggested he might have changed his mind about wanting to get to know her after all. Which wasn't necessarily what she wanted, but she still wasn't ready to play nice. However, she did lighten up, at least a little.

"So, Ron Thompson, what do you do for a living?" Brenna asked as she took her drink from the bartender.

"I'm in the Marine Corps."

Yeah, she could believe it. He definitely had an air about him that said he was in charge and in control. Probably was one of those drill sergeant types she'd seen in the movies.

"How long have you been in?"

"Twenty-four years."

She nodded, acknowledging that was a long time, and begrudgingly said, "Well, thank you for your service."

"My pleasure." He smiled and cocked his head. "What about you, Brenna Roberts? What do you do?"

Fuck she hated that question. She was never sure how to answer it. Once she'd stopped writing, her whole identity became being Mrs. Danny Roberts and Danielle's mom. Even though she made more money from her movie residuals than Danny did, she'd reply she was a wife and mother. But being a wealthy stay-at-home mom and wife had nothing to do with running the household; they'd had hired help for that.

And now... well now, when she was asked the question, she still didn't know what to say. She could no longer say wife or stay-at-home mom, considering her kid was a state away at school, and her almost ex-husband was dead.

She still created storylines in her head sometimes, just never full stories, and she never actually wrote them down. Lately, she'd been figuring out ways a bond trader could meet his death. Looking at the bastard with his wife, maybe making him penniless and impotent might be better than killing him off.

She decided writing stories in her head counted, and since she still got residual checks from movies she'd written...

"I'm a screenwriter."

Ron surprised her by not asking the usual next question, *any movies I'd know?* and instead, asked her if she enjoyed what she did. He seemed genuinely interested if she liked being a screenwriter.

"I loved it." She hoped he didn't catch her slip using the past tense.

His interest softened her, and she asked, "What about you? Do you like being a Marine?"

His demeanor told her the answer before his words did. "It's what I was born to do."

"I think there's probably quite a few things you were born to do," was out of her mouth with a playful grin before she had time to think about what she was saying.

*Goddammit, no flirting, remember?*

Her comment seemed to surprise him, but he didn't miss a beat when he looked her up and down and replied, "You have no idea how many of them I can do quite well."

*Oh snap!* Her belly did a little flip.

Was she holding her breath?

He grinned at her. "Dancing happens to be one." He gestured to where other couples were dancing during cocktail hour.

She caught sight of Ray and his wife still at the bar as Ron led her to the dance floor, and she remembered that men were not her favorite group of people right now. As determined as the Marine seemed to charm her, she was equally determined not to be swayed, but those two whiskeys she'd had were not helping her resolve. Neither were Ron's amazing shoulders or the strong hand she was holding while he moved her around the floor.

As he held her at the waist, he pulled her closer to whisper in her ear, "You are breathtaking."

She pulled back to look at his face and smirked. She wasn't falling for another guy's line of bullshit.

"I'll bet you say that to all the girls."

He stopped dancing right in the middle of the floor and lifted her chin so she had no choice but to look at him.

"Brenna, you need to understand something about me. I don't play games, and I mean everything I say."

His serious expression, and the fact that his eyes never left hers, let her know he was telling the truth. She was suddenly intimidated by him and felt very small next to his large, muscular frame.

In a strangely good way.

Her smirk must have changed to a look of surprise because he chuckled when he pulled her back in tight against him and resumed dancing.

"So let's try this again," he said in her ear. "You are breathtaking."

She lay her head against his shoulder and whispered, "Thank you."

He stroked her back and she felt a smile on his lips as he murmured against her hair, "Good girl. That's better."

She should be offended as fuck for being told she was a "good girl," so why the hell was she so turned on?

# Chapter Four

*Ron*

He liked the way Brenna felt in his arms. So much so that when she leaned her head against his shoulder, he felt things jump below his belt. This woman brought out something primal in him. He enjoyed talking and laughing with her, but he also kinda wanted to drag her to a hotel room by her hair and fuck her until the sun came up.

He should probably stick with the former, for now.

The song ended and they made their way back to the bar to refresh their drinks before dinner. The married man glared at them from his spot at the end of the bar.

"So what's his story?" Ron gestured toward him while they waited for their cocktails.

Although he guessed she knew who he was referring to, Brenna turned and looked, and was met with a death glare from the man.

She looked back at Ron. "Well, we went out on a few dates until he stood me up a few weeks ago, and I hadn't heard from him since, until tonight. At this point, I'm not really sure if anything he told me is true but he said his name is Ray-*mond* Reitmeier," she emphasized the second syllable in Raymond. "Apparently he's a bond trader by day, and a whoring husband by night."

"Where'd you meet him?"

Brenna looked a little squeamish but said with conviction, "I met him online."

Ron looked at her, trying not to convey what he was thinking, which was, *Seriously? What the fuck is wrong with you?*

Brenna must have read his mind because she defended herself. "It seemed like a safe way to weed people out. I even did a background check on him. There was no mention of him being married. Just a Jeanie Reitmeier who co-owns property with him, but when I asked him about her, he said she was his sister."

Ron didn't say anything, just subtly shook his head at her, and she continued. "Nope, not his sister." Glancing at the woman at the end of the bar, she groaned. "Yes, in hindsight, I'm a complete moron, but he was so charming and nice."

She put her hands at her eyebrows as though she was blocking out the light, then starting laughing and peeked up at Ron. "I almost want to go back over and tell him, well played, because I honestly did not see that one coming."

At least she had a sense of humor about it.

Still, Ron didn't like the way the guy was staring at them and moved his body between Brenna and the man.

With the corners of his mouth turned up, he said, "Maybe you should just stick to meeting men the old-fashioned way. Like at weddings."

"Why do I get the feeling that could lead to my broken heart?"

He drawled, "Oh no, darlin'. I'm going to do a lot of things to you, but break your heart is not one of them."

****

*Brenna*

*Fuck.* Maybe she should just hand him her panties and room key now. She seriously could not remember the last time she was so attracted to a man. It was as though he oozed masculinity. He was definitely a man's man. She didn't think they made those anymore. Apparently they did, and one was standing right in front of her looking amazing in his tuxedo and promising to do things to her.

Her toes curled.

Literally.

Curled.

*So much for not flirting.*

Brenna tilted her head and gave a slight smile. "I can't decide if that sounds delightful or ominous."

She hoped he couldn't tell how fast her heart was beating.

Ron leaned down and kissed her right below her left ear before growling in it. "It will be nothing but delightful, I promise."

She tried to disguise her gasp.

Taking her hand, he led her back to her seat, where she proceeded to glance over at him every two seconds from across the table. Each time, she found him looking back at her, even while appearing engrossed in a conversation with the lovely Davenport couple. He seemed really interested in their daughters' lacrosse accomplishments.

She, on the other hand, might have just agreed to marry Mrs. Sewell's grandson; she wasn't really sure.

The only thing Brenna was able to concentrate on was the handsome Marine's infectious smile, which he readily gave her every time she peeked over at him. She also wondered if he looked as amazing naked as she imagined he would. And what it would feel like to be thoroughly kissed by him.

*Oh my God, is dinner ever going to end?*

Fortunately, she was put out of her misery when Ava and Travis cut their wedding cake and Ron brought her a vanilla slice. Sitting in Mrs. Sewell's empty seat, he offered her a bite of his chocolate piece.

"I wasn't sure which you'd prefer, so I got one of each."

She placed her lips around the fork he offered and closed her eyes once the confection touched her tongue. She murmured "mmm" as she pulled her lips off slowly and opened her eyes.

"I think this is what heaven must taste like."

He didn't even attempt to be subtle when he looked her up and down.

"Somehow, I imagine it tastes like something else."

*Oh.*

*My.*

*God.*

Shouldn't she be offended? He was coming on too strong. *Way* too strong.

But it wasn't in a, *here's an unsolicited dick pic* kind of way. It was *I'm all-man and I'm claiming* you kind of way.

And fuck if she didn't want to be claimed by him.

Perhaps if she hadn't felt the chemistry, she would be offended. Actually, she knew damn well had any other man tried that with her, she'd tell him to go to hell and mean it. But at the moment, all she felt were her panties getting damp.

She wanted to respond with something coy and witty, but worried if she opened her mouth to speak, nothing more than strangled gibberish would come out. Instead, she just looked up through her lashes at him and noticed his eyes seemed to match his light brown hair almost perfectly—the color of coffee with a lot of cream.

Once she was semi-composed again, she asked, "Are you sure you're a Marine? Aren't you supposed to have a buzz cut or something? Isn't that a requirement?"

He smirked at her attempt to defuse the sexual innuendo. "Nope. I could wear it a whole half inch longer if I wanted," he said as he offered her another bite of cake.

She happily accepted the forkful of decadence and sighed with delight as she tasted it.

"I have to find out who made this cake and make sure I always have one in stock. You are turning me on just watching you eat it."

Ron's eyes twinkled as he offered her yet another bite.

Brenna couldn't help but laugh when she took one more mouthful then pushed the plate away and told him, "No more! I'm going to slip into a sugar coma!"

"Aw," he teased. Standing up, he offered her his hand. "Well how about another dance then?"

*Be held in those strong arms as he moves me around the dance floor? Gosh, if he insists!*

# Chapter Five

*Ron*

There were a few things he knew at the moment.

One, he wanted Brenna more than he'd ever wanted a woman.

Two, he needed to chill the fuck out. He was a goddamn two-star general in the Marine Corps for Christ's sake, and he was acting like a hormonal sixteen-year-old boy.

And three, there was no way he could play it cool with her.

They danced, talked, flirted, and laughed well into the night, and hadn't realized it was almost twelve o'clock until someone interrupted the song they were dancing to in order to make the announcement for guests to get their party hats and horns to usher in the New Year.

The countdown to midnight started, and they watched each other until confetti fell down on them while people shouted, "Happy New Year!"

He took her in his arms and said, "Happy New Year, Brenna," before leaning down to kiss her gently on the lips. He felt her sigh when he broke away.

She looked up at him, smiling wider than he'd seen her do all night.

"What?" he asked with a raised eyebrow.

She shook her head. "I was just thinking I can't remember the last time I've enjoyed myself so much. Thanks for talking me into staying. What a great way to start the New Year."

Ron smiled as he put his cheek against her temple and began to dance with her again. Holding her tightly against him, he whispered in her ear, "I'm glad you're having such a good time. Do you have any idea what effect you have on me?"

"Well, if it's the equivalent of wet panties, I'd say the feeling is mutual."

One side of his mouth lifted in a wicked grin when he drew away and looked at her in mock surprise.

"Wet panties? I've only kissed you once." Pulling her back into him, he drawled, "Damn, I'm good."

Brenna looked up at him, amused at his faux arrogance. "So you keep saying. I'm starting to wonder if you're all talk."

He twirled her off the dance floor and held her hand as he led her back to their table.

"Get your purse," he advised, standing next to her chair.

She silently obliged, and he placed his hand at the small of her back while escorting her out the ballroom doors.

# Chapter Six

*Brenna*

She was nervous as they waited for the elevator. She didn't think she'd ever been this turned on before, but it'd been a while since she'd had sex. Even longer since she'd had really good sex. What if he was disappointed with her performance? Or possibly worse, what if she was disappointed with his?

The fact she was aching to touch him and wet merely from dancing, flirting, and one innocent kiss told her that wasn't going to be the case. She couldn't wait to taste his mouth again.

The elevator doors opened, and they stepped inside the empty car. As if reading her mind, the minute the doors closed, he swept her up in his strong embrace and gently lowered his mouth on hers. Taking his time, he sucked on her lips before his tongue explored her mouth, looking for hers. Their kiss got more frenzied, their breathing heavier. She had just wrapped her arms around his neck when she heard a *ding* and they separated as the doors opened again.

He'd almost made her forget where she was, and it took her a minute to remember her room number.

"Are you sure you're staying here?" he teased as they walked down the carpeted corridor.

She went along with his kidding. "I think this is where I got ready. It looks vaguely familiar."

He took her key card and opened the door, gesturing for her to go in first. The door hadn't even latched, and he pulled her back in his arms and brushed her hair from her face as he stared into her eyes.

"My God, you are stunning," he said before capturing her lips again with his.

She let out a whimper while her arms wrapped back around his neck. His mouth was cool and tasted like peppermint, and she could smell sandalwood cologne mixed with his deodorant. Everything about him was intoxicating, and she couldn't get enough. She wanted to feel his body against hers and pressed as close to him as she could, hoping to convey just that.

He was kissing her neck and starting to unzip her dress when he suddenly stopped and pulled away from her, his face full of concern.

"Brenna, am I moving too fast?"

Her mind screamed, *what the fuck are you talking about? Why are you stopping!?* Panting and confused, she said, "I don't understand. Have you changed your mind?"

He held her by her shoulders at arm's length. "Oh, make no mistake, darlin', I want you. More than anything. But the last thing I want is you waking up tomorrow morning with regrets. I don't want to rush you. If you're not ready, I can wait. You're worth the wait."

She was frustrated at this point and frowned. "Ron, why would you think I'm not ready?"

"Because you're trembling, sugar."

She looked at her hands. So she was. She noticed her legs were a little shaky, too.

Embarrassed, she offered, "I guess I'm kind of nervous. It's been a while since I've done this."

*Actually, I just really want you!*

Ron pulled her back into his arms, and simply held her while stroking her hair. "It's been a while for me, too."

She let out a contented sigh as she enjoyed how safe and warm she felt. His arms around her were lovely, really, and she closed her eyes for a minute while he held her close. But truth be told, she had been looking forward to getting fucked, like maybe against a wall.

She rubbed his half-erect cock over his suit pants and pressed her chest against him.

"This is what I want," she whispered, and turned her face up at him, smiling like she had a secret. He groaned and brought his mouth down hard on hers.

He was completely erect against her hand, and she kept stroking him while returning his kiss. She felt herself being guided backward until he had her pinned with his clothed body against the wall.

Ron ran his hands up her sides until they found her breasts, and he squeezed before tugging the top of her dress down to free her tits from the confines of her bra. He pulled his lips from hers and leaned over to suck on her nipples. Brenna tilted her head back and closed her eyes, clinging to him like he was a lifeline as he suckled on her boob. She felt him start to inch her dress up her thighs. She was so freaking wet.

Just then, an unfamiliar noise cut through their sounds of passion. She didn't comprehend it was his phone until he pulled away from her to retrieve it from his inside jacket pocket.

*Is he really answering his phone right now?*

She felt relieved when he looked down at the screen but didn't take the call. She then realized he was merely trying to steady his breathing, because he inhaled deeply and said, "I'm sorry, I have to take this," before stepping onto the balcony.

*He just had his lips around my tit and he's taking a call? Seriously?*

Maybe he wasn't as turned on as she was because there was no way in hell she would have answered her phone. Her pussy ached to be filled, and she knew he was hard, so she was pretty sure he wanted her, too.

*Why on earth did he answer his phone? And what's so secret that he had to leave the room?*

She tugged her dress and bra back up over her chest.

*Oh fuck.*

*If he's married, I swear I'm going to throw him off this balcony.*

She didn't have time to stew because he stepped back through the door, but she could tell by how his mouth was set, she wasn't going to like what he was about to say.

"I have to go to work."

He looked genuinely upset. At least there was that.

"Right now? You have to go to work, *right now?*"

He looked like he was about to embrace her, then thought better of it. "Brenna, I am so sorry."

She didn't say anything and looked away. The wetness in her panties now nothing but an uncomfortable reminder of what they were doing just thirty-six seconds ago.

He sighed. "I feel like I've completely blown it with you."

She wouldn't say that. She did want to see him again, even though she wasn't exactly thrilled with how their night was ending.

Shaking her head, she said quietly, "You haven't blown it with me. I understand, your work is important. The government needs you."

*Apparently more than I do.*

She hoped there wasn't any bitterness in her voice.

"Fuck." He exhaled as he ran his fingers through his hair. "If I weren't up for this big promotion..."

Brenna touched his arm. "You go do what you need to do. I'm going to Tucson tomorrow for a few days to visit my daughter, but I'll be back. I'm not going anywhere." She grinned. "I'll even give you my phone number."

He didn't seem convinced.

"God, Brenna, I don't think the timing of this could be any worse. I wish I could stay."

"You need to go. The last thing I want is to feel guilty because you didn't get your promotion." She shrugged her shoulders. "Besides, the mood's kinda ruined anyway. There will be another time."

Ron scanned her eyes. "I will make this up to you. I promise. Thank you for understanding."

He proceeded to kiss her so completely, she was having second thoughts about caring if he got his promotion, as long as he was with her tonight.

"You need to go," she whispered when they came up for air.

He leaned his forehead against hers. "I know." He swallowed hard as he caught his breath. "But I don't want to."

Brenna smiled. "I don't want you to either. But you have to."

She kissed him as they walked toward the door.

"I will make this up to you," he said while his lips were still on hers.

She laughed when she pulled away. "You said that already! I'm going to hold you to it."

He kissed her again and opened the door. "Please do."

"Goodbye, Ron. Be safe."

Once he turned to walk down the hall, she reluctantly closed the door, then leaned against it with her eyes closed and touched her mouth as she relived their make-out session. She really hoped he meant it when he said he'd make it up to her. Right now, she was going to get in bed, pretend her hands were his, and finish the job he had started.

Just then there was a knock on the door. She smiled wide and flung it open. Maybe she could live with the guilt of him not being promoted.

Only it wasn't Ron on the other side of the door.

# Chapter Seven

*Ron*

He almost ran into Ray Reitmeier as he was getting off the elevator. The other man stumbled as he tried to get on while Ron was still exiting the car. When the bond trader recognized Ron was the man dancing with Brenna, he leered and said, "Bitch wouldn't put out for you either, huh?"

Ron ignored him but then turned around and held the doors from closing. "Fortunately, when I do get Brenna in my bed, I won't have to worry about getting home to a wife, so I'll be able to take my time and enjoy her thoroughly."

He stood back to let the doors close. The drunken man flashed a menacing smirk. "We'll see about that," he sneered just as the doors shut.

*Fuck, this night has been amazing.*

He hoped he hadn't blown it by having to leave her so abruptly. She seemed like she understood. But she also seemed hurt.

*Goddammit, this better not be a fucking bullshit call based on inaccurate information or heads were gonna roll.*

Ron could practically still feel her in his arms.

He caught a whiff of her perfume on his shirt as he walked through the lobby, and it was all he could do to keep from turning around. Then his thoughts turned to Ray. Something wasn't sitting right with Ron; the way the other man had said, "We'll see about that." It felt *odd.*

He picked up his phone and dialed her number. He smiled when he saw how she had entered her name into his phone. *Breathtaking Brenna.* She was fucking breathtaking.

No answer. Maybe she was in the shower? He made it to his truck and got in before dialing her again. Still no answer. Was she was upset with him? Is that why she wasn't picking up? He started his F150 and made it onto the main road before dialing one more time. When she didn't answer again, he turned his truck around and headed back to The Plaza. His head was telling him he needed to go to the base, but his gut was telling him something was wrong at the hotel.

He replayed his run-in with Ray the entire elevator ride to her floor. He tried to come up with what he was going to say to her when she opened her hotel door in a towel with wet hair. He didn't think he could resist leaving her if she answered the door like that, but he would have to.

*Maybe this was a mistake?*

He was sure she was fine, and he should just turn around. He didn't want her to think he was playing games. He had told her he didn't do that, because he didn't. Him showing back up would contradict that, wouldn't it? Still, his instincts wouldn't let him turn around, and he found himself knocking on her hotel room door.

No answer, just like her phone.

He knocked a little louder and soon he found himself pounding on the door. "Brenna! Open the door."

He finally heard her say, "Go away, Ron."

"Brenna, open the goddamn door or I'm going to break it down."

After what seemed like an eternity, he heard movement on the other side of the door, and she opened it a crack with the chain on. She'd been crying, and at first he thought it was because of him, then he looked at her again and saw terror in her eyes.

Thinking of a way to communicate to her that he knew something wasn't right, he said in a loud voice, "Look Brenna, I know you said you weren't interested, but you gotta give me a chance. You have to get over Ray; he's married, and he doesn't want you."

She shifted her eyes to the right, as if to indicate Ray was standing next to her. Her mascara was smeared and in a soft voice, she said, "You can't be here."

"I *want* to be here. Open the door."

She shook her head no and when she did, he could see a bruise starting to form on her cheek.

Ron continued pleading with her while he motioned for her to step back. Using his fingers, he counted down from three, and kicked the door when he reached one as she jumped back.

# Chapter Eight

*Ron*

He kept her within arm's reach the entire time the police were there. When she explained to them the reason she opened the door was because she thought it was Ron coming back, he sucked his breath in through his teeth and ran his hand up and down her back as he whispered, "I'm so sorry." He felt like he'd been punched in the gut.

She turned to him, and in front of the officers said, "Why are you sorry? You saved me. If you hadn't known something was wrong and come back, he would have..." Her voice trailed off. Her bottom lip started to quiver while the tears threatened to stream down her face. He pulled her against him and held her once they began to fall. He didn't want to think about what may have happened any more than she did.

He let the police take pictures of her bruises but drew the line when they wanted her to go to the station to give a statement.

"She can give it to you now. If you need her for anything else, she'll come down in the morning."

The officer gently asked her, "Is there anyone you want us to call? You probably shouldn't be alone tonight."

Before she could respond, Ron put his arm around her waist and interjected. "I'll be here with her."

She tilted her head. "I thought you had to go?"

He held her gaze. "You're my priority right now."

It was all he could do to keep from kissing her in front of everyone when her eyes welled up with tears. He couldn't get rid of everybody fast enough.

The hotel had moved them to the presidential suite, next to the bridal suite. It had a stunning view, and he stood with his arms around her while she leaned back against his chest as they looked out over the city.

She turned to face him and smiled weakly. "You really don't have to stay. I know you're needed on base. I can call my sister, she—"

Ron cut her off as he gently put his index finger to her lips. "Brenna, I told you, I'm not going anywhere. This is where I need to be."

She looked so vulnerable, he couldn't help but lean down and kiss her on the lips he had just silenced. The woman before him was a stark contrast to the tigress he'd almost taken to bed right after midnight. He couldn't decide which he was attracted to more. Even though the circumstances were awful, he felt honored she'd allowed him to see both sides of her tonight.

She returned his kiss before burrowing her face against his chest and nuzzling her body as close as she could against his. He held her for a few minutes then whispered, "Come on darlin', let's put you to bed."

He groaned out loud when she looked up at him and said in a soft voice, "Only if you're coming with me."

Gathering her in his arms, he carried her to the bedroom.

Ron lay Brenna on the bed and slid on his side next to her, facing her. He stroked her arm while looking at her face; she was going to have a handprint across her pretty cheek in the morning.

He still wasn't sure how he'd managed not to kill that bastard. Lucky for Ray, the hotel had hired extra security because of all the high-profile people at Travis and Ava's party, and they were there in a matter of minutes once Brenna called for help. Otherwise, Ron was pretty sure he would have hurt the man far worse than he did.

Ray seemed to have drank his troubles away and convinced himself his marital problems were all Brenna's fault, and he was going to teach her a lesson. Fortunately, Ron followed his instincts and came back. He had learned long ago to trust his gut. It hadn't failed him yet.

Right now, his gut was telling him the beautiful woman he was in bed next to was pretty damn special. His heart was telling his head, 'don't fuck this one up.'

"Darlin', I think you need to rest tonight. You've had a pretty traumatic experience."

She didn't respond with words, instead, kissed along his jawline and down his neck to his chest. Unbuttoning his shirt slowly, she kissed him down his core until the last button was undone. With his shirt pulled open, she smiled like she approved. He wasn't too hairy, but he was forty-five years old. That came with a little body hair.

She traced her index finger from his chest to his stomach, her head rested against his shoulder. He reached for her hand, brought it to his mouth, and kissed her fingers.

"Brenna..." He kept her hand at his lips.

Withdrawing her palm from his, she caressed his face.

"I don't want to rest," she whispered as she ran the back of her fingertips along the outline of his jaw.

Not waiting for a reply, she rolled over onto him and slithered her body down his until she was nestled between his legs.

He didn't know how to respond. *Shouldn't I be stopping her?* She couldn't be thinking clearly. He should be thinking for both of them.

But holy shit, she felt good.

As if reading his mind, she breathed, "I just need to be close to you."

Well, how the fuck could he argue with that?

Easily undoing his belt and opening his pants, she found his cock semi-erect under his boxer briefs. He protested when she tugged on his trousers, but then his brain overrode his mouth, and he shut up and lifted his hips so she could remove them. She even took the time to take off his socks before laying her head across his hip and outlining his bulge over his underwear.

"Thank you for being there for me tonight."

Ron took a deep breath as he felt himself getting more aroused. "I'm glad I was."

"I'm sorry I kept you from work. I know you're needed on base."

He sat up, so by default, she did too. Cupping her face in his palm, he kissed her furrowed brow.

"Darlin', I'm needed here more, and here is where I'm staying."

With a pout, she replied, "I hope I didn't ruin your chance for promotion."

"You didn't. They understood why I couldn't make it."

The weak smile she offered let him know she wasn't convinced. He needed to reassure her.

He winked. "If anything, I think I earned points for staying with you. Chivalry is important, ya know." His lips kissed her exposed shoulder. "Besides, they knew if I were there, I'd be worthless because all I'd be thinking, and worrying about, is you."

He lowered his lips to her neck, and she drew a sharp breath in, tilting her head to better expose her throat and pulling him closer.

*Fuck, she smells good.*

With one hand at the base of her neck, his other hand slid up her side until it found her breast. He massaged and squeezed her through her dress as he remained lost in the crook of her neck. He could have feasted on her for hours, but her hand rubbing his cock made him want to move on to other things.

He reached behind her to unzip her dress and noticed it was torn. If he ever saw that motherfucker again, he wouldn't be responsible for what he did. Ron didn't say anything about the tear while he moved the zipper down and slid the dress off her shoulders. Kissing her throat, he pushed the garment all the way off her, while he caressed her arms and sides, and pressed her to lie down, whispering how beautiful she was as he did.

He about came in his boxer briefs when he saw her displayed before him, bruised face and all. Matching black lace bra and panties, and black thigh highs, she looked like she belonged in *Maxim*, not his bed. That image alone would be worth not making lieutenant general this time around.

# Chapter Nine

*Brenna*

*Oh my God, he is so hot!*

She loved Ron's lean, strong body, and how it felt against hers. She wanted to get to know every inch of him. It'd been a long time since she was with a man. And even longer since she'd been with one who looked at her with as much desire as Ron was.

He obviously kept in shape. His body came to a delicious V at his waist, his core wonderfully defined. His arms wrapped around her were perfect —muscular but not bulging. She noticed the Marine logo on his right bicep. Brenna had never thought tattoos were sexy until right then. And damn, his was sexy.

He really was her hero, her very own Superman. She had been off-the-charts attracted to him before. There weren't even words to quantify how sexy she found him now, and Brenna was dying to show her appreciation to him for saving her.

Ron stared at her; his eyes full of pure lust as she lay on the bed. She was glad she hadn't skipped any workouts lately.

He observed her without saying a word for what felt like hours. "You are so goddamn sexy," he finally muttered before enveloping her body in his, kissing her with passion as he pressed his hips against hers. She grinded against him, feeling his body heat as she pressed her tits into his toned chest. He thrust back hard. They were basically fucking with their underwear on. Her panties were pushed inside her as his cock tried to find its way in, despite the cloth barrier between them. Her moans of desire grew, and she bucked against him. Her need to be filled by him almost overwhelmed her. When he grabbed her face in both his hands, she winced in pain.

"Oh fuck, Brenna, I'm so sorry!"

That slowed the pace back down, and he was extra gentle when he kissed both cheeks.

"Let's take these off, shall we?" He gestured to her undergarments. She sat up and moved to slide her nylons off when he grabbed her hand. "No, leave those," he said with a wink and evil grin, then reached behind her back and undid her bra, kissing her below her ear as he pulled the garment off.

He glided his hands down to her hips and outlined the waistband in her panties before sliding them to her ankles. He worked his way back up her body, kissing every inch along the way.

*Hey, I wanted to do that to you!*

When she felt him cupping her right breast in his palm while he rolled her nipple between his fingers, she decided not to protest; there would be time to explore his body later.

He kneaded both her tits in his hands and jiggled them, as if he were trying to determine their weight while he did. His mouth found its way back to her sensitive nipples, and she arched her back underneath him, offering more of herself to his mouth. He seemed to take delight in making her rosy peaks stiff, and they were standing at full attention for him.

Ron trailed his hand back down her stomach until he was between her lower lips and smiled as he rubbed her slit.

"You're so wet, darlin'."

*Yeah, well keep calling me darlin' in that southern drawl of yours and I'm only going to get wetter.*

He watched her face closely when he slowly slipped a finger inside her. Brenna raised her hips to thrust against his hand.

*Fuck, that feels good.*

He continued watching her while sliding another digit in and was met with the same reaction. He moved in and out of her in a slow rhythm, and she whimpered, moving her hips in time with his fingers. He lowered his head and licked her labia while his fingers continued their steady pace. She gasped out loud and bucked against his face when his tongue found her clit. When he sucked on her magic button, she moaned and grabbed a handful of sheets.

"Oh my God, Ron. That feels so amazing," she cried out while arching her back again.

The vibrations from his *mmm* almost sent her over the edge. She reached down and touched his face with both hands until he looked up at her, his face glistening with her juices.

"Please stop. You're going to make me come," she begged.

He smiled devilishly and dove back into her pussy with fervor, flicking his tongue on her clit while his fingers plunged in and out of her at a faster pace. Her moans and the wet noises from between her legs seemed to echo in the room.

Just as she predicted, she came. And it was heavenly. She lay there savoring the first orgasm she'd had with another person in as long as she could remember, feeling his warm skin on hers. His arms protectively around her made her want to stay like that forever.

She felt his cock enter her while she was still euphoric.

He felt so damn good inside her. He was thick and the sensation of being filled while he skillfully thrust in and out of her, made her feel like she was going to come again. When he picked up the pace and was balls deep inside her, she begged him not to stop.

He grunted and held her hips tight as he rammed into her hard. The impact of the thrusts against her already sensitive nub sent her over the edge as he filled her with his cum. Her entire body convulsed with orgasm number two.

Not that she was keeping score.

But if she were, by the time they finally fell asleep, the score was a lop-sided four to two, in her favor.

# Chapter Ten

*Brenna*

She woke up when she felt movement in the king-sized bed. It was a feeling she hadn't experienced in a while, and it caused her brain to recognize something was different. She looked over at the clock to see it was after ten. Five hours of sleep—she could get by on that.

Ron had obviously already been up; she could smell coffee. but his skin was warm against her bare thigh. She happily recalled he wasn't wearing any clothes when she fell asleep. When he noticed she was awake, he stroked her hair.

"Good morning," he said in a low voice.

"Happy New Year." She rolled onto her side in order to nestle her butt against him so they could spoon. She immediately grimaced when the side of her face hit the pillow and turned back over to face him. He lightly traced his finger over her bruise.

"That looks like it hurts. I'm sorry I kept you from putting ice on it last night."

She grinned and brought the sheet around her mouth when she answered him. "I'm not."

"Does it hurt?"

She shook her head no, then spoke into the sheet. "As long as I don't touch it."

"I'm sure you're going to get some looks on the plane. What time is your flight?"

She gestured for him to hang on one second; she was not going to carry on a conversation with him without having brushed her teeth. Sliding out of bed, naked, she made her way to the bathroom.

\*\*\*\*

*Ron*

Ron loved she didn't try to cover up her body and instead walked nude freely in front of him. He put his hands behind his head and leaned back against the pillows to enjoy the view.

With her hair brushed, she came back wearing his tuxedo shirt. He liked that view, too.

Smiling, she snuggled in next to him and put her arms around his waist, her head on his chest. He could smell toothpaste.

"To answer your question, I decided I'm not going to Tucson today after all. I'm just going to lay low for a few days and let myself heal before I venture out again. I have to remember to text my daughter and let her know I'm not coming. What about you? Do you need to be anywhere?"

He leaned over her and started unbuttoning his shirt she had on.

"I think I need to be right about here," he said as he kissed in between her breasts.

Brenna giggled at first but was soon gasping when he swirled his tongue around her nipple while kneading her other boob in his hand. She ran her fingers through his hair and pulled his head closer to her chest.

Her tits were amazing. He knew they were fake, but whoever her plastic surgeon was, he deserved some kind of award, because they damn sure felt real.

When he sucked her nipple, she pushed him off her. With a seductive smile, she purred, "I need to shower."

Ron waited in bed a few minutes until he heard the shower start. That was his cue.

He picked up the bottle of her body wash off the shower bench as he stood naked in the glass-block entrance, admiring her backside while the water sprayed her front.

"Need any help washing your back?"

She turned around and grinned, her wet hair slicked back on her scalp. "As a matter of fact..."

Ron couldn't help but notice her hard nipples when he stepped in and the mist started to wet his body. She took the bottle from him, poured body wash on a green bath sponge, and lathered his chest. It smelled like flowers.

Brenna seemed to take her task very seriously, carefully studying his body while caressing it as she soaped up his skin. Chest, arms, chest again, stomach—she stopped to pour more body wash on her sponge, then turned him around to wash his back. He felt her tits rubbed against his spine when she washed his shoulders. He turned around and slid his arm around her so she was pressed against chest.

"I think you might have missed a spot."

Playing along, she gasped, "Oh my gosh, I'm so sorry," and squeezed the green, mesh ball from shoulder to shoulder so soap ran down his chest, then playfully used her tits to rub it around.

"Is that better?"

His cock was so stiff it was sticking straight up. "Oh, yeah," he said with a sharp exhale.

After adding more soap, she grazed his dick with her boobs when she knelt down to wash his calves, taking her time to work her way up to his thighs. Using long, firm strokes, she reached the crease between his leg and hip.

Ron groaned when she reached over and carefully started to clean his balls, moving the loofah in gentle circles around each one and reaching under to lightly scrub there, too. She stood up and squeezed the sponge over his cock to drop more soap bubbles on him, grinding her pussy ever-so-slightly against his thigh as she did.

Using only her hand, she caressed up and down his sudsy shaft. Her fingers were small, and he liked the way they looked wrapped around his dick.

She knew exactly how to stroke him to the point he was about to explode, rubbing the sweet spot under the head with her thumb until precum dribbled out. She watched his face while she fondled him and rubbed herself harder against his thigh when he pulled her in for a long kiss.

Brenna continued stroking him while they kissed, and his hands wandered over her wet body. She was soft and curvy in all the right places, and he reached between her legs to find her wet from her juices, not just the shower. Grabbing her ass and lifting her up, he pushed her against the shower wall and thrust hard into her. Ron loved watching her tits bounce as he penetrated her over and over. Her back was flat against the tile with her legs around his waist, and her face contorted in pleasure while the shower continued cascading over them. She felt fucking amazing.

He had an idea and lifted her off him. Turning the shower head to *jet spray*, he adjusted it so it blasted the shower bench, then he sat down and pulled her onto his lap, her back against him. Moving her legs apart, he slid his cock back inside her to fuck her from underneath. Brenna moaned loudly and threw her head back against his chest when he spread her pussy lips apart with his hands so the jets would hit her clit. Ron held her firmly in place, splayed wide, when she started to wiggle from the intensity of the spray. It was obviously a brilliant idea because it didn't take long before she started coming—hard. He pumped her furiously when her pussy spasmed and milked his cock, and soon felt his balls draw up. With a roar, he coated her inner walls with rope after rope of his cum.

Pushing his hips further back onto the bench, he leaned his head back against the wall and tried to catch his breath. She slid off him then turned around to straddle his lap, her knees on either side of his thighs.

"Oh my God, that was amazing," she murmured against his lips while pressing her forehead to his.

He hadn't quite caught his breath so all he could do was nod in agreement.

She smiled as she climbed off him, turned the shower head back to *spray,* and got under the water to clean herself. Watching her kept him from going flaccid, and he sat on the bench admiring her while she ran the soapy pouf all over her body.

Damn, she was incredible to look at, to feel, and to talk to. Someone he could have an intelligent conversation with at dinner, then take home and fuck senseless. Hadn't he just wished for exactly that last night?

*Don't eff this up, Ron.*

When she reached for the shampoo bottle he stood up and took it from her hand. Pouring probably too much into his palms, he rubbed them together, then massaged her scalp with it as it lathered in her hair. He took his time working it through the blonde strands, enjoying being able to watch her with her eyes closed and head tilted back, an occasional "mmm" coming from her lips.

Ron turned her to rinse the suds out, running his fingers through her long hair to make sure all the soap was gone.

When the water ran clear from her hair, he put his arms around her waist from behind and nibbled her neck. His hands slid up her belly to palm both her tits, gently squeezing while he pushed them together. Her boobs looked sexy as hell in his hands, and he would happily play with them all day. His cock grew hard at the thought. With a soft moan, Brenna leaned back against his chest, eyes closed, her arm curled behind his head while the shower rained down on them.

She turned around to pull his face close then nip at his lips. Ron closed his eyes as he returned the favor. When she pulled her mouth off his, he opened his eyes and found her looking at him—her eyes full of passion.

He gripped her face to kiss her harder, and she drew a sharp breath as if in pain.

*Fuck! Her bruise.*

"Oh God, darlin', I'm so sorry!"

The corners of her mouth curled up. "It's okay."

Ron leaned down and kissed her cheek then grabbed the bottle of her fruity shampoo. He quickly washed his hair before shutting the water off and stepping out with her. He softly, but thoroughly, dried her from head to toe using a towel he had pulled from the rack. With a smirk, he made sure her tits and pussy received extra attention before draping the cotton cloth around her middle and tucking it in at her chest, swatting her butt as he did.

"Are you hungry?" He wrapped a towel around his waist after running it swiftly over his body.

"I am, but I think we should just get room service," she replied, pointing to her bruised cheek.

"Good idea."

# Chapter Eleven

*Brenna*

Ron ordered them room service while she texted Danielle that she wasn't able to make it that day. Fifteen seconds later, her phone was playing the ringtone for her daughter.

"Hi sweetie," Brenna answered.

"Mom, is everything okay?"

Not wanting to upset her daughter, she downplayed the incident.

"I had a run-in at Ava's wedding reception with someone I had been on a few dates with."

"The guy who stood you up?"

*Cassie has a big mouth.*

"Yeah, him."

"What happened?"

Taking a breath, Brenna answered, "We had a bit of an altercation, and he went to jail."

Danielle's voice rose an octave. "Oh my God! Are you all right? Did he hurt you?"

Brenna tried reassuring her daughter. "I'm okay, really, I'm just a little shaken up so I'm going to stay in San Diego today. But I'm still planning on coming to Tucson at the end of the month to look for a place, so I'll see you then."

"Are you sure you're okay, Mom? Is Cassie with you?"

Brenna shook her head, even though Danielle couldn't see her doing so. "No, this happened at the hotel pretty late.

The Plaza moved me to the Presidential Suite so I'm just going to take my time and probably go home later this afternoon." She avoided answering her daughter's second question.

*Maybe she won't notice.*

Nope, she noticed.

Danielle repeated, "Is Cassie with you?"

*Hmmm. What to say...*

Brenna knew when she told Danielle that Cassie wasn't there, her daughter would be worried and want someone with her. So how did Brenna say she wasn't alone, without explaining too much?

"No, she's with Zona at the house. The person who came to my rescue is here with me."

Her daughter paused, then drew her next words out. "Annnddd, does this person happen to be male?"

"Quite a nice looking one, as a matter of fact." Brenna glanced over at Ron sitting on the couch. He winked at her.

Danielle began whispering, although Brenna wasn't sure why, since she was on the phone, and he couldn't hear her anyway. "Mom! Did anything happen? Are you going to see him again?"

Brenna lied. "Okay, honey, room service is here, I have to go."

"You got room service?" Dani squealed.

"Goodbye, Daughter. I love you." Brenna hung up while Danielle was still peppering her with questions. Seven minutes later, Cassie's ringtone started playing.

Brenna groaned, "It's my sister."

Ron chuckled. He had obviously overheard her conversation with Danielle.

"Aren't you going to answer it?"

She sighed. She knew if she didn't, her sister would just keep calling her.

"I'm fine, I'm coming home later today," was how she answered.

Cassie was practically shouting. "What the hell happened? Are you okay?"

"Didn't you just hear me? I said I was fine. I'll tell you about it when I get home." She sounded more exasperated than she felt.

Her tone didn't deter Cassie. "And who is this mystery man Danielle said you're with? He came to your rescue? How?"

"Cass, can we please talk about this when I get home?"

Once again, her sister didn't take the hint. "Do I get to meet him?"

Brenna hadn't thought about him meeting her family. "I don't know. Maybe."

"When?"

Her persistence brought a smile to Brenna's lips. "I said I didn't know!"

"You sure you're okay?" Cassie really was worried about her.

"Just a little bruised and shaken up."

"*Bruised?* You're *bruised?*"

Brenna took a deep breath. "Yes, I'm bruised. And if you tell Danielle, I swear, I'm never telling you anything again. I have to go, but I will see you later. If you run into Luke, will you tell him I'm going to be home tonight, and he doesn't have to worry about staying?"

Cassie's voice sounded odd when she answered. "Um, yeah. If I see him, I'll let him know."

\*\*\*\*

They spent the rest of the morning in the white fluffy robes the hotel provided. Ron had ordered way too much food from room service, and they sat around the glass-top dinette set in front of a floor to ceiling window in the suite, nibbling, talking, and looking out at the city below them.

Ron seemed very secretive about his work, so after just a few questions that he gave vague and one-word answers to, Brenna decided not to pry and left it alone. She was having second thoughts about him being a drill sergeant. She did learn, however, that he grew up in South Carolina, hence the Southern drawl.

"It's gotten a lot less noticeable since I moved out here. But you should hear me when I go home."

"Where do you consider home?"

"Charleston."

That piqued her interest.

"I have a place on Sullivan's Island." Brenna told him, happy they seemed to have something in common, as the island was just outside of Charleston.

The beach house and the house in South Carolina were the only two places she kept after Danny died. The house on Sullivan's Island had been in Danny's family for a couple of generations, and she just couldn't bring herself to sell it. Plus, she really loved the property. It was as old-school Southern as you could get. White plantation-style with columns and wraparound porches on the first and second levels. Mature trees lined the long drive. She sometimes would escape there when the tabloids had sniffed out one of Danny's new conquests. Since his death, she had only been back a handful of times. The upkeep was costing her a pretty penny, but she liked that it somehow connected Danielle to her dad—whom her daughter missed terribly—so it was money well spent, as far as Brenna was concerned.

Ron grinned. "Sullivan's Island, huh?"

She knew houses were expensive there, but she passed it off like he somehow knew her maiden name was Sullivan, and that was what he was referring to. "Yes, Sullivan, but no relation."

He chuckled. "So you were Brenna Sullivan growing up?" he asked as he looked her over. "It suits you," then quickly interjected, "not that Roberts doesn't."

She smiled and cocked her head as she popped a grape in her mouth. "What were you like growing up?"

Ron sat in thought for a moment. "Probably a lot like I am today, only more stupid. I've always been a risk taker, pretty much have always known right from wrong, although I sometimes didn't make the right choices even when I knew better. I've always been in charge, ever since I can remember. My younger brother hated that about me," he said with a laugh.

Risk taker, ethical, leader... she could live with those qualities, although the risk taking thing might turn out to be a deal-breaker down the road.

"Any other siblings?"

"Just my kid brother, Greg. He's a commercial pilot and also single. My poor mother is beside herself wanting grandbabies."

"Do you think you're ever going to give her grandkids?"

"Well, I'm not. When I turned forty-two, I decided there was no way I was going to my kid's high school graduation when I was sixty—or older—so I took steps to make sure that didn't happen."

"Really? You did?" She was genuinely surprised someone with no kids would undergo a vasectomy.

"Brenna, you didn't think I would be so careless otherwise, while we were sleeping together, did you?"

"Well, I hadn't really thought about it, since I had a hysterectomy ten years ago."

He nodded his head once. "Well, I guess we're on the same page when it comes to procreation then."

"I guess we are."

There was a slight lag in their conversation, and he sat there with his head tilted, looking at her and smiling.

*Damn he is sexy.*

"Do you want to watch some football in bed?" She hoped he understood that was her forty-four-year-old version of *watch Netflix and chill.*

If he did understand, he didn't let on. Standing up, he offered her his hand, "What game do you want to watch?"

*Um, your tongue in my pussy game?*

That'd probably be a bit too crass.

Shrugging her shoulders, she replied, "I don't know, let's see what's on." *Or off.*

She walked into the bedroom ahead of him and dropped her robe in a heap on the ground. With a knowing smile, she walked naked to the bed.

He didn't move from the doorway, just watched her slowly crawl toward the headboard on all fours. She glanced over her shoulder at him leaning against the doorjamb with an appreciative smile for what he saw.

She turned onto her back and asked, "Do you have the remote?" as she put her index finger to her lips and gently bit down. She hoped her lack of subtlety was taken in the playful spirit it was intended.

She got her answer when he dropped his robe and pounced on her. At first, he tickled her briefly. She was glad it was briefly because she hated being tickled, then wrapped his arms around her and fell back on the bed with her in a bear hug. Rolling over to straddle her stomach, he then grabbed her two wrists together in one of his large hands and pinned them over her head.

"Let's see how *you* like being teased."

She braced herself to be tickled again, but instead was delighted to learn what his form of teasing entailed.

Hint—it wasn't tickling.

Her chest was heaving from the brief wrestling on the bed, but mainly from the excitement she felt as he leaned over her. He focused on her mouth, tracing the outline of it with his middle finger—taking his time doing so before leaning over and kissing her. It was a slow, passionate kiss that took her breath away. The kind that when he pulled away, she whimpered because she didn't want it to end. He released her wrists, but she left them above her head and savored the moment with her eyes closed.

She opened them and found him watching her, like he was waiting for her to look at him. Brenna was startled at the exchange of unspoken words as they gazed at each other. She drew a breath in; it was like a jolt of electricity shot through her, and she felt her nipples get stiff as goosebumps traveled down her entire body.

*What the hell was that?* Her stomach felt like it had butterflies in it, a feeling she hadn't experienced in almost twenty years.

Just like she knew last night she should have been offended at how strong he was coming on to her, but wasn't, she knew these feelings she was having were too fast, too soon, and she should get the hell out of there.

But she didn't.

She reached up behind his head and pulled him back into her for another kiss instead.

Brenna gently sucked on his bottom lip, tugging as she did, before Ron parted her lips with his tongue to seek hers out. As their tongues tangled, their kisses alternated between light and gentle to hard and urgent. They had a twenty minute make-out session where all they did was kiss. Any time she tried to touch him below the waist, he'd pull her hands away and hold them in place. His fingers lightly traced her body as their tongues intertwined, and she remembered how exciting she always found necking to be when she was a teenager. Somewhere along the way, it had gotten pushed aside in favor of *other* things. She realized what a travesty that was. Kissing Ron was as intimate, if not more, than anything they had done together so far.

However, she didn't object when he decided to escalate things.

He massaged her right breast when they came up for air. "My God, darlin', I want you so damn badly."

She knew the feeling.

Brenna pushed him back onto the bed and wasted no time mounting him, sliding his cock inside her. She was so turned on, it had no trouble finding its way in.

He sat up and kissed her more while she started rolling her hips on his. When he bent over to suck on her tits, she leaned back and bucked a little faster, stimulating her clit against his pubis bone as she clung to the back of his head and pushed her tit further into his mouth. Ron tugged her nipple away from her chest with his teeth then lay back to rub her clit with his thumb. With her hands on her thighs, back arched, and head thrown back, she started to moan.

Soon she was stuttering her words. "Oh-oh my Ga-God! Oh, yes! Oh, please don't stop. Don't st-stop, don't stop, doooonnnn't stoooopppp!" as she bounced on him faster. She went still and silent, then cried out in pleasure and convulsed as the orgasm ripped through her. It was as amazing as the first one he gave her. Which was saying a lot, because that had been pretty damn awesome.

Well, they all had been rather fantastic.

Ron kept rubbing her until she fell forward onto his chest.

Flipping her onto her back, he immediately began to fuck her, which only served to heighten her orgasmic sensation, and she knew she was going to come again.

*Goddamn he is good!*

He grunted as he thrust into her harder. She gasped with every push and soon they were both moaning. He seemed to be trying to hold out for her to climax again and once she started to, he let out a long grunt as he came deep inside her; holding her hips tight as he gave short thrusts while emptying his seed in her pussy. He fell forward to the left side of her.

They both lay there, gasping for breath, swallowing hard.

With his forehead resting on the mattress, he finally spoke. "Oh, Brenna. Sugar, you have no idea what you do to me."

She had a hand on her stomach, feeling it rise and fall while she gulped for air. Looking at the ceiling she managed, "Oh my God. That was so incredible. *You* are so incredible."

He was still inside her and made no effort to remove himself as he wrapped his arms around her and nuzzled her neck. Brenna gave a contented sigh when he hugged her tight.

She was thinking her year was off to a wonderful start when her face began to throb. She must have released a lot of endorphins because she did not notice it hurting during their make-out or lovemaking sessions, and she remembered he was holding her face a lot.

Well, it was making up for it.

He noticed her wince and immediately attended to her; cleaning her up and getting the ice pack the hotel had given her last night while insisting she remain lying down.

"I have some pills in my purse to help with the pain." Although they might be expired, but she was willing to try anything at this point.

They were expired, but still worked like a charm, because the next thing she knew, Ron was standing before her fully dressed in the previous night's shirt and trousers.

Shaking her gently, he said in a soft voice, "Come on, darlin'. Let's get you home."

# Chapter Twelve

*Brenna*

She woke up in her bed and had no idea how she got there.

Was it dusk or dawn?

Another reason the prescription bottle didn't get emptied before it expired.

She made her way downstairs and found Cassie sitting on the window seat in the kitchen that faced the ocean. Except she wasn't looking at the water, she was looking at her phone and smiling.

"Hey, Cass," Brenna said in a shaky voice.

Her sister looked up. "Hey, sleeping beauty. How are you feeling?"

"A little disoriented. Um, what time is it?"

"Just after six. You want me to make you some dinner?"

That answered the dusk or dawn question.

"How—how did I get home?"

Cassie smirked. "Your hero brought you home."

Brenna tried to sound nonchalant. "He did?"

"He did." Cassie got up and started toward the fridge. Over her shoulder, she called out, "He's kind of bossy."

"Why do you say that?" Brenna chuckled as she slid onto a barstool at the kitchen island and watched her sister pull ingredients from the refrigerator.

Cassie closed the stainless-steel door. "I told him to just lay you down on the couch, so he didn't have to haul you up the stairs. He told me no, he was putting you in your bed. Then he handed me an ice pack to fill and wouldn't let me put it on you; he did it himself. *Then* he wanted to make something for you to eat in case you woke up. Like I wouldn't feed you or something."

Brenna tried to disguise her smile. *He was looking out for me.*

*Again.*

It was a wonderful, strange feeling.

She'd had people who used to take care of her professionally: an agent, publicist, studio executives, and a part-time assistant to name a few. But, personally, she was the one taking care of everyone else. Danny sure as fuck never took care of her. This was kind of nice. Although she wasn't sure how comfortable she was being so vulnerable, especially so soon after first meeting him.

She needed to be sure and return the favor when she saw him again.

*Wait. Was* she going to see him again?

\*\*\*\*

*Ron*

Ron appreciated the ride back to the hotel from Luke, the guy who watched Brenna's dog. He learned Luke was a former Marine and now a SWAT sergeant for the San Diego police department. Ron liked hearing about former Devil Dogs who went on to prosperous careers outside the Corps.

Although, he had to remind the guy a few times he didn't have to call Ron *sir*.

He was surprised to learn Luke knew who he was, but Ron had been organizing the Tower Challenge on September eleventh for several years, and a lot of guys from the San Diego emergency services participated, so it made sense. It was a big fundraiser for the Wounded Warrior Project, and something he felt worthwhile to give his time and energy to.

As they pulled into The Plaza's parking lot, Luke asked, "Are you going back to Brenna's?"

*Am I going back?* Shit, he wasn't sure what the right thing to do was. He didn't want to smother her, but he also wanted to make sure she was okay. Plus, he needed to reiterate to her that last night wasn't just a one-night stand for him.

Luke must have sensed his hesitation, because he put the truck in park, looked down at his phone and said, "Cassie says Brenna's awake and asked about you."

That made his heart beat a little faster.

Since he begged off last night's mission, he would have a few days before he had to be back on base. He'd love to spend them with her.

*Slow down, leatherneck. Don't fuck this up. Play it cool.*

Still, he couldn't help but feel like playing it cool with her would be what fucked it up.

He needed to trust his gut. It had yet to steer him wrong.

Ron hopped out of Luke's Jeep. "I need to go home and change, then I'll be by."

The former Marine grinned. "I'll let them know."

"Thanks for the ride, man. I appreciate it."

"No problem. Have a good night." And with that, Luke pulled away.

****

Ron decided to call Brenna to make sure she was up for his company.

She answered with, "Hey, you."

He smiled the minute he heard her voice.

"Hey yourself. What are your thoughts about me coming back over?"

"Luke said you would be coming by. Do you still want to?"

"Hell yes, I do."

He could hear the smile in her voice. "Good. You should probably bring your toothbrush, you know, just in case you need it for some reason."

Another night holding her? It was his lucky day. He was too busy thinking about how much he was going to enjoy falling asleep with her in his arms and didn't realize he hadn't responded until she said, "I mean, unless you can't stay over."

"Oh no, I can stay. I was just thinking how spoiled I'm going to get, waking up in bed with you two mornings in a row."

She teased, "It'll be rough, but I think I can manage lying next to you all night again."

He smirked. "Well, at least I don't hog the bed."

She feigned offense. "What? I do not hog the bed! Next thing you're going to tell me is I snore!"

"Well, now that you mention it..."

"I'm told I have a very comfortable guest bed, if I get too loud."

"Darlin', it would take a lot more than a little snoring and bed hogging to get me out of your bed. I'll see you shortly."

She giggled. "Can't wait."

Neither could he.

# Chapter Thirteen

*Brenna*

When she hung up with Ron, she turned to find Cassie watching her.

"What?" Brenna asked as she walked around the island, carefully keeping her back to her sister.

Cassie didn't answer, so Brenna finally turned around to find her smirking.

"*What?*" she questioned a little more emphatically this time.

"Oh nothing." Cassie pretended to busy herself with rearranging the fruit in the black wire basket on the counter. "I just can't remember the last time I've seen you smile so much while talking to a man."

Brenna tried to make herself stop smiling. It was impossible. She conceded with a giggle, "He is pretty great."

"I can see that. So tell me about him. What do you know?"

Leave it to Cassie to rain on Brenna's parade. She didn't know much about him, but she could still think he was pretty great.

She tried to sound casual as she answered. "He grew up in South Carolina, graduated from The Citadel, and joined the Marines right after. He's been in for twenty-four years. No kids."

"Divorced?"

Brenna shook her head.

Cassie's eyebrows raised. "*Never* been married?"

The two had talked more than once about if a man had never been married by the age of forty, it was a red flag that something was wrong with him. She knew where her sister was going and intended to head it off at the pass. That red flag did not apply to Ron.

"No, he's never been married," she replied firmly.

Cassie opened her mouth to make a comment and Brenna shot her a hard look, daring her to respond. She theatrically closed it and raised her eyebrows again, as if to convey even though she was shutting up, she didn't approve.

"And, he had a sixth sense which saved me from a very bad situation last night."

Brenna said that to squelch her sister's judgement about Ron, but immediately realized her mistake because by doing so, it opened up the discussion about what transpired with Ray. Something she didn't want to talk about.

"What happened last night?"

Brenna took a deep breath. She really had no desire to relive this, but knew she had to at least tell her the basics.

She shrugged. "Ray assaulted me because he was angry I let his wife know he was dating other women."

Cassie's eyes got big, and she shook her head, almost like a cartoon character would after getting hit in the face.

"*His wife?!*"

"Yeah, his wife."

The younger woman sat staring straight ahead, trying to absorb what she'd just been told.

"So *he* hit *you* because…" She was pointing her fingers back and forth as if keeping track of the events. "He was dating other people and his wife found out about it, but somehow he thought you were the one in the wrong?"

"I'm sure his inebriated state didn't help his thought process." Brenna didn't like saying that because it felt like it was somehow helping justify what he'd done. "He went to jail, although I'm sure he's already bonded out. Can we talk about something else, please?"

To her surprise and relief, Cassie dropped it.

It was Brenna who kept it going when she added, "I'm serious about you not telling Danielle. I mean it, Cass. I don't want her worrying about me."

Her sister nodded her head and said, "Okay."

Brenna's raised eyebrows conveyed she didn't believe her.

"I said okay!" Cassie then tried to lighten the mood and giggled, "I won't tell her that her mother looks like she should be in the next *Rocky* movie."

The description made Brenna smile. "Shut it."

The doorbell rang. Both Zona and Rex raced to the door to greet Luke as he walked in, calling "Hello?" as he did.

"We're in here!" Cassie replied, trying to disguise her own big grin.

Brenna tilted her head, and her baby sister avoided her stare.

*Hmmm, what's going on here?*

She knew Cass would tell her when she was ready to, so Brenna opted to remain silent. For now.

Luke appeared in the kitchen, followed by the canines who worshipped him.

"Just came to pick up Rex."

Brenna grabbed some money out of her purse and handed it to Luke.

"Thanks for going out of your way. Sorry I wasn't gone like you expected."

He narrowed his eyes and held up his hands as if he were offended.

"Brenna, when you adopted Zona and I told you I would always be available to dog sit, I meant *for free.*"

Her embarrassment was obvious. "I didn't realize that's what you meant. But to be honest, Luke, I don't think I can ask you to stay here if you won't let me pay you."

Cassie chimed in, "Oh, but you have no problem not paying me!"

"That's different. You know—"

Luke interrupted the sisters. "Brenna, I love your place. Being on the water in this house is payment enough. Trust me." He glanced over at Cassie and smiled. "And the hot tub is a nice bonus."

Brenna didn't say a thing about her sister's red cheeks. She knew better than to push Cassie.

Later, when they were all sitting outside, even Ron noticed the chemistry between Luke and Cassie, commenting, "Is there something going on with them?" when the two conspicuously got up from the fire on the patio and decided to leave at the same time.

"I'm not really sure. I'm not imagining it though, right? They are acting strange? I think for right now, I am going to mind my own business."

They sat in comfortable silence, and she leaned her head against his shoulder with his arm possessively around her, as they watched the boat lights in the distance. She liked how warm he was when she cuddled up next to him and closed her eyes while breathing in his scent.

A yawn escaped her. Ron bent down and held her chin as his mouth lightly touched hers.

"Let's go to bed," he whispered while looking into her eyes.

\*\*\*\*

*Ron*

Ron stood up and offered Brenna his hand. She called for Zona and shut the lights off on their way to her bedroom. As they walked up the stairs, he grabbed his bag he'd left at the foot of the landing.

He'd seen her bedroom earlier today when he brought her home from the hotel. It was large but minimally furnished. The ocean view from her bed seemed to be all the decoration she needed. She hit a few switches when they walked in and her blinds began to close as the lights turned on.

He smiled. "Well, that's convenient. But don't you like to lay in bed and look at the ocean?"

Gesturing to the blinds on the sliders leading to her glass-walled balcony, she said, "I'll open those once we're in bed and the lights are turned off."

Before disappearing into what he assumed was her bathroom, she pointed to a door. "There's a bathroom for you to use."

*Two master baths?*

He was glad Danny at least left her monetarily taken care of. When Ron walked in the room, he looked to his left and noticed a large walk-in closet which was completely empty, except for a few boxes that looked like they held Christmas decorations. The bathroom décor was masculine, but void of any indication it had been used.

He was in bed wearing only his boxers when she walked back in the bedroom. He caught his breath at the sight of her rubbing lotion over her hands and wearing a silky, light green nightgown that came to her mid-thigh.

*Damn, I am one lucky bastard.*

The simple act of them getting ready for bed together was so intimate, yet not necessarily sexual, and he couldn't think of anywhere else he'd rather be than there with her. He wasn't going to even attempt anything with her tonight; she needed to rest, and he shouldn't have kept her up as late as he did last night. She paused and looked at him before hitting the switches that shut off the light and opened the sliders' blinds.

When he felt her arms around his middle and her head against his bare chest, he could tell she was smiling. She smelled like lotion, and he could feel her silk nightie against his stomach and thigh. They looked out at the moon shining on the ocean waves, neither speaking as he stroked her hair. Before long, her breathing let him know she was asleep, but he continued petting her hair, lost in his own thoughts. He couldn't remember the last time he'd felt so content. How was that fucking possible after less than thirty hours with her?

Still asleep, she rolled over and stretched out. He had been teasing her earlier about hogging the bed, but it was obvious from how much she spread out, she slept alone. Fortunately, it was a big bed, however, he made sure his hand was on her silky hip as he drifted off. The last thoughts through his head before he fell asleep were, *she's not wearing any underwear,* and *I can't wait until morning.*

# Chapter Fourteen

*Brenna*

She woke as the sun came up with Ron next to her, and her mood was happy. Who wouldn't love waking up and finding a bare-chested, amazing looking man in her bed? Unlike yesterday morning, it didn't even take her a second to register she was in bed with him; it was like he'd always been there.

She rolled onto her side, put her hands in a prayer pose underneath her face, and watched him sleep. His hair was wavy and light brown, and she had an urge to run her fingers through it, but refrained. Instead she studied his handsome face and wondered how his nose had become crooked. Probably by saving someone's life or some other heroic thing. Or maybe he pissed off one of his recruits when he was yelling at him. Although it was becoming harder and harder for her to picture him yelling at anyone.

What *did* he do for the Marines?

Her eyes fell to his tattoo. It suited him. It was understated, not at all flashy, but it exuded masculinity on his strong arm.

She looked back at his face and found him with his eyes still closed but grinning.

Opening one eye, he peered at her. "Do you like it?"

"Like what? Your tattoo?"

"Yeah." He had both eyes open and there was a twinkle in them.

She nodded her head and focused on the design on his bicep.

"Normally, I wouldn't. But I think yours is sexy."

With her index finger, she lightly traced its outline on his arm.

"What does *semper fidelis* mean?"

"Always faithful," he said in a low voice as he moved his gaze from her finger caressing his arm to her face.

She continued tracing the tattoo while softly repeating to herself what he said, "Always faithful."

She glanced up and found him watching her expression.

"Do you think that describes you or the Marine Corps in general?"

He brushed her hair away from her face. "Both."

Her finger stopped tracing the tattoo and her eyes narrowed. "And *you've always* been faithful?"

Looking her in the eye, he flatly stated, "Always."

Brenna looked down and tried not to smile too wide. His answer made her almost dizzy.

She didn't know exactly what was going on between them, but she did know there was a yummy, half-naked man in her bed who was always faithful, had taken care of her yesterday, and had been her hero the night before last. She needed to take advantage of the situation and show him just how much she appreciated him.

Her lips planted feather-light kisses on his chest, and she noticed his nipples stiffen, so she swirled her tongue around the brown tips and sucked gently. Sitting up on her knees, she continued down his core, her hair splayed across his chest and stomach while her lips moved down his body. When she reached his boxers, she wasted no time in removing them. He was completely naked—and hard—in front of her.

As she kissed his inner thigh, she stroked his balls with her hand. He let out a small moan, letting her know she was on the right track. Pushing his legs further apart, her breasts brushed his thigh as she rubbed her cheeks against his sac, savoring how smooth and soft it felt against her face. Moaning as she slipped one ball in her mouth, she swirled her tongue around it before sucking gently. She pulled his skin with her lips before moving to the other one. Her hand pushed them higher on his cock so she could lick underneath.

He groaned when her attention focused on his shaft. From the base, she ran her tongue up his cock until she reached the tip. There, she twirled her tongue around the smooth helmet before licking back to the base. She did this several times and then without warning, completely engulfed him in her mouth.

He cried out, "Oh fuck," when her nose hit his stomach, and she held him in her throat before slurping off him.

"Mmm," she said as she jerked his shaft while sucking him in unison with the rhythm of her hand. His cock was amazing.

*Like, fucking amazing.*

His length was perfect. So were his soft, suckable balls. And the manscaping he did was appreciated.

She tasted his precum as he grabbed a handful of her hair to guide her head up and down on his dick. He wasn't rough as he maneuvered her, although she didn't think she would have minded if he was. But he wasn't exactly gentle either, and she moaned at his aggressiveness. He held her head down on him deep for a moment, then thrust his hips against her face. His breathing became irregular, and he let go of her hair when he warned with a harsh whisper, "Brenna, I'm gonna come."

She kept up the pace he had set when he had her hair in his fist, and he told her again he was going to come while touching her face, not quite pushing her mouth away but getting her attention, before he grunted, "Oh God, yes!"

He gushed in her mouth, and the warm, salty cum flooded her tongue. She held her head still while he emptied himself between her lips and let it dribble out the sides of her mouth. She stroked him until she couldn't feel anything more from his cock, then bobbed her head twice for good measure.

"You taste so good," she said as she swirled her tongue around his tip and squeezed any remaining cum out.

Ron lay panting with the back of his hand to his forehead.

"Goddamn, darlin'," was all he could manage between breaths.

Brenna smiled and crawled up his body to kiss his neck before disappearing to get him a towel.

He cleaned himself off then threw the towel on the floor toward the bathroom while she watched from the edge of the bed. Reaching over, he tugged her back toward him, and she sighed when he wrapped his arms around her as she nestled against his naked body.

A thought popped into her head: Danny would have already been up and in the shower if she had done that to him. Which she stopped doing after she learned about his affairs. Being her husband's second—or sometimes even third—choice didn't exactly put her in the mood to have his cock in her mouth. When they did fuck, there wasn't a lot of foreplay, and it was always the same; doggie style so they didn't have to look at each other in an intimate way, and she could get herself off while it was happening.

She had tried to be a good wife to Danny. They had a lot in common and were good friends, which made him easier to live with in the end. She made sure she always looked nice, even as things were falling apart. Before she knew about the others, she loved sex with him. She'd worn lingerie on a regular basis, and she enthusiastically came on to him while willing to try anything he suggested if she thought it would make him happy.

About eight years into their marriage, right after she'd had a boob job, she found a woman's card in his pants pocket and realized she could have been perfect and it still wouldn't have been enough. He had too many options available to him, and she couldn't compete with variety, try as she might.

Right about the time she came to that realization was when she stopped writing; something she probably resented

Danny most for. What had once come so easily to her became non-existent.

Sex with Ron was, dare she say it, the best she'd ever had. He was dominant and in-charge, yet attentive to her needs, and he left her no doubt how much he desired her. Which was probably what turned her on the most, being Ron's first choice.

His perfect cock didn't hurt either.

\*\*\*\*

*Ron*

*Holy fuck, what did that woman just do to me?*

He'd had good blow jobs, he'd even had great blow jobs, but how she just sucked his cock was in-fucking-credible. She acted like his dick was the greatest thing she'd ever seen or tasted. Like she couldn't get enough of it.

Talk about an ego boost.

He rubbed her slit, and found her drenched.

*Holy shit! She wasn't acting, she loved sucking my cock!*

She just might be the woman of his dreams.

While he was caressing her pussy, she massaged his junk.

*If she gets me hard again already, I'm marrying her.*

After just a few minutes, he decided, *June weddings are nice.*

"Mmm, Ron, I want you to fuck me," she breathed into his ear.

Yeah, there wasn't gonna be a problem with that.

# Chapter Fifteen

*Brenna*

They fell back asleep after more mind-blowing sex, and she woke up alone in bed. She laid there for a few minutes with a big smile on her face as she relived her time with Ron since meeting him.

He was... What was he?

*Dreamy.*

She giggled at how school-girl the description sounded.

*Too good to be true.*

*Fuck!*

He *was* too good to be true. When was the proverbial other shoe going to drop?

She listened to see if he was in 'his' restroom but didn't hear a sound, so she got up and brushed her teeth and hair, then checked how her bruise was healing. It had started to turn a greenish-yellow color and didn't hurt nearly as bad, but it was still ugly. She couldn't believe Ron found her the least bit attractive with her face looking like she'd gone a few rounds in the ring. And maybe he really didn't, but he sure made her feel like he did.

She was still in her nightie when she made her way downstairs. She wouldn't be surprised if Mr. Too Good To Be True was making a gourmet breakfast.

She walked into an empty kitchen, not at all what she expected. There was no sign of life anywhere.

*Did that bastard leave and not say goodbye?*

That didn't seem like him.

She walked out the front door and saw his black truck still in her driveway.

Weird.

Calling for Zona as she filled the dog dishes, she paused. *This really was weird.* Zona was usually skidding around the corner when she heard her bowls get picked up, and she also was nowhere to be found. *He must have taken Zona for a walk on the beach.*

Brenna made some chai tea and took her cup outside to enjoy the gorgeous San Diego morning. She was curled up in her favorite oversized blue chair with her eyes closed and face to the sun, when she realized she was feeling happy.

Her.

Happy.

Yeah, that confirmed it. He was definitely too good to be true. Something had to be wrong with him.

She opened her eyes just in time to see Ron running up the beach with a very ecstatic Zona at his side.

*Goddamn he is hot.*

He looked sexy as fuck as he ran toward her. His running shorts showing off his toned legs, and she loved how his gray USMC tee-shirt clung to his chest and arms. His skin glistened with sweat.

*It fucking glistened.*

Would he think she was a total pervert if she jumped his clammy body right there on the patio? Because she should *not* be attracted to him when he was all sweaty and yet she was. She really, really was.

Ron smiled at her as he stood on the wet sand and peeled his shirt off before toeing out of his shoes. He jerked his head toward the ocean with raised eyebrows, as if asking her to join him. She was still panty-less in her chemise, not to mention the ocean was freezing this time of year, so she just shook her head no and grinned when he shrugged his shoulders at her, like it was her loss, then ran and dove in the water.

He came out of the water looking like a god. She couldn't look away from his swagger as he slicked his wet hair back and walked against the waves towards the beach.

*Oh Brenna, this is bad.*

Zona had found one of her toys and bound into the surf to show her new best friend her prize. He rubbed her face when she dropped the red ball at his feet, then he picked it up and threw it into the waves for her to fetch. He didn't realize Brenna's dog would be relentless now while trying to get him to throw the ball, because he laughed and tossed it again when she dropped it on his shirt and shoes he was picking up off the sand. Zona got him to throw it three more times before he made it back to the house.

He immediately came to where Brenna was seated on the patio and leaned down to put his arms on both sides of her chair before kissing her on the mouth, making her lady parts tingle. He was dripping wet and shirtless, which only exacerbated the tingling.

"Hi darlin'," he said in his sexy drawl with his lips still only inches away from hers.

She felt giddy.

*Giddy.*

*Yeah, Brenna, this is very, very bad.*

"How was your run?"

"Terrific."

He kissed her again, then stood up and grabbed one of the beach towels she kept on the outdoor shelves to dry off.

"I could get used to running on the beach every morning."

*I could get used to watching you every morning.*

Zona, who had dropped the ball at his feet minutes ago, impatiently nudged the back of his knee with her muzzle. He picked it up and told the pup, "Last time," before making a long throw with it.

"I'm going to go hop in the shower," he said, then turned to head in the house with a wink. "I'll leave the door unlocked." Then he disappeared inside.

"I'm not joining you!" Brenna called after him.

Ron reappeared at the door with a hurt look.

"Wh-at? Why?"

She stood up and walked over to where he was standing. Kissing him as she slipped her arm around his neck, she said with mock sternness, "Because if I join you, it will be another two hours before we eat, and I'm starving. I'm going to make us a late breakfast."

She kissed him again then smiled. "It should be ready by the time you come back down."

He pulled her chemise up and squeezed her bare ass, snarling, "I'd rather have *you* for breakfast."

Zona came springing back with her ball, and Ron reached down to pick it up, one hand still on Brenna's naked bottom. He threw it, telling the dog once again, "Last time."

Brenna smirked. "You already told her that."

Grabbing a handful of flesh from her butt, he said through clenched teeth, "Don't judge me," then kissed her hard on the mouth before continuing, "I can't ever tell a beautiful woman no."

And just like that, the wind was knocked out of her sails. She'd found out what was wrong with him and suddenly didn't want him touching her anymore. She'd already been with a man who couldn't tell a beautiful woman no. It didn't matter Ron was teasing about a dog. It wasn't funny.

"You sure you can't join me?" he asked with a smirk.

She pushed him away and grumbled, "Positive," as she sulked past him.

\*\*\*\*

*Ron*

From upstairs, Ron heard Brenna loudly taking pots and pans out of the cupboard and banging them down on the counter.

*What the fuck just happened?*

One minute he had her gorgeous ass in his hands and was kissing her, the next she was pissed off and storming by him. He wracked his brain in the shower trying to figure it out, replaying what transpired right before she got mad.

He didn't have a clue.

Clad only in a pair of Levis, he went back downstairs. Her mood was still surly as she motioned for him to sit down at the kitchen island, and he ran his fingers through his wet hair in frustration. Even Zona seemed to have made herself scarce.

*At least she isn't one of those, "everything's fine" types.*

She clanked his plate down in front of him. Burnt sausage and toast with runny eggs. The glare she gave dared him to comment about it, then she poured herself a bowl of granola cereal. Instead of milk, she used yogurt and sliced up a banana to put on top. He'd rather have what she was having.

They ate in silence until he couldn't take it anymore.

"Can we rewind about thirty minutes so I can figure out what the hell I did wrong?"

You could have knocked him over with a feather when she told him. He thought for sure he'd have to play the pry it out of her game.

"I'm being completely irrational and I'm ashamed of myself because of it, but I'm sorry, I didn't like hearing you say you can't ever tell a beautiful woman *no*. I was married for sixteen years to someone who couldn't tell *any* woman *no*."

*Oh fuck.*

Okay, yeah on the surface, she was right; she was being irrational, however, he understood why. But he wasn't like her dead husband and the comparison was a little insulting, because frankly, the only beautiful woman he wouldn't be able to tell no was standing right in from of him with a bruised face and tears in her eyes. The bruise reminded him she hadn't exactly had the best luck with men.

He touched her hand and she jerked it away from him.

"Brenna, look at me."

When she wouldn't, he tried tilting her chin toward him. She still wouldn't make eye contact with him.

She was fucking stubborn. And gorgeous.

He tried another tack. Standing up and wrapping his arms around her waist, he pressed his forehead against hers.

"Brenna," he uttered in a low voice. "Look at me."

This time she did, just as a tear spilled out onto her cheek. Then another. And another.

He put his hands around her face, careful of her bruise, and looked into her eyes.

"I'm not Danny."

She glanced away again, and he leaned his head over in front of where she was looking, so she had no choice but to return his gaze as he continued.

"I'm not Danny. There are only two females I couldn't say no to, and they both happen to live in this house."

Her tears continued to fall and it seemed like an eternity before she whispered, "I know you're not Danny. I'm sorry," then choked back a sob. "I'm so embarrassed for getting this upset over something so stupid."

A gorgeous woman, with a bruise on her face, who he'd made love to repeatedly over the last few days was standing before him crying because she was embarrassed for getting upset with him. Braless, in a nightie that barely covered her naked ass, no less. What the hell was he supposed to do now?

Kiss her, of course.

So he did. Thoroughly. Trying to leave her with no doubt about how he felt about her.

*Shit.*

How *did* he feel about her?

As his tongue sought hers out, he conceded.

He fucking adored her.

# Chapter Sixteen

*Brenna*

She couldn't believe she hadn't scared Ron away with her little tantrum that morning. Sometime while she was in the middle of cooking breakfast, she knew how ridiculous she was behaving and was embarrassed. Then she didn't know how to fix it, so she acted even more like a petulant child.

But instead of getting mad, Ron kissed her.

And kissed her.

And kissed her.

Still ashamed of herself, Brenna broke the kiss and walked over to the refrigerator—for what, she had no idea, she just needed to distance herself from him. As she opened the door, Ron's arms came around both sides of her with his palms flat against the panel, her body caught between his muscular frame and the cold stainless steel.

She felt his bare chest against her back and his warm breath on her neck.

"I wasn't done with you," he growled in her ear.

She closed her eyes when he grabbed both her tits in his hands and pulled her into him so her body molded to his. Kissing her neck while kneading her breasts, he grinded his hips against her ass.

His cock was hard under his jeans, and she wanted nothing more than to set it free. When she tried to turn so she could unbutton his Levi's, Ron tightened his grip on her tits.

"Stay still," he whispered against her cheek.

He tugged on her nipples over her chemise before releasing her breasts from his firm hold. She gasped when he clutched her under her jaw with one hand, but did as he told her and didn't move.

"Good girl," he whispered in her ear, then slipped his other arm around her body and pulled her nightie up around her waist.

Why the fuck did she like it when he told her she was a good girl?

He slid his hand up and down her slit, and she couldn't believe how wet she already was. He explored her folds with authority before gruffly plunging two fingers into her wet pussy, still rubbing his denim against her backside.

She tried, really, at least for a second, not to respond, but she couldn't help but moan while pushing back against him as his fingers deftly worked at a furious pace between her legs.

In and out, over and over, hard and deep inside her.

Maybe it was the angle and swiftness of his hand inside her pussy, or his commanding grip under her jaw, or her emotional state of mind, whatever it was, in minutes she felt her impending orgasm creep up from her toes. Her breathing came in short gasps.

He pressed his palm down hard on her clit, which was all it took to send her shuddering. He released his grip from her jaw and wrapped his now-free arm around her waist in a bear hug, bending his body with hers as she writhed in ecstasy, his fingers continued to thrust into her dripping pussy until she pushed his hand away.

The next sound she heard was his zipper, followed by his jeans being pushed down. He spun her around, grabbed her under her bare bottom, and lifted her body. She wrapped her legs around him, and felt the smooth refrigerator door against her back while he pushed his cock into her. Her mouth was agape while she watched his face as he fucked her hard.

*Hard.*

Her tits bounced with every thrust, the sound of his balls slapping her ass rang out in the kitchen.

She loved how deep he rammed into her and wondered how long he could go in that position. Surprisingly, it took a while before he spun them around and deposited her on the nearest counter surface.

He continued his deep strokes, but they were longer and slower. Cupping her face in his hand and bringing his lips to hers, he continued to plunge into her. His tongue explored her mouth, and he groaned when she lifted her legs higher for him. He held her under her knees and increased his speed. Brenna looked him in his eyes just before he climaxed and closed his, all while holding her hips tight against him.

His breathing stilled and he lifted her off the counter, still inside her, then dropped down in a table chair with Brenna straddling him. He continued kissing her like he had after she apologized, while his hands gently stroked her back.

If this was his version of makeup sex, she was going to pick a fight every day.

# Chapter Seventeen

*Ron*

"Can we order takeout later for lunch?"

Ron grinned at her when she walked back in the kitchen after her shower.

"I really can cook, ya know," was her offended reply.

Ron arched his eyebrows but didn't say anything else.

"Who do you think made those cookies you've been munching on for the past few days?"

Her words prompted him to grab another from the plate on the counter and take a bite.

He turned the football shaped cookie over, examining it.

"You made these?" he said after he swallowed his bite. "They're delicious!"

"I know my way around a kitchen. I was just having an off morning."

Her evil smile let him know his breakfast was no accident.

He smirked.

*Note to self, no fighting before meals.*

At least not if she's preparing it.

Actually, he didn't consider today a fight as much as a need for reassurance on her part. What kind of a dick had her husband been that he made her that insecure?

Jerking his head toward the door, he asked, "Feel like a walk on the beach?"

"I'd love to. Let me grab a sweater."

While Brenna went upstairs to her closet, Ron whistled for Zona, and when the dog heard the patio door open, she came sliding around the corner. It was hard for her to get traction on the wood floors, and she reminded him of Scooby-Doo.

"Come on, girl!" he called, and she bound out the door past him onto the patio.

While they waited for Brenna, he kneeled down to scratch the dog behind her ears and told her she got him in trouble earlier.

"So *last time* really means *last time*, from now on."

"Aw, don't do that because of me," Brenna said from the doorway.

Ron smiled and stood up. "Ready?"

Brenna slipped her arm through his. "Ready."

He kissed her hair. "There's a lot I would do because of you."

With her head on his shoulder, she hugged his bicep with both arms, and they made their way to the sand.

"Have I told you today how beautiful you are?"

She touched her face at her bruise and snorted, "Oh yeah, gorgeous."

"You are. Both inside and out."

He meant it. Even with her discolored face, she was stunning. He loved his time with her. She was smart and witty, but the more he got to know her, the more he sensed an air of sadness about her.

"So, are you working on a screenplay now?"

She gave a fake smile when she shook her head. "I've had writer's block."

He nodded in understanding until she added, "For about the last eleven years."

"Eleven years is a long time."

"Yeah," she said wistfully. "I lost my mojo somewhere along the way."

Kissing her hand, he smiled. "Well, I hope you find it again soon."

He couldn't quite read her expression when she answered, "You never know, stranger things have happened. Sometimes inspiration hides in plain sight, and you just need to look at things differently to rediscover it."

They strolled farther along the sand, and she picked up sea glass while they walked and chatted.

Storm clouds started to move in so they turned around, making it back just as the first raindrops hit the ground.

It must have been serendipity that they decided to spend the rest of the day snuggled up on the couch watching movies with wine and snacks. Ron was flipping through the movie channels when a film popped up he was familiar with, so he paused and asked, "Do you want to watch this one?"

Brenna gave him a sideways glance like he was teasing her.

"You want to watch this one?"

He didn't understand why she didn't believe him. "Well, yeah. I know it's old, but it's kind of a classic."

She tilted her head at him. "A classic, huh?"

"Why? Don't you like it?"

"Oh, I didn't say I didn't like it. I love it. I'm just surprised you do."

Ron still felt like he was missing something. "Why does that surprise you?"

She laughed. "Because I wrote it."

"*You* wrote *Blue Oasis*?"

She seemed embarrassed at his reaction and just nodded.

"Do you know how many times in my life I've quoted scenes from that movie?"

"Probably a few," she acknowledged.

"Brenna, I've literally been saying things that you wrote for years. That blows my mind."

She chuckled. "So do you want to still watch it?"

"Hell yes, I do!"

Watching the movie was bizarre now. He'd had to have seen it at least a dozen times, but this time, sitting next to her, knowing she was responsible for the story and the dialogue, made it so much different. He tried to imagine what was happening in her life when she wrote the story; what made her create certain scenes? What inspired her?

He stopped her when she tried to turn it off before he saw her name in the credits. When it appeared, he couldn't stop smiling at her.

*My breathtaking Brenna is brilliant.*

*Say that five times fast.*

"I'm just awestruck. What else have you written?"

She cast a thoughtful glance upwards and breathed a heavy sigh. "Well, let's see. *Warning Track*, and—"

His voice went up an octave. "You wrote *Warning Track*?"

Nodding her head slowly while biting her bottom lip, she replied, "I did. It was my first story ever picked up by a studio. I met Danny when I was doing the research for it."

He'd been curious about how they'd met but hadn't felt it was an appropriate question to ask yet. He also realized he was probably wrong in assuming she needed Danny to make sure she was taken care of financially. She probably was doing just fine on her own.

"How long were you together?"

He hoped it was okay to be talking about her deceased husband, but since she brought him up, Ron thought it was safe.

"Technically, seventeen years total. Sixteen married and we dated for a year before we got married. I should have left after nine."

Thinking of her unhappy for eight years made him sad. He gathered from her outburst earlier that Danny hadn't been faithful. Why had she stayed with him?

"We were in the middle of a divorce when he died."

*I guess she hadn't.*

He was glad. Not that she was getting divorced, but that she wasn't going to stay in a shitty marriage. Although, eight years was far too long to be unhappy without doing something about it.

Brenna didn't offer anything more, and he didn't want to pry, so he returned his attention back to her accomplishments.

"So why didn't you tell me you are a famous screenwriter?"

Brenna burst out laughing. "Well, for one thing, I'm more of a has-been than I am famous. And secondly, it's not something you can easily work into a conversation."

He smiled and shook his head in awe of her. "I honestly had no idea. You're kind of a big deal."

"You thought I was just another pretty face who married well," she teased as she got up to refill her wine glass.

He hated to admit it, but yeah, that's exactly what he'd thought.

She poured more wine and asked him if he wanted more. He finished the contents of his glass and stood up, making his way to the sink.

"I should probably get going before I wear out my welcome," he said while he rinsed his glass.

The frown on her face indicated that was not the case.

"But I haven't even made dinner! I need to prove I really can cook."

He walked over to her and wrapped his arms around her waist to pull her into him.

"She writes, she cooks, she's amazing in bed... what *can't* you do, you beautiful woman?"

She grinned. "Well, I can't sew."

Ron threw his head back and laughed. "Ah, I knew you had to have a flaw somewhere."

Her face was solemn when she looked up at him. "I'd love it if you could stay. Do you have to go?"

"I just don't want you to get sick of me, darlin'."

She laid her head against his chest. "Not possible," she whispered.

# Chapter Eighteen

*Brenna*

She was ecstatic when Ron said he could stay. She needed this dinner to be perfect to make up for the awful breakfast she'd served him that morning. She wasn't sure why, but she wanted to prove her domestic worth to him.

"What can I make you for dinner? You must be starving."

They'd opted for movie snacks instead of lunch.

"*You* aren't making me anything. *We* can make something together," he countered.

*What the heck? He wants to cook with me?*

*Yep, too good to be true.*

"Well, what are you in the mood for? We could grill some filets with baked potatoes and veggies, or we could make stir-fry with chicken, veggies, and brown rice, or spaghetti and salad? Or if you have something else in mind, I'm open to that too."

He gave her a sly grin.

"*For dinner*," she scolded.

"Okay, okay…" He kissed the back of her neck and murmured, "You'll be dessert."

They decided on steak. The prep work was easy, so his part was wrapping the potatoes in tinfoil.

While he was outside putting the potatoes on the grill, she decided to set the table in the formal dining room. She rarely ate in there, except for holidays and parties, but for some reason, she felt being with him tonight was a special occasion that warranted the good china.

As she arranged the silverware around the place settings, she looked up with a start to see him leaning against the doorjamb watching her.

"Oh my goodness! I didn't see you there," she said with her hand over her heart.

Ron cocked his head. "I'm sorry, I didn't mean to scare you. I was just enjoying watching you."

She furrowed her brow. "You were enjoying watching me set the table?"

He walked into the room and took her in his arms.

"Yeah, I was. I love that you're going to the trouble to sit us in here. It makes me feel special."

With a shy smile, she confided, "You are special."

In her head she screamed, *So hurry up and let me know what's wrong with you before I fall head-over-heels in love!*

He kissed her lips softly, then whispered, "You are too."

They finished preparing dinner, and he came in from the patio with the steaks and potatoes on a platter and headed straight to the table while she put the vegetables in a serving bowl in the kitchen.

When she walked in the dining room, she found he had lit long taper candles and dimmed the lights.

"What a perfect touch," she said as she sat down.

They had a wonderful meal; wine and conversation flowed easily, and it wasn't until they noticed the candles had burnt all the way down that they realized how long they'd been sitting there.

She rinsed the dishes to put in the dishwasher while he cleared the table. When he brought the last plates from the dining room, he stood behind her at the sink with his arms around her waist and his chin on her shoulder.

"Thank you for dinner. And for a wonderful day," he murmured as she leaned back against him.

She smiled at his omission of her outburst earlier. "Thank you for letting me make breakfast up to you. I'm glad you were able to stay."

What she wanted to say was, *thank you for not letting me scare you off this morning. You're wonderful, and I've loved spending time with you.*

"Me too," he whispered, squeezing her middle.

# Chapter Nineteen

*Ron*

They had a spirited conversation on their way to her bedroom about who they considered the best musical artists of all time. He made his case for the Beatles and followed her into her closet.

"I don't disagree with you about the impact they've had on music," she countered as she shimmied out of her jeans. "But I think you're discounting the effect solo artists like Michael Jackson and Elvis also had."

When the denim was at her thighs, Ron sat down on an upholstered bench and watched her finish taking her clothes off. Looking at her creamy skin, he no longer gave a fuck about the point he was trying to make and stopped talking; instead just watched, mesmerized by her.

*God, she's beautiful.*

She must have realized he was no longer talking when she got down to only her bra and panties and cocked her head at him.

Holding out his hand, Ron gestured for her to come to him. When she was within arm's reach, he pulled her onto his lap and nuzzled her hair. It was soft and smelled like her shampoo. He took a deep breath in, trying to fill his lungs with her scent. Slowly stroking one hand up and down her spine, he smiled when he felt goosebumps spread over her body.

His fingers continued caressing her back, and he pulled away from her hair to silently watch her face. Her lips were parted and her eyes closed.

"You really are breathtaking," he murmured against her skin while gently sucking on her shoulders. Remembering how she had put her name in his phone, he whispered, "My breathtaking Brenna."

He was happy when she sighed and whispered, "Thank you."

"Mmm, that's my girl."

He loved how silky her skin felt and was in no hurry to stop caressing her body. When her hand slid down to his crotch, he pulled it away.

"Just let me enjoy you, sugar."

Brenna closed her eyes again and mewled at his touch, but soon he felt her body stiffen and she shifted in his lap. She seemed uneasy with all the attention he was giving her.

He pushed her hair behind her ear. "What's the matter, darlin'?"

The corners of her mouth turned upward when she confessed, "I feel selfish just sitting here. Like I should be giving instead of taking."

With that single statement, he felt he had a good idea of what her love life must have been like with her husband. The man could play second base, Ron would give him that, but it seemed he didn't have a clue when it came to appreciating his hot wife.

He raked his fingers through her hair and in a low voice told her, "Brenna, you are giving to me by letting me hold you. I am getting so much pleasure from having you in my arms. Being able to touch your skin."

He kissed her shoulder. "Smell you."

Moving his lips toward her neck, he continued. "Taste you. Feel you. You are amazing."

He buried his face in her hair as he simultaneously ran his fingers down her spine and between her breasts.

"It'd be selfish of you to deny me this," he breathed in her ear.

He heard a soft whimper.

"Just let me experience you," he whispered in her ear.

The clasp of her bra was undone in a second, and he slid it down her arms to casually drop on the ground. Maneuvering her bottom so she was straddling him, he looked up into her eyes before feasting on her breasts.

His touch was gentle at first. He ran his index finger along the underside of her boobs and planted soft kisses above her chest. When he felt her breathing quicken, he cupped one tit firmly in his hand and kneaded it while he continued to kiss her above her chest. With her soft flesh pushed up toward his mouth, he heard her gasp when he sucked on her stiff nipple.

Again, she tried to rub his cock through his pants.

Grabbing her wrist, he growled, "Brenna, don't make me tie you up. Because I will and I'll rather enjoy it."

He couldn't tell by her reaction if the idea turned her on or scared her. Maybe both. But she didn't try touching him again, and he continued his enjoyment of her tits.

She grinded her hips against his when he flicked his tongue over her rosy peaks.

*Mmm, what is that wonderful smell?*

He reached between her legs and found the satin fabric of her panties completely drenched.

"Fuck, darlin'. You are so wet."

She swallowed hard and nodded. "That's what you do to me."

Ron groaned and pressed his hard cock against the wet material covering her pussy.

"That's what you do to me."

"Please let me touch you," she begged. "Please."

Ron smiled and stood up. With her legs wrapped around his middle, he carried her out of the closet and into the bedroom, where he deposited her at the head of the bed and stepped back to take his jeans off.

"Unless you don't mind those getting ripped off you," he said as he gestured to her underwear. "I suggest you take them off."

She must have been related to Houdini, because the next time he looked, her panties had disappeared, and she was completely naked with her elbows propped back on the pillows while she watched him finish stripping.

He crawled up the bed on all fours, almost as if he were stalking her, and pulled her by her ankles to slide her onto her back. Continuing his ascent up the bed between her legs, he licked her thighs as he went. When he reached her sex, he spread her apart with both hands and groaned when he saw how slick with her juices she was.

"Mmm mmm mmm," he hummed, pressing his lips together. "You look delicious. I can't wait to taste you," he said right before he dipped his tongue between her pussy lips.

With long, flat strokes, he licked her up and down her entire length, pausing to move his tongue in circles around her clit before returning his attention to her folds. The next time he came to her clit, he sucked on it, and she cried out, thrusting her hips into his face. He worked on her little nub with his tongue while he moved a finger in and out of her. Her breathing changed, and he slid two fingers in deep to locate her g-spot. Ron wiggled his fingers as he thrust them inside her. His mouth continued its assault on her clit. She arched her back off the bed, and he felt her getting wetter.

"That's it, darlin'. Come all over my face."

She gasped in between moaning his name.

He flicked her clit faster with his tongue while pumping his fingers deep into her pussy. The sound of how wet she was as he finger fucked her was immensely satisfying.

Brenna cried out as she bucked her hips and he felt her come; her pussy contracted around his fingers while her delicious sweetness flooded his hand.

He licked her thighs where her wetness had smeared.

"You taste like candy," he moaned as he eagerly lapped at her legs. "So fucking delicious."

She grabbed both sides of his face, drew him up to her mouth, and kissed him passionately. He hadn't thought it was possible for his dick to get any harder.

Apparently, he was wrong.

He positioned himself at her entrance, and when she sucked his tongue into her mouth, he pushed his cock inside her. She felt just as fucking good as the first time he got his dick inside her sweet little pussy. She had the goldilocks of pussies... not too loose and not too tight. His cock fit inside juuuust right.

She met him thrust for thrust with her hands in his hair as she looked into his eyes.

"You feel so good," she whispered. "Your cock is amazing."

They had a nice, steady rhythm as he continued fucking her. He didn't want to come; he was enjoying it too much. But when she raised her legs in the air and commanded, "Fuck me harder," all bets were off.

Sitting up on his knees, he grabbed the back of her thighs and increased his tempo. Her tits jiggled with every push, and she moaned, "Oh my God, yes! Don't stop!"

He knew she climaxed again, and he continued thrusting into her, pulling out just in time to pump his load on her chest. He'd been envisioning his cum all over her tits since the first minute of meeting her. She didn't seem to mind as she smeared it all over her boobs like expensive lotion with a smile.

*Is this woman for real?*

# Chapter Twenty

*Brenna*

She got a phone call the next morning from Cassie.

"What's up, little sister?"

"How's the face?"

She absentmindedly touched her bruise. "Better, thanks."

"Have you heard from your hero?"

Brenna glanced over at Ron next to her in bed, reading email on his phone.

"Um, I have," she answered cryptically.

With a smile, Ron leaned over and kissed her, whispering, "I'm gonna take Zona for a run."

Brenna put her hand over the microphone and mouthed, "Okay."

"*Oh my God*, he's still there isn't he?" Cassie said loud enough so when Brenna glanced at Ron, he grinned and gave her a wink.

"Maybe," was all Brenna would answer. At least in front of Ron.

"Has he even gone home?"

"No."

"This is so awesome!" Cassie squealed. Then chanted like she was on the playground, "Brenna's got a boyfriend."

Brenna couldn't help but laugh at her sister's juvenile behavior.

"How old are you?" she chastised.

"Old enough to know what you've been doing the past few days," Cassie lobbed back.

She had no retort, so Brenna simply asked with a huff, "Is there a reason you called?"

"There is, but I want to know more about G.I. Joe. How is he in bed? How many times did he make you come? Is he a good kisser? Is he—"

Brenna cut the younger girl off. "Fantastic. I lost count. And definitely."

"*You lost count*? Are you fucking serious? I hate you, you bitch."

"Anyway…" Brenna wanted to change the subject. "Why are you bothering me so early in the morning?"

"Well, I hope I wasn't interrupting *anything*."

Brenna didn't take the bait. "You weren't. Yet."

"You are such a whore! I'm telling Mom!" Cassie teased.

"Go ahead, and I'll tell her about Dr. Feelgood."

"Aw, why'd you have to go and bring him up? He broke my heart."

"Cassandra Jo Sullivan, if I thought for a second that were true, I'd feel bad. But I know you. It was not *your* heart that got broken in that relationship."

"Well, he kinda broke my heart. I mean, we were having so much fun, and then he had to start talking about feelings and shit. It broke my heart to stop seeing him! He's a sexy pediatrician who deals with kids all day long, what the hell did he need any at home for?"

That was her sister. Serial dater. The minute anyone got too attached, she was outta there.

"Um, probably because he was in love with you, you moron!"

"Yeah, well, I dodged that bullet. I heard he got married, had three babies, and then got caught having an affair with his nurse."

"Really?" Brenna asked incredulously.

"No. He would never do that, come on. But he did get married and has a kid."

"You are such a shit. Why did you call me?"

"Well, funny that we are talking about dating...." Cassie began.

"Yeah?"

"Do you happen to know if Luke is dating anyone?"

*Victory*. Could Brenna call 'em or what?

"Well, I'm not one hundred percent sure, but I don't think so. I'm assuming you want me to find out?"

"If you can without it being obvious you're asking for me, then yes. If you can't, then no."

"I'll see what I can figure out."

Cassie giggled into the phone. "God, I feel like I'm sixteen, asking you to find out about a boy for me."

"He's a good guy, not to mention he's gorgeous. I don't blame you. I think you two would really get along great."

"Hey, speaking of getting along. I want to hang out with you and G.I. Joe, and make sure he's good enough for my big sis."

"Okay, A) stop calling him G.I. Joe, his name is Ron, and B) what are you doing for dinner tonight?"

"*Really*? I was just kidding. I didn't think there was any way you'd really say yes."

Brenna conceded, "Well, I like him, and I want you to get to know him."

"Oooh, this sounds like it's getting serious! I am available for you to feed me tonight. What time?"

Brenna hung up the phone and wondered how she was going to ask Ron to have dinner with her sister. She hoped it wasn't too soon, and she didn't freak him out.

"Only one way to find out," she muttered as she headed to the shower.

****

*Ron*

Brenna was standing at the kitchen island, cooking and humming when Ron walked up from the beach, wet from his quick plunge into the ocean to cool down. Zona, excited from their run, tried to get him to play fetch again.

He loved that goofy dog. She seemed to still be growing into her body and hadn't gotten used to her long legs. Yet, for still being so young, she obeyed his commands really well. Hell, she listened better than half of the new recruits.

Brenna was showered and dressed, and it looked like she had makeup on because her bruise was barely noticeable.

"Hey beautiful, do you have plans today?" he asked from the doorway as he grabbed a towel from the rack on the patio and briskly rubbed it over his body before stepping inside.

"No, I just felt like getting up and around. Are you hungry?"

He stopped on the other side of the island and watched her stir what looked like pancake batter.

"I am. Let me hop in the shower, and I'll be back down. I think I better head home later, I'm sure the mail is piled up and the poor cat is probably starving."

*"You have a cat?!"*

He cocked his head and shot her a look that said she should know better.

"Brenna, I go overseas for months at a time, of course I don't have a cat. I was teasing you."

"Oh," she replied with pink cheeks.

He came around the island with a smirk and rubbed between her legs. "I only want one pussy in my life."

She shook her head and returned his smirk. "You're incorrigible!"

He kissed her softly on the mouth and caressed her hips while whispering, "Maybe you can redeem me."

She stood on her tiptoes and kissed him back. "Maybe."

With his eyes twinkling and his face inches from hers, he gave her a wink. "I think you should at least try. You owe it to your country."

She played along. "Well, I am a good patriot. If it's for my country..."

The corner of the right side of his mouth lifted. "Mmm, you are definitely a good..." He paused as he kissed her neck. "Patriot. The best patriot I've ever known, as a matter of fact."

He gently tugged on her bottom lip with his mouth.

She pressed her body against his. "Well how can I not be? You're such an amazing... Marine."

Their kiss got more intense, and his tongue slipped between her lips. She grinded against him harder, and he knew she could feel how aroused she made him.

Pulling away, he groaned, "You keep kissing me like that darlin' and I won't be going anywhere but back upstairs to bed."

With a devilish smile, she retorted, "Would that be so bad?"

"Not in the least. It's a shame you've already showered."

"Mmm, that is a shame. But it is lucky for you because I'm going to make you a nice breakfast while you take yours. Do you like pancakes? Eggs? Sausage?"

He grinned. "Well, yes, I normally like all of those things, but yesterday..."

"I already told you! I was having an off day! I'm going to redeem myself this morning. I promise."

She did redeem herself. Breakfast was delicious, and he felt a little melancholy helping her clean up; he was going to be leaving soon.

As he loaded the last dish into the dishwasher, she asked him, "Can I talk you into having dinner tonight with me and my sister? I'm making lasagna."

Dinner with her again tonight? Fuck yeah, she could talk him into that. She could pretty much talk him into giving her a kidney at this point.

"Sounds great. What time?"

"I was thinking about six-thirty, but you can come any time before that you want. The lasagna takes a while to bake."

"I'll bring the wine and dessert."

That made leaving her a helluva lot easier. Knowing he was going to be back with her in less than six hours put a spring in his step, but he still wasn't going to pass up a chance to give her a proper farewell kiss.

They stood in her foyer for at least ten minutes as they said their goodbyes. Every time he made it a step closer to the door, one of them would go in for "just one more kiss."

He smiled the whole drive home, and when he looked into the rearview mirror and saw her lipstick on his face, he didn't wipe it off. He considered it a badge of honor. Better than any medal he'd ever received, that was for damn sure.

Ron spent his afternoon putzing around his house and thinking about Brenna. They'd been spoiled with the amount of time he was able to spend with her. How would she react when he was gone for a whole month? Not only would he be gone, but there were times when it would be impossible for him to even communicate. Then what?

He couldn't tell how much maintenance she was going to need from him, but he knew she deserved whatever amount she required. He'd just have to make sure to pamper and spoil her when he was home and hopefully that would make up for his absences.

Fuck, he prayed that was enough.

Because he was a goner when it came to her.

# Chapter Twenty One

*Brenna*

The doorbell rang and Zona raced to the door. Cassie had just left to go to the store for her, borrowing Brenna's sports car in the process, of course. In the middle of layering lasagna noodles, she yelled from the kitchen, "Come in!"

Zona gave her welcoming howl, the one she reserved for the people she loved. Brenna couldn't help but smile, thinking Ron had come back early. So when it was Luke who walked through the kitchen doorway, she jerked her head in surprise. She wondered if his ears were burning from her earlier conversation with Cassie.

"Hey! What are you doing here?"

"Sorry to come over without calling. I'm out running errands and realized I took Zona's leash home by accident the other night, so I thought I'd drop it off."

"You didn't have to make a special trip, but that was very sweet of you. You're all dressed up." This seemed like the perfect time to subtly ask if he was seeing someone. "Got a hot date?"

Luke grinned and shook his head. "No, meeting some friends from work at the bar later. I'm not going home before going out, so I got ready before I left."

"Well, you look very handsome. Women are going to be fighting over you."

He shrugged but kept his grin. "I hope not. I don't wanna have to arrest anyone tonight." He looked around. "Is Cassie here? I saw her car out front."

"She just ran to the store for me."

Zona whined at his feet, so he bent down to pet her.

"Does she need to go out?" he asked when the pup kept whining.

"She might. Would you mind? My hands are a little dirty."

Luke took Zona out without leashing her up. No one ever leashed Zona, she was such a good girl and stayed close.

*That's odd. So how did he end up with Zona's lead? And isn't it a coincidence my sister's car is parked out front when he decides to stop by?*

He and the dog walked back inside just as Brenna put the dish in the oven.

"My mom used to make lasagna every Sunday when I was growing up," Luke said as he slid onto a barstool.

"Do you want to stay for dinner? It's just me, Ron, and Cassie so there's plenty."

He shifted in his seat at the sound of her sister's name. "Cassie's staying?"

Brenna turned around to hide her grin. "Yeah. She should be back pretty soon." Glancing at the clock, she added, "I'm kind of surprised she's not yet."

And as if on cue, the door from the garage opened, and her baby sister yelled out in her best Ricky Ricardo impersonation, "Lucy, I'm home!" Zona sprinted to the door. The lab mix was in heaven; all of her favorite people were there at the same time. The pup started sprinting laps through the house; she was excited and needed to burn off energy. She zoomed past Cassie and almost knocked her out at the knees.

"Goddammit, Zona!" Cassie yelled while grabbing the doorjamb to keep from falling.

Luke was up to help her sister before Brenna could bat an eye.

"Oh, hey. When did you get here?" She asked as she took the hand he offered.

"I just stopped by to drop off Zona's leash. I took it home by accident."

Brenna gave a small smirk.

*Sure you did. By 'accident.'*

"I invited him to stay for dinner, but he never answered me," Brenna teased.

Luke turned his attention to Brenna. "I'm sorry. I'd love to stay."

Zona sprinted by yet again, and Luke knelt down to grab her collar and calm her down.

Cassie gave her sister an excited smile with raised eyebrows.

"Wow, I didn't notice earlier, but your face looks good," she said as she passed Brenna on her way to the refrigerator. Opening it, she called with her head inside the door, "Now can I have some wine?"

"Yeah, no more errands for you. It's on the shelf to your right. Pour me a glass too, will you? Luke? Wine? Beer? Water? Soda?"

"I'll have a beer."

The doorbell rang, and once again Zona bound to the door.

Brenna quickly washed her hands and dried them on her apron as she walked toward the front door. Zona must have seen Ron through the side windows because she barked excitedly, urging her owner to answer the door and let him in.

*I know the feeling, girl.*

Brenna opened the door with a smile and without a word, Ron kissed her at the threshold before stepping inside.

He was holding wine and a pink box from the bakery when he walked in and broke out into a big grin when he saw her eyeing it.

"Is that what I think it is?" she asked in a hopeful voice.

He winked and said, "I told you I was going to keep these in stock." After kissing her again, he looked her up and down, and smirked. "Nice apron." Moving closer to her ear, he lowered his voice to murmur, "I wouldn't mind coming home to you in nothing but that and a pair of heels."

"Oh, I'd have to have pearls on, too," she said over her shoulder as she turned toward the kitchen.

He threw his head back and laughed then followed her.

Cassie pounced on Ron the second he walked in the room, kissing his cheek and taking the wine and dessert from him. He nodded his head at Luke sitting at the island.

"I wondered whose car was in the driveway. No Jeep tonight?"

"Nah, not tonight. It's supposed to get cold later."

They had a terrific dinner, and Brenna couldn't help but notice the electricity in the air between Cass and Luke. The dishes were loaded in the dishwasher, and they all sat at the table, laughing and drinking while they waited to have dessert, when Ron's phone rang.

He looked down at the screen and grimaced. Brenna recognized the ring tone. It was the same one she'd heard on New Year's Eve, when he was called away right as things had started to heat up between them.

"I apologize. I have to take this," he said as he stood up from the table and walked toward the patio.

*Why can't he answer the damn phone in front of me?*

She smiled at Cassie and Luke, trying not to convey she was bothered. She was a master at pretending she didn't care; she had done it for so many years with Danny. Except her sister knew her too well and eyed her suspiciously.

She needed to get away from Cassie's hard stare, so she emptied the contents of her glass and got up from the table, asking, "Anybody want more wine?" and not waiting for a reply.

With the phone still to his ear, Ron peeked his head in the door. "Hey Bren? Do you own the property between the house and the water?"

*What an odd question.*

"Yes... why?"

He ignored her and just said, "Thanks," then stepped back out on the patio.

Brenna and Cassie traded an unspoken *what the hell?* Luke said nothing while he observed the two women.

Ron came back inside as Brenna poured another glass of wine. She knew what was coming next.

He came over and wrapped his arms around her waist from behind and murmured against her hair, "Darlin', I have to go."

The corners of her mouth turned down as she set the bottle on the counter next to her glass, but she nodded her head and sighed. "I figured."

He turned her around and pinned her between him and the counter. She rubbed his arms while offering a weak smile. "Do you have time for dessert, or do you have to leave right now?"

He studied her face carefully. "I do have time. They're going to come get me. Is it okay if I leave my truck here?"

Brenna stood on her tiptoes and kissed his jawline. "Of course."

He smiled and stroked her back. "Thanks. I need to grab a few things out of it; I'll be right back."

Cassie walked into the kitchen and pulled the cake Ron had brought from the refrigerator.

"All right, what's so special about this cake?" she asked as she lifted the lid on the pink box.

Brenna set a stack of small plates on the counter and offered Cassie a knife and cake server. She had a handful of dessert spoons in her fist while she smiled at the memory of the first time she tried it.

"It's from the bakery that made Travis and Ava's wedding cake. Ron and I shared a slice at their reception, and I practically ate the whole thing."

Her sister giggled. "Yeah, it's chocolate, I can definitely see you doing that."

"See her doing what?" Ron asked as he came through the door with a military duffle bag.

Brenna shook her head. "Eating the whole piece of cake I was supposed to be sharing with you."

He walked over to the patio door and set the bag down, chuckling. "I gladly gave up my half. I got more enjoyment watching you than I ever would have from eating it. Why do you think I brought more over tonight? I couldn't wait to see you have more."

She remembered he had said at the wedding that watching her eat it turned him on.

"I'll be sure to save a piece for when you get back," she purred.

Ron stared at her for a beat, then took her by the hand and pulled her into the hallway. As soon as they were around the corner in the darkened corridor, he held her tight against him and planted his mouth on hers, grabbing a handful of her hair in the process. She eagerly parted her lips as his tongue looked for hers. When he pushed her against the wall and ground his clothed cock against her pussy, all she could think was, do we have time for a quickie?

She got her answer when he pulled away from her.

"We need to stop before I take you upstairs and have my way with you. And get court marshalled because I refuse to get out of your bed and go to work."

With her chest heaving, she nodded her head in agreement. He put his forehead against hers.

"Darlin', I hate having to leave you. I'm not sure when I'll be back."

She touched his cheek with her hand and caressed it up and down. "It's okay. I understand the government needs my boyfriend."

As soon as she said the words, she was mortified they had come out of her mouth.

*My boyfriend? Oh my God, can the earth just swallow me up, please? How the fuck do I recover from this?*

She didn't want him to freak out because she called him her boyfriend after less than a week of dating.

*Who does that?*

Only needy, clingy women, that's who. She did not want him to consider her clingy.

"I mean, not my *boyfriend*. I meant, just my friend who—"

He cut her off by leaning down and kissing her gently.

"Believe me, I'd much rather be here with my *girlfriend*," he said with a tender smile, his lips inches from hers.

His mouth had enveloped hers again when Cassie's voice interrupted from the other room. "Hey lovebirds, are you going to have some of this cake, or should we start without you?"

They broke the kiss laughing, and Brenna called out, "We'll be right there!"

His lips found hers one more time before they went back to the table.

Ron held her chair out, then sat down.

"I apologize for being rude," he directed his attention to her sister who was plating their desserts. With a twinkle in his eye, he continued, "I didn't think you'd appreciate watching me kiss your sister goodbye."

Cassie rolled her eyes as she approached the table, but smiled at Brenna when she set their cake slices in front of them. "Thanks for sparing me."

Ron grinned and grabbed Brenna's hand. Looking in her eyes, he brought her knuckles to his mouth and murmured, "Anything for my girlfriend's sister."

Brenna felt her cheeks flush when she noticed Cassie's eyes go wide, but Brenna didn't say anything, just smiled back at Ron.

Suddenly, she heard what sounded like a helicopter hovering over her house.

*What the hell is going on?*

"My ride's here," Ron said as he stood up.

Brenna stood up with him. "Your ride is a *helicopter*? They're picking you up *in a helicopter*?"

He winked at her. "They're kind of in a hurry to get me back on base."

She walked him to the doorway, where she stared at him with her eyebrows raised and lips pursed, as she slightly shook her head in disbelief. "Um, you're kind of a big deal?"

It was more of a question than a statement. He had said those same words to her just yesterday, except, it appeared he was really the one who was the big deal.

One side of his mouth lifted yet he didn't say anything, just leaned down to try and kiss her one last time, but she pulled her head back.

Furrowing her brow, she asked, "Shouldn't that be something a girl knows about her boyfriend?"

She was only half joking she was upset. But part of her *was* bothered. How did she not know this about him?

He picked up his bag with one hand, then grabbed her tight around the waist with the other and yanked her into him.

"Stay inside. The wind is going to kick up a lot of sand," was all he said before kissing her thoroughly on the mouth.

His kiss made her knees go weak, and she was glad he was holding her close against his strong frame. Luke politely tried not to stare, but Cassie blatantly watched with her mouth agape.

"Take care," he said with another wink when he looked down at her disoriented state. She could only look up at him with a dazed smile.

Ron nodded his head at Luke and told Cassie it was good seeing her, then was out the door.

They all three stood at the French doors to watch the chopper land and Ron get on board. It took less than a minute between when it touched down to when it was airborne again.

After it took off, they were quiet until they could no longer hear it in the distance. Finally, Luke broke the silence.

"*Kind of* a big deal? Brenna, he's a huge fucking deal. He's a two-star general on the rise. Did you really not know?

Cassie looked at her in disbelief, "How could you not know something like that?"

Brenna turned to look at the two. She was wondering the same thing.

# Chapter Twenty-Two

*Brenna*

It'd been a week since Ron had been picked up by helicopter at her house, and she hadn't heard from him since that night. He'd sent her a text three hours after leaving, telling her what a great time he'd had with her, and that he was leaving the country, unsure when he would be back or when he could contact her. That was the last communication she'd received.

She thought about all the things she didn't know about him. How could she care so much for someone she knew so little about?

Then worry about him took over. Was he in danger? What would she do if something happened to him? Their relationship was just getting started, what if the universe decided to play a cruel joke on her and take him away? The very idea made her feel sick to her stomach.

She found herself crying in the shower one morning as her writer's imagination took over, and she envisioned him hurt. She tried not to even allow herself to think anything worse.

It was odd she could miss him as much as she did, considering they'd only met on New Year's Eve. Yet she did. Every morning when she woke up, she wished he were there to wiggle her butt against, and every night she dreamed of him holding her. Oh, and drinking her tea while watching him on his morning run... she got damp just picturing how he looked coming out of the ocean—bare chested, with the swagger of a man who was definitely in charge. He needed to make it back safely to her, and soon.

Apparently, she wasn't the only one who missed Ron. Zona chewed a pair of her favorite shoes the previous night. The dog hadn't ruined anything of hers since she was pissed off when Danielle left for college. Brenna couldn't even be mad at her. She understood the pup was upset and that was her only way of expressing it. Brenna would have chewed up a pair of shoes too, if she'd thought it would make her miss him any less.

He was constantly on her mind. Remembering how they made love, and, well, fucked, but also how she loved just being with him—his laugh, his intelligence, how he always called her darlin', and how he always, always made her feel taken care of. Not to mention the chemistry between them was unlike anything she'd ever experienced.

One quiet afternoon, after she'd taken a walk on the beach, grinning the whole time she thought about him, she did something that surprised the fuck out of herself.

She sat down and started writing.

Brenna knew she needed an outlet for her feelings. Even though she was sad she wasn't physically with Ron, and missed him to pieces, she was also happy. Really happy. He had made her feel wanted and desired. Maybe loved even? She hadn't felt that way in such a long time, and in doing so, he had awoken something inside her, something she had feared was lost forever.

She couldn't believe it when she looked up and realized it was almost midnight. She'd been writing for eleven hours straight. Her muscles ached after working for so long, but it was a good kind of ache. The kind an athlete would feel after an intense workout. She had missed that feeling. Even if nothing more happened between them, Ron had somehow helped her flip a switch, and she was incredibly grateful to him for it.

Thinking about him made her smile. He was the kind of man who made those around him better just by knowing him. She felt privileged he had called her his girlfriend.

Now, whether he really meant it or not might be another story. The more time lapsed from when she last heard from him, the more she began to wonder. She hated feeling insecure, but she was only human.

She came home from the grocery store one afternoon to find his truck gone from her driveway. Part of her was happy he was home safe, but part of her was sad he didn't seem to want to see her. And there was also a tiny part of her that was pissed he hadn't called her.

The tiny pissed off part got a little bigger with every passing day she didn't hear from him. She thought about texting or calling but elected against it. She had her pride; if he wanted to see her, he knew how to get in touch with her. On the fourth day, she was in disbelief he still hadn't reached out to her. Had she imagined the connection? Was it really just an extended one-night stand for him? She would have sworn there had been something special between them

She was really off her game. First Ray, now Ron.

After what seemed like the millionth time of checking her phone, she muttered, "Fuck this," and decided to move her house hunting trip up. She wasn't going to sit around San Diego waiting for him to want to see her. He obviously wasn't as into her as she was him.

"How could I have been so stupid?" she whispered misty-eyed she packed her luggage.

What did she expect? He'd arrive back in the States and want to pick up where they left off? That he'd want to spend every moment of his spare time with her?

*Well, yeah.*

That was exactly what she'd expected. She definitely hadn't anticipated being ignored once he got back. She thought she deserved at least a text or a phone call. Hell, even a booty call would have been better than being ignored altogether.

\*\*\*\*

*Ron*

Ron couldn't wait to have Brenna in his arms again. He had to keep from tapping his foot furiously during his debriefing, then practically ran to his truck once it wrapped up. He'd had one of the majors arrange to get his vehicle from

Brenna's and back on base so it would be waiting for him when he got off the plane.

He wanted to surprise her so he hadn't called, and on his drive to her house, was second-guessing that decision. What if she wasn't home, or worse, had *company?* She didn't seem like the type to label him her boyfriend, then see other men once he left. She hadn't had sex since Danny died. Waiting for him for three weeks should have been a piece of cake.

Unless he woke the beast.

Because she was a wildcat in bed, that was for sure, and she seemed to enjoy sex as much as he did. Which was saying a lot because, fuck, he loved it. Especially with her.

He rang the bell at the beach house and waited, smiling when Zona came charging to the entrance, barking excitedly when she recognized him. Cassie opened the door with a frown and grasped the black lab mix's lime green collar.

"Brenna's not here," she said coldly as she tried holding the pup back.

"Oh. When do you expect her?" Ron kneeled down to pet Zona, so Cassie released her hold and the dog lunged toward him, whining and wiggling while licking his face.

"Um, next week. She's in Tucson." Cassie said it like he was an idiot and should know better.

He stood but kept his hands on Zona's head. "I thought that was next week?"

She appeared to be weighing whether or not to tell him anything. He didn't understand what her problem was.

*Whoa, Brenna's little mini-me. Chill out.*

With a snide tone, she told him, "She decided to leave early. You'd know that if you would have called her when you got back into town."

Being gone for long periods of time was part of his job, and he sure as fuck wasn't going to answer to Brenna's sister for doing his job.

"I got back into town two and a half hours ago. When did she leave?"

She seemed confused and still gave him attitude.

"Yesterday morning. How is it possible you got back two and a half hours ago, when your truck has been gone since last week?"

*Ah, that's why she's being a snot.*

Still, part of him didn't feel like he owed her an explanation. But the part of him that adored her sister knew she was just looking out for Brenna.

"I sent instructions to have it picked up so it'd be waiting for me when I arrived. They should have talked to Brenna when they came to get it. I'm guessing they didn't."

*Someone was going to hear about that.*

His explanation seemed to lighten her up, and she bent sideways at the waist to scratch Zona's back. "No, they came while she was out. She thought you were back and just couldn't be bothered to see her."

"Cassie, I haven't even been to my own house. I came straight here after debriefing, that's how bothered I am to see her."

She couldn't suppress her grin. "Well, she's staying at the Starr Pass JW Marriott, Room 436."

Ron frowned and shook his head. "I can't, I have to be back on base tomorrow at noon."

Cassie offered no sympathy. "Well, at least call her so she knows you didn't blow her off."

*Did she really think I blew her off?*

He could kind of understand why she would think that—kind of. But she should also know him at least well enough to know he would never do that to her. Although, he was just worrying on the way over if she might not be alone.

This was the part about new relationships he hated.

"Oh, by the way." Cassie was looking at her phone. "It's a forty-five-minute flight to Tucson. There's one leaving in ninety minutes, and another that comes back in the morning. Plenty of time to get there, take her dinner, and be back before noon. I'm just sayin'."

He kissed her cheek. "I guess I better get going then."

After one last head scratch for Zona, he turned on his heel and headed back to his truck. With any luck, he would make it to the airport in time to catch a flight to Arizona.

# Chapter Twenty-Three

*Brenna*

She was worn out after another day of house hunting with Graham Turner, a realtor Ava Sterling had recommended. He was a nice-looking man in his early thirties who was very hip and stylish, and eager to sell Brenna a much bigger home than she wanted.

After the third McMansion, she refused to get back in the car until she was sure he understood if he showed her another house like the ones he'd been showing her, he was fired. She wanted a house with character that had a view of the city and the mountains, or a loft downtown in a dog-friendly building, and anything over 2,500 square feet was out of the question. She knew with her budget, Graham was not going to have a problem finding exactly what she wanted.

They'd looked at five that fit precisely what she was looking for, and she narrowed it down to three. She was sitting at the desk in her hotel room, creating a list of pros and cons for each property, when there was a knock on the door. She was a little wary of answering it after her run-in with Ray on New Year's Eve, so she asked, "Who is it?" before sliding the lock.

"It's Ron."

A million thoughts surged through her brain at once.

*Am I imagining things? Did he say Ron?*

*I hope he said Ron.*

*I think I have butterflies!*

*Wait, I'm pissed. Should I open the door?*

And finally, *what the fuck is he doing here?*

"Brenna..." He sounded ominous, like he was warning her she better let him in.

She unlocked the door and found her gorgeous Marine with his hands on either side of the doorjamb, looking down while waiting for her to open the door.

He brought his eyes to hers and fuck if his camel-colored shirt didn't match his hair and eyes perfectly. He looked hot in his camouflage pants tucked in his laced up boots. And oh man, those muscular arms with his tattoo peeking out from under his short sleeves was sexy as hell.

She couldn't help but smile at him standing there. In one movement, he was inside the entry with her face in his hands and his mouth on hers. He kicked the door closed behind him and kissed her like she was his oxygen supply.

She knew she was supposed to be angry at him for blowing her off, but it felt so good to be in his arms again, she decided she could be mad later. Right now, she was just going to enjoy his body against hers and his mouth as it caressed her lips. After all, he did come a long way to see her.

"Darlin'," he said between kisses.

She didn't respond verbally, just kept arching herself against his frame and pulling him closer.

"Brenna."

*Nope, can't hear you. La la la. Just keep kissing me.*

Finally, he pulled away.

*Damn.*

With her face still in his hands, his eyes scanned hers. "I missed you so much," he whispered.

Tears welled in her eyes.

*If you missed me so much, why didn't you call or come see me sooner?*

She knew she couldn't speak without breaking down in a sob.

Ron pulled her tight against him and caressed her back as he kissed her head through her hair.

"I talked to Cassie. Brenna, I haven't been in town. I just got back this afternoon and came straight to see you. How could you think I'd be able to stay away from you for even one day, let alone five?"

Tears rolled down her cheeks. Deep down in her heart, she knew he wouldn't have done that. She just didn't trust her instincts anymore.

"I didn't know what to think," she said in a hushed tone. "All I knew was your truck was gone, and I hadn't heard from you."

He stepped back and tilted her chin to look at him. Through her tears, she could see he was smiling at her and shaking his head.

"Darlin', I don't think you realize the spell you have me under. You're the first thing I think of when I wake up in the morning, and the last thing I think about before I go to sleep. There's no way in hell I wouldn't have been on your doorstep if I were in town. Hell, I'm at your doorstep, and you're not even in the state."

She sniffled and smiled, then hugged him tighter. "I'm so glad you're here."

"I promised your sister I'd take you to dinner. I need to catch a nine-a.m. flight tomorrow, but you've got me all night."

Brenna gave a sinful grin. "How about room service?"

As he unbuttoned her blouse, he sighed. "God, I was hoping you'd suggest that."

She closed her eyes when she felt his mouth at the base of her throat. He groaned as he worked down to her chest. "Fuck, you smell so damn good."

Running her fingers through his hair, she countered, "You *feel* so damn good."

He took her blouse and bra off and pulled her toward the couch. She thought about teasing him but quickly quashed that idea; she needed to feel him inside her too badly. After briefly rubbing his cock over his pants, she had him unbuttoned, unzipped, and naked before pushing him on the couch. She lifted her skirt to her waist and straddled him. He pulled her panties to the side while she eased down on him, moaning as he filled her pussy.

She rode him for about thirty seconds before he growled in her ear, "Sugar, I'm gonna last about five more seconds like this."

He lifted her off him and laid her on her back, then slid her panties off, before taking over to dictate the pace. While controlling the tempo and rhythm, he reached down and rubbed her clit as his delicious cock slid in and out of her. He moved his hand in circles over her nub, quickening the speed in response to her cries.

"Oh my God, baby, just like that," she moaned as she edged toward the cliff.

"I have missed fucking this wet pussy," he growled and increased the pressure of his fingers. Thrusting into her, over and over, he worked his hand in unison with his cock.

Flinging one leg over the couch so she was completely spread out in front of him, Brenna lifted her hips to meet his. Ron leaned over and sucked on her tits while maintaining his attention to her pussy. He felt so fucking good, and she felt her stomach muscles tighten when her impending climax started to creep from her toes.

"Oh God, Ron, don't stop!" she gasped.

When he gently bit down on her nipple, she arched against him and clung to his back while crying out in ecstasy. Her movements became uncoordinated, and she convulsed as she came.

"Ohhhh yessss!" she moaned repeatedly.

He continued fucking her and buried his head in her neck, holding her close while she rode her orgasmic wave. She kissed his mouth and met his thrusts again. Every nerve ending in her body was sensitive, and she relished the feeling of his skin on hers as he continued plunging deep inside her.

Ron sat back on his knees and held her legs as he pumped furiously into her. She could tell by his breathing and his moans that he was going to come. He slammed into her hard then grabbed her hips and went still before letting out a roar. She felt the streams of cum hit the inside of her walls and took great delight knowing she'd caused him to orgasm.

He lay still and silent for a few seconds with his eyes closed, then smiled when he opened them and leaned down to kiss her on the mouth.

"Thanks for coming all this way to see me," she whispered when he broke the kiss.

"Darlin', I'd crawl here to see you."

She couldn't help but smile. He had a way of making her feel so important and special. She wondered if she made him feel the same, because he was definitely important and special to her. She hoped she did half as good a job as he did conveying it.

"Come on, baby, I need to feed you. I'll bet you're starving and tired from traveling all day."

He gave her a grin as he stood up. "Guilty."

They ordered room service and ate in their pj's. Well, Ron was in his underwear, and Brenna put on a royal blue silk cami and boy shorts pajama set.

When they finished their meal, they lay down on the bed. Ron wrapped his arms around her middle and put his head on her chest while she stroked his hair.

He couldn't tell her much about where he'd been or what he'd been doing, so that part of their conversation was brief. He did tell her he wasn't sure when he'd have to go again, but knew it was going to be soon.

The idea of him leaving again made her melancholy, so she changed the subject.

"I've found a few houses in my search. I wish you could stay and let me show them to you tomorrow."

He hugged her tighter and absent-mindedly kissed the skin on her chest.

"Come home with me in the morning. We'll come back together Friday night and look at them Saturday," he suggested.

It was tempting, Friday was only the day after tomorrow. She wanted to spend more time with him, especially if he was going to be gone again soon. Not seeing him for three weeks had been torture.

"I want to, I'm just worried they'll be sold before the weekend."

She felt him nod his head. "I get it."

They laid there in silence until he lifted his head, "So when are you coming back to San Diego?"

He had such a lost, little boy look on his face that her heart melted.

"How about if I show you online the ones I've narrowed it down to, and you and Danielle can help me come up with a decision tonight. I'll put an offer in first thing in the morning and fly home with you. I will need to come back this weekend though, if you're still willing to come with me. I'd like to show you the house in person, as well as introduce you to my daughter."

He was grinning like a happy kid on Christmas morning. "I think that is a terrific plan."

****

*Ron*

Brenna showed him the properties she was interested in. The woman had impeccable taste. He liked that she knew exactly what she wanted and pointed out each place's strengths and flaws. There was one she was obviously leaning toward, even if she didn't realize it herself.

"I think you should go with the one on the mountain. You've not only got amazing views from your backyard, but spectacular city views, too. The house and yard seem like there's relatively little upkeep, which could be especially important if you're not here all the time to take care of it. And I think you'll want the pool in the desert heat."

He could envision himself there with her, looking at the city lights at night from the patio while holding her close, having breakfast by the pool, or lounging around on the couch reading in the great room facing the mountains.

"That's Danielle's favorite," she beamed.

Ron leaned over and kissed her cheek. "Darlin', it's yours, too. You should hear how you've talked about it."

She shrugged sheepishly. "Yeah, I think you're right."

He hugged her around the shoulders. "It's a great place. I can't wait to see it in person."

She said she was going to write an email to her realtor, Graham, outlining her terms, and explain she'd need him to come to the office early so she could sign the paperwork before getting on the plane. He closed his eyes while she tapped away on the keyboard. He must have fallen asleep because the next thing he knew, she was snuggling in next to him, and the lights were off. He heard her whisper, "I've set the alarm, so sleep tight, baby."

With her in his arms, he knew he finally would be able to. It'd been three long weeks since he'd had a good night's sleep.

# Chapter Twenty-Four

*Brenna*

They were waiting to board the plane when she got a text from Graham telling her the contract had been accepted.

Ron smirked. "You should have offered less."

Brenna shook her head. "No, my offer was fair, and was the most I was willing to pay. Graham must have a done a good job conveying that, which is probably why they didn't counter."

He slid his arm around her waist and kissed her temple.

"Well, congratulations." He lowered his voice and said in her ear, "I can't wait to help you christen every. Single. Room."

"Even the laundry room?" she asked with a raised eyebrow.

"*Especially* the laundry room, are you kidding me? The washer is the perfect height to sit you on for a little spin cycle of your own."

She shook her head with a giggle. "Oh great. Now every time I do laundry, I'm going to get turned on thinking about that."

"Wait until you're actually remembering it, not just imagining it."

"You must have some dirty clothes in your duffle bag," she teased.

"At least two loads worth. Wanna go to my place and wash them before I head to the base?"

"I can't think of anything I'd rather do than help you with your laundry."

He leaned closer to her again. "We are talking about having sex, right?"

"Your whites will never have been so white, General," she whispered in his ear.

She smiled when she heard him mutter under his breath, "Fuuuuck."

"Yeah, baby, that's the idea."

The corners of his mouth turned up, and he shook his head. "Darlin', I think I'm in trouble when it comes to you."

She sighed and grimaced slightly. "Likewise, baby," she whispered. "Likewise."

Ron grabbed her hand and kissed it. "Hey, that's not a bad thing. At least not for me."

With a slight smile, Brenna squeezed his hand. "Not a bad thing at all."

Yet, she wasn't convinced her heart was going to make it out in one piece.

****

Their plane arrived early in San Diego, and they were at Ron's home in no time. It didn't hurt he sped the whole way.

She hadn't been sure what to expect of his house, but looking around, she realized, as with everything of his, it suited him perfectly. It was very masculine with dark wood and rich colors; a sharp contrast to her bright and light beach house. His study was by far her favorite room, with its floor-to-ceiling bookshelves; it even had a rolling ladder you slid around the walls to reach different books from higher shelves.

"Oh my God. I would never leave this room!" Brenna exclaimed as she walked in and spun around to take it all in.

Browsing through his collection, she found the majority of his books were nonfiction with historical and political references. Also, very fitting of him. There were also several classics, and she wondered if they were placed there to make him look less one-dimensional with his tastes.

"*Pride and Prejudice?*" she teased.

"Hey, I had to read it in college, and it turns out I really enjoyed it, much to my surprise. It had some valuable life lessons about not judging too soon or behaving too proudly." He paused with a smirk. "And how to find a happy medium when peoples' lives are vastly different."

He continued with a wink. "Would you like to borrow it?"

*Point taken, General.*

"No, I've been busy. *Writing.*"

He grinned from ear-to-ear as he picked her up and spun her around. "Brenna, that's terrific! Definitely cause for celebration. How about Evangeline's tonight?"

She cocked her head, her feet still dangling off the ground. "Don't you have to work late since you're going in late?"

Kissing her before setting her down, he replied, "No, I'll be done at five. Trust me, Uncle Sam has gotten more than his fair share of my time these last few weeks."

He continued the tour of his home, with the next stop being his bedroom. The first thing she noticed was the beautiful four-poster bed, sans the canopy.

"It's been in my family for a few generations. I don't know if I would have necessarily picked it otherwise," he told her when she ran her fingers over the smooth wood in obvious awe.

Tracing his plaid comforter behind her as she walked around examining the bed, she said, "Really? I think it suits you."

He jerked his head at her. "Oh? How's that?"

Brenna smiled. "It just fits with the rest of your décor. Very masculine, but still elegant. It's an amazing piece that catches your eye the minute you walk in the room, and when you get closer, you can really see the craftsmanship. You know it's the real deal and not a knock-off."

She ran her hand up the column at the foot of the bed. "No wonder it's lasted for generations."

His eyes twinkled while he watched her admire his bed, and he closed the distance between them.

"I know I promised you the spin cycle, but you've just convinced me there's no better place than my bed. I think we should lie in it and admire the craftsmanship. Naked, of course."

Rubbing his growing bulge over his pants, she teased, "I don't think I'll be able to admire anything but *your craftsmanship* if we're naked."

Ron wrapped his arms around her waist and pulled her against him. "Oh yeah? So you like my wood?"

She giggled.

*Boy this conversation has gone south fast.*

Trying to sound sophisticated, she managed, "Mmm hmm, it's a most impressive piece."

He was smirking when his lips found hers. In between kisses, he uttered, "Well, it is a hardwood, they tend to be quite durable.

They were naked in no time, and as she turned to climb up on the high bed, he stopped and bent her over the mattress with her feet on the side rail, as he kissed her neck and shoulders. She realized how exposed she was, and at the perfect height for him to fuck her when he pressed his cock against her center. His mouth trailed down her spine and ass while he caressed his hands over her body in a wide circular motion.

"Mmm, that feels nice," she murmured with her eyes closed.

He plunged his face into her pussy from behind.

*This is new.*

*And oh my.*

As he lapped in between her folds, she found herself pushing back against his mouth; prompting him to use both hands and spread her apart while his tongue went to work.

*Oh damn, that feels good.*

She gasped out loud when he began to fuck her with his tongue. The things he was making her feel were incredible, and she just laid there, not caring her ass was in the air and her legs spread wide for his face to dive deeper into her pussy. At that moment she understood what it truly meant to have no inhibitions. How odd and wonderful that she felt this way with a man she'd known less than a month but never once did with the man she was married to for sixteen years.

And she hadn't even been drinking.

Ron reached up and massaged her clit with his middle finger. She felt her entire body relax, and she melted against him, feeling like a puddle of jelly on his bed. Everything he was doing to her felt... perfect. Would he mind if she asked him to do this for, say, the next two hours before he went to work? Because holy hell, she didn't want him to stop. Maybe ever.

*How does the saying go? All good things must come to an end?*

Fortunately for Brenna, the consolation prize for it ending was an orgasm.

He darted his tongue faster in and out of her pussy while his fingers picked up speed. Her previously relaxed body tensed as the sensation of coming overtook her entire being. With a deep plunge of his tongue and rapid stroke of her clit, the most amazing orgasm of her life took hold of her. Her body shook at the peak of her climax, and it felt like it lasted forever. In a good way.

What the fuck had he just done to her? Besides ruin her for any other man.

And how the hell was she supposed to match that for him?

He bit her ass before she felt his cock enter her.

She lay with her eyes closed and relished how wonderful he felt inside her. She almost felt guilty for being such a lazy fuck. Almost. But it was his own fault for doing what he had just done to her.

He put her legs together while he continued to move his cock in and out of her. Just that simple change made everything feel differently. But still *ah-mazing*. Maybe even better?

Her clit was being stimulated in a whole new way and seemingly out of nowhere, another orgasm overcame her.

*That's it—this bed is definitely magical. He is never getting rid of it.*

His grunts were ones she had come to know meant he was going to climax. He pushed into her hard and harshly whispered, "Fuck!" a few times before she felt him spill his seed deep inside her.

Falling forward on top of her, he enveloped her body with his and held her. As he kissed her back, shoulders, and neck, he murmured how sexy she was before pulling out and retreating to the bathroom. She didn't move until he brought her a towel to clean herself with, then scrambled under the covers once she had.

Ron joined her and, as always after sex, he held her.

Which is when she started to cry.

*What the hell is wrong with me?*

He had to be wondering the same thing, but just hugged her tight and let her continue without saying a word as he stroked her back and hair.

Finally, she stopped.

"Better?" he asked.

"Yes," she said sheepishly as she wiped her eyes with the sheet.

"Want to tell me about it?"

Not really, but she probably owed him some kind of explanation.

"I don't think I realized how much these last few weeks had affected me; how worried I was—not only about us—but about your safety, too. Or just how much I'd missed you." She hesitated. "Or how much I care about you. It all kind of hit me at once and, I guess, that was my brain's way of handling it."

He frowned and seemed to choose his next words carefully.

"For the record, however much you missed me, I missed you ten times more. But I hate you were worried, and I wasn't able to reassure you I was okay. That *we* were okay. Unfortunately, I don't see my situation changing in the near future. I'm concerned I'm asking too much of you to stick with me."

She sat straight up like a shot.

"What are you saying?"

"Darlin', I know this life isn't for everyone—"

She interrupted. "Don't you dare do this to me, Ron Thompson. If you break up with me after I just told you how much I care about you, that would be the cruelest thing anyone has ever done."

He reached up and stroked her face, then sat up to be closer to her, smiling in a way she had never seen him do before. Tracing her bottom lip with his thumb, he appeared lost in thought and didn't say anything.

*Oh fuck. Did I just screw this up royally?*

Finally, he spoke.

"Brenna, you mean more to me than I ever thought possible. But I want you going into this with your eyes wide open about what being with me is like. This past month would be considered pretty typical. Yes, sometimes I know ahead of time I'm going to be leaving, and sometimes I am even able to communicate while I'm gone. But there are a lot of times I'm called out and leave the country within a matter of hours. I don't want you to resent me six months from now when I've missed your birthday, or when you're alone again for weeks at a time without a word from me. I'd rather we end as friends now than have you hate me in a year."

She knew exactly what he was saying, but her soul wanted to believe she could be satisfied with what he could give her. That she was strong enough to handle his absences. She had done it with Danny all those years. Yes, it was different, because all she had to do to know he was safe was turn on ESPN, but she spent many nights worrying—just for different reasons. Wasn't being with Ron worth all the other stuff?

Or was he just going to break her heart in the end, too?

"I'm not going to lie, you being gone was torture. Partly because I didn't know if you were okay, but mostly because I missed you. I can't imagine my life without you in it. But I'll admit I'm not exactly sure what having you in my life looks like going forward. Do I play the part of the dutiful major general's girlfriend and roll bandages while pining for my Marine? Or do I carry on with my life, and when we're both free, we're together? And if so, what does that mean? Are we monogamous? Can I even ask that of you, not knowing anything about the conditions you live in when you're gone? When you're home, are we dating, meaning you're calling me and asking me out, or are we living together to take advantage of our limited time? If we're living together, where are we doing that, and what does that look like?"

He took a deep breath. "Damn, woman, you sure do like to have your ducks in a row."

"I just need to know where we stand."

He looked at the clock on the bedside table. "I'm sorry to do this, but can we talk more about this tonight? Let's both take the afternoon to figure out what we want from each other and how we can make this work. You channel your inner Elizabeth Bennet and I'll channel Mr. Darcy and we'll find a happy medium."

She gave a weak smile and nodded.

"Brenna, I care about you, but I want to make sure you understand what being with me entails."

She closed her eyes and sighed. "I care about you, too. I know this will be hard."

"It doesn't have to be. We just need to get things figured out. I know I'm asking a lot of you, given my position with the Corps, but if you're up for it, I think what we have is worth the effort to make it work."

She snuggled against his chest. "It is."

He held her and stroked her hair until she was half-asleep. She felt him get out of bed but was too emotionally exhausted to follow suit.

After a few minutes, he whispered against her cheek, "I'm going to the base but sleep as long as you want. I'll call you later about dinner."

She gave a groggy acknowledgment she'd heard him, then rolled over and burrowed into the covers. She didn't want to think anymore, she just wanted to lie in his beautiful bed that smelled like him and not worry about anything.

Which was exactly what she did. At least for an hour.

# Chapter Twenty-Five

*Ron*

*Yeah, she's going home with me tonight.*

He watched a group of businessmen checking Brenna out the minute she walked in the lobby of Evangeline's. She didn't pay them any attention as she entered the bar and looked around, then smiled wide when she found him sitting at a high-top table.

He didn't blame the men for eyeing her. She looked like a model as she glided toward him; her blonde hair complimented by the button-up emerald-green cashmere sweater. He wondered if it would be expensive to have someone sew all those buttons back on because he was having visions of ripping her sweater open. Her tailored cream colored slacks weren't going to fare much better. She could leave the four-inch heels on though. And the necklace.

She approached where he sat on the barstool, and he slid his arm around her waist when she kissed him on the mouth. He hadn't expected that, but he sure as hell wasn't complaining.

She didn't move toward the empty seat and stayed in between his legs where she was eye level with him.

"Have you been waiting long?" she asked as she brushed the hair above his ear.

"I just got here. Our table should be ready shortly."

"Oh good, I was worried I'd kept you waiting. I didn't expect traffic to be so heavy at this time on a Thursday night."

"The way you look, darlin', I'd wait all night."

She stroked his freshly shaven face. "Aw, flattery will get you everywhere."

Ron grinned. "I'm counting on that."

"You look very handsome yourself."

He was glad she had said that. He never knew what to wear when he didn't go out in uniform, which wasn't very often anymore. Most of the dinners and events he'd been to lately were when he represented the Marine Corps, so that made picking out what to wear pretty easy. Should he wear his dress blues or his other dress blues? He was a little rusty when it came to civilian wear. He thought black slacks and a plain gray sweater with the expensive watch his brother bought him were a safe bet.

The hostess appeared to tell them their table was ready, and Ron drained his Scotch. He was apprehensive about what tonight's conversation was going to bring. His intention was a clearer understanding for her about what being involved with him meant so there weren't hurt feelings down the road. He knew, however, no matter what was said tonight, inevitably there were going to be hurt feelings at some point. It seemed to be a by-product of the job and was probably one of the main reasons he was still single.

Except she was different. He wasn't going to be able to take solace in the old standby of "I warned you from the beginning" when she was upset. He'd hated watching her cry earlier, and had felt helpless, unable to fix everything to make her happy. The fact he couldn't weighed on him heavily. If she wanted to leave because she was unhappy, instead of shrugging his shoulders like he normally would, he'd move heaven and earth to make her stay.

If you were to ask him why she was different from the rest, he wouldn't have a good answer. She just was.

He came to that realization one night when he was trying to sleep in a tent somewhere in the Middle East. He'd tried to pinpoint exactly when he think he fell for her and decided it was the night she came out of her bathroom in her light green nightie while rubbing lotion on her hands. He didn't know why that moment stood out, maybe because at the time he remembered looking at her and thinking there was nowhere else in the world he'd rather be than right there with her or anyone else he'd rather be with.

They were seated in a discreet corner booth of the restaurant. The maître d' seemed to recognize Brenna and changed his mind about their original table where they would have been more visible.

Ron didn't know how to start the conversation, so he opted for small talk.

"Did you have a good nap?"

"Oh my God, yes! Your bed is magical." She gave a sly smile. "In more ways than one." She looked around and lowered her voice. "That was the best orgasm I've ever had in my life. It might be part of the reason I started crying. I've heard of people doing that."

"Well, I'd much rather that be the reason than because you were upset about me or us."

She reached for his hand. "I'm new at this. I'm going to be insecure, it's just who I am. And I'm going to worry about you. How could you expect me not to? I have no idea where you are or what you're doing, and to top it all off, I have a pretty vivid imagination."

He squeezed her hand. "I know it's silly for me to think you're not going to worry. I will try to do a better job of at least getting word to you on a regular basis that I'm all right."

She smiled. "Well, that's a start."

*Here goes everything.*

"I need to know you're going to be okay when I'm gone. I can't be distracted worrying about you. Too many Marines' lives depend on me being one hundred percent focused on the mission. I can promise you though, when I'm home, I'm with you and you will have my complete attention. That's the best I can offer you right now. You need to be honest with yourself if that will be enough for you for the time being."

She paused as if letting what he just said sink in.

"Ron, I already told you I want to make this work. You said to take the day and channel Elizabeth Bennet and decide what I needed. I guess in a nutshell, I need you. However I can get you."

He shook his head. "You need to be sure about this. Sure you can accept me being gone for weeks at a time, sure that—"

She put her index finger to his lips. "Mr. Darcy, stop talking. We're trying to find a happy medium, remember?" She leaned over and kissed his cheek. "I'm sure I want to be with you; that's what I'm *sure* of. All the other stuff, not so much. But you, yourself, said it doesn't have to be that difficult. There are two things I can promise you. I promise I will be fine when you're gone. I was married to a professional ballplayer, being alone is not new to me. And I promise I'm probably going to need a lot of reassurance."

He had his doubts, but he'd take it for now. It sure as hell beat the alternative.

****

*Brenna*

She had woken from her nap in Ron's bed and decided he was right; it didn't have to be complicated. She didn't need to have all the answers that second. Besides, love conquered all, right?

They ended up at her beach house after dinner. Ron had been a doll to take her out and celebrate the fact she was writing again. After their discussion about their relationship, which really only turned out to be a commitment to try to make things work, he wanted to know all about what she was writing.

Unfortunately, she was secretive when she was working on something new.

*Secrets suck, don't they, Mr. Marine-Man?*

She told him exactly that, and he had the nerve to act offended and not know what she was talking about.

"Really, babe? A goddamn helicopter landed at my house without me even knowing it was coming. You aren't exactly an open book."

"Well, there's a lot of things I can't talk about, and frankly, there's a lot of things you don't want to know."

"Well, there are some things I do want to know," she countered.

"Like what?"

"Is it true you're going to be a lieutenant general by the end of the year? Is that the big promotion you talked about on New Year's Eve?"

"That's what I was talking about, and I'm still not sure what's going to happen."

"What will that mean? Will you have to move? Will you travel less?"

"I won't have to move, but I'll probably travel more. Except I will be traveling mostly to Washington and only occasionally overseas."

"Will you get a place in D.C.?"

"I might. Just think of all the places we'll have to choose from to stay. San Diego, Tucson, Sullivan's Island, Washington D.C., Grand Forks..."

"Grand Forks?"

"My ranch in North Dakota. Well, the closest town is Grand Forks."

"You have a ranch? With horses and everything?"

He laughed. "My brother and I bought a thousand-acre cattle ranch about ten years ago. It turns a small profit, and we have a great rancher overseeing things so we don't have to be hands on."

"Is that where you want to retire?"

"Well, when we bought it that was the plan. But the older I get, the less I'm convinced I want to spend my retirement shoveling snow in the winter."

Brenna grinned. "No, let's go somewhere closer to the equator. Maybe Belize or Costa Rica."

"I don't know," he teased. "I think I might enjoy getting snowed in with you."

"Yes, but I'll wear much less clothing if we're somewhere warm."

"Darlin', if we were snowed in, you wouldn't be wearing *any* clothing."

The way he said it, like she'd have any say in the matter, turned her on, and that was such an enigma to her. She prided herself on being independent but found it hot as fuck when he was in control. Especially in bed.

# Chapter Twenty-Six

*Brenna*

She and Ron made it back to Tucson on Friday night in time to take Danielle out for dinner. She was nervous to have her daughter meet Ron, worried Danielle would not like Ron out of loyalty to her dad. Turned out, she had nothing to worry about; the two were as thick as thieves by the end of the night. Watching the two of them banter back and forth made Brenna's heart smile.

Danielle wanted to go with them when they went to look at the house in the morning.

"How about we pick you up for breakfast?" Ron suggested.

"That sounds great." Danielle replied.

"That sounds great? *Great*? Since when do you get up for breakfast?" Brenna chided.

"Since I became a grownup."

"You weren't a grownup over Christmas vacation?"

"That's different, Mom. When I'm home with you, I feel like a kid, but when I'm here in my own apartment and have to take the spiders outside myself, well, that makes me an adult."

Ron interjected. "You take the spiders outside?"

Brenna laughed. "Of course! There's no need to kill them, they eat other bugs."

Ron didn't say anything more, just hugged Brenna around the shoulders and kissed her temple.

"Don't judge me!" she scoffed.

"Darlin', that's just one of many things I love about you."

Danielle's eyes widened at the phrase, 'I love about you,' and she looked at her mom with a smile.

"So as I was saying, Mr. Thompson, before my mother interrupted, I'd love to have breakfast with you two."

"You need to call me Ron, and we'll pick you up at eight-thirty."

They made sure Danielle got to her car safely, and on the way to their rental, Ron squeezed Brenna's ass.

"You might have a hard time yourself being ready for breakfast by eight-thirty, Ms. Roberts, because I plan on keeping you up all night."

Brenna smirked. "I'm not worried, General. I plan on wearing you out before midnight. There will be plenty of time left to sleep."

He leaned in to growl in her ear, "Oh sugar, challenge accepted."

****

*Ron*

Brenna didn't wear him out until closer to one. He took great pride that he had made her come so hard, multiple times, that she was out like a light.

Ron enjoyed meeting her daughter. She was beautiful like her mom, but he could see Danny's features in her, too. Danielle was the first real proof that Brenna had actually been in love before she met him. He wasn't necessarily jealous, the man was dead, but it served as a reminder of how different their lives had been.

He wondered what he would be doing right now if he had decided not to go to Ava and Travis's party. *Nothing better than this,* he thought as he kissed her hair.

She nuzzled closer to him. She'd gotten better at sharing her bed, but he knew it was only a matter of time before she turned over and sprawled out. He loved it when she did that. That was when she was totally oblivious to the world, and he got to see her completely vulnerable. He'd only seen her vulnerable while awake twice—after she got upset and made the bullshit comparison of him to Danny, and on New Year's Eve. He'd rather have not seen her like that on New Year's.

On the plane she had told him the district attorney called earlier that day to let her know Ray had pleaded *no contest* to the assault charges and was given probation. The news infuriated Ron, but Brenna shrugged and said his wife filed for divorce and his reputation had been ruined, so that was justice as far as she was concerned.

*Yeah, no, it wasn't.*

He thought about how she had been able to let it go; he wasn't sure if he admired her or was angry at her for it. The whole ordeal had shaken him up, he could only imagine what she must have been feeling as she experienced it.

Thinking about it got his blood pressure up, and he knew he wasn't going to be able to fall asleep anytime soon. He looked over at Brenna sleeping peacefully. Maybe she was onto something with letting it go.

Carefully sliding out of bed so not to disturb her, he picked up his phone and scrolled through email. There was one sender that immediately caught his eye.

Sarah Jennings.

His ex. They'd ended things civilly enough and continued to talk on occasion; the last time ended with them in bed again. Then she became upset with him the next morning when she realized he wasn't ever going to change and be what she wanted, no matter how great the sex was. Their communication all but stopped after that.

He often wondered if he'd made the right decision; if he should have tried to change for her. Sarah was smart, funny, beautiful, and good in bed, but he still hadn't been willing to make sacrifices for her. He recognized if he had, he wouldn't have Brenna in his life.

And he was willing to turn his world upside down for that woman.

He clicked on Sarah's email. It was her usual inquiry as to how he was, if anything new was happening, and a synopsis of the events that had occurred in her life since the last time they had seen each other. It ended with an invitation to cook him dinner, which he was pretty sure was code for spending the night.

He was about to hit reply when he heard Brenna say quietly, "Babe?"

He shut the screen off and put his phone back on the desk.

"I'm right here, darlin'."

He got back in bed next to her.

"Everything okay?" she asked.

"Oh yeah, everything's fine. I just couldn't sleep so I made the mistake of checking email."

She giggled as she nestled closer to him. "Now you're never going to fall asleep, silly."

"Nah, nothing too important that can't wait until Monday."

"Good," she said in a pouty voice. "I want you all to myself this weekend." He smiled when she added, "Well, I'll share you with Danielle."

"Go to sleep," he whispered, "I'm all yours until Monday."

He was all hers, but not just until Monday. Until she was tired of him, or he was dead, whichever came first.

# Chapter Twenty-Seven

*Brenna*

They were together every night for almost two weeks and she loved every minute of it. Sometimes they'd stay at the beach house, and sometimes they'd bring Zona to his place. Ron even bought a dog bed for the pup.

He was called to D.C. early on the morning before Valentine's Day.

She got a text from him.

**Ron: Bren—en route to DC; will catch a flight back tomorrow a.m.**

**Brenna: Good! I'm cooking you Valentine's Dinner.**

**Ron: Will you cook it naked?**

**Brenna: You don't even know what I'm making! What if it's fried chicken? Or bacon?**

**Ron: Don't cook fried chicken or bacon then. You could make me oatmeal for dinner, as long as you're naked doing it.**

**Brenna: SMH. Talk to you tonight?**

**Ron: SMH?**

**Brenna: Shaking my head (at you! you naughty man.)**

**Ron: I'm going to be shaking something else at you tomorrow.**

**Ron: Talk to you tonight. xoxo**

Damn, he made her happy.

\*\*\*\*

*Ron*

He called Brenna once his plane touched down in San Diego.

"Hi darlin'. I'm back in town."

"Hey babe! How was your trip?"

"Exactly what I expected."

She sighed. "Oh, there's my open book."

Ron laughed and changed the subject. "What time do you want me there for dinner?"

"I think everything should be ready by six. Call me when you're on your way?"

"I'll bring dessert, and yeah, I'll call you when I leave the house."

"Okay. Can't wait to see you and hear *all* about your trip!" she teased.

"Happy Valentine's Day, you little minx," he snarled before he hung up.

He hoped she liked what he got her for Valentine's. In addition to the cliché roses that should be delivered to her anytime, and the racy, red lingerie that, let's face it, was more for him than her, he found a tennis bracelet that reminded him of the sea glass she liked to pick up on their walks along the beach.

He had gone to the jewelry store to look for her present and felt like a deer in headlights; their relationship was too new for a ring, and she wore the same diamond stud earrings every day, so he thought maybe a necklace. As he browsed the display cases, a bracelet caught his eye. It looked like it belonged in the bowl of sea glass that sat on Brenna's entry table. When he saw the price tag he concluded it probably was not made of glass. The salesgirl told him the jewels were emeralds, rubies, sapphires, diamonds, and a bunch of other stones he couldn't remember the names of. Hopefully Brenna would know.

On his way to the bakery for the cake she loved, he thought about how he never had been able to understand why people fretted so much about this day and how he had tended to agree with those who leaned on the side of disliking the "holiday made up by Hallmark," which is what he had always referred to it as.

Chuckling to himself, he conceded that Brenna had definitely done a number on him, because he now understood what the big deal was.

He called her from the car to tell her he was on his way.

With a beer in hand for him, she greeted him at the door in her apron.

And pearls.

And heels.

And nothing else but a smile.

She was the porn version of Barbara Billingsley, the mom in *Leave It to Beaver,* and was playing the part perfectly as she handed him his drink and took the cake from him.

"How was your day, dear?" she inquired while pecking him on the cheek.

"It just got infinitely better," he replied with a grin as he openly leered at her.

"I was just about to put dinner in the oven. Do you need anything?"

She turned and strutted towards the kitchen, and he followed with his eyes transfixed on her naked bottom.

"As a matter fact, I do."

"What can I get you?" she asked over her shoulder, then pressed her lips together as if trying to suppress a cocky smirk.

He took a sip of his beer while he debated what to do next and decided he was going to have a little fun. Walking to a chair in the adjoining family room, he called to her. "Would you mind bringing me my slippers, sugar?"

She turned to him with a knowing grin. "Of course, dear," then disappeared into the hall, only to return with a gift bag in hand, which she promptly brought to him.

Inside were a pair of new house slippers.

*Oh, she's good.*

He pretended to struggle taking his shoes off. "Darlin', could you help me?"

She dropped to her knees in front of him, providing him with an exceptional view of her bare tits under her apron, and took her time removing his shoes.

Running her hands along the inside of his thighs, she asked, "Anything else while I'm down here?"

He didn't say anything, and she stroked him higher, seductively biting her bottom lip as she looked up at him.

"Well now that you mention it, I could go for a nice blowjob."

"Mmm, I thought you'd never ask," she purred while unbuckling his belt. She pulled his zipper down, and he lifted his hips for her to remove his pants and boxers. When he felt her hand on his shaft, he leaned back and closed his eyes.

*People who don't like Valentine's Day are crazy.*

She stroked him up and down and dipped her head between his legs to lick his balls. He loved when she did that; not many of his former lovers paid any attention to his balls, so the first time she licked his, he thought he'd died and gone to heaven.

He felt her push his legs up.

*What the fuck is she doing?*

Her tongue was flat against his taint, and he let out a long moan.

*Damn, that feels amazing.*

She kept licking him—fast, then she would slow down and swirl her tongue before sucking on his skin. Her soft moans made him more turned on; he loved that she wasn't timid when pleasuring him. She dragged her tongue back to his balls, up his shaft, and back down again. With his sac in her mouth, she looked up at him and stroked his cock with her right hand.

"Fuuuuck," he groaned when she took him between her lips. "Oh that's it, darlin', suck my balls."

"Mmm," she responded as she sucked, making a *popping* noise with her lips as she released one and replaced it with the other.

"Oh my God," he snarled and threw his head back with his eyes closed. Her mouth was nirvana.

She trailed her lips to his shaft and pulled his leaking cock in her mouth. He thrust his hips against her face.

"Yes, sugar, take me deep."

When he felt his tip in her throat, he moaned, "Mmm, that's a good girl. Just like that."

She bobbed her head up and down on his slippery rod, jerking him in unison with her mouth. He grabbed a fistful of her hair as he grunted.

"Suck it. Oh yeah, suck my cock," he said through gritted teeth.

His excitement seemed to spur her on because she increased her tempo while wiggling her ass.

"Oh fuck," he groaned when he sensed his orgasm. His body tensed. "You're going to make me come."

"Oh, come on my tits," she moaned.

*Um, what? Come on your tits?*

And that was pretty much all it took. He stood up and stroked his cock as she untied her apron and let it fall to the floor.

"Mmm, yeah baby. Come all over them," she said while squeezing her round orbs together and offering them up to him.

Happy motherfucking Valentine's Day to me, he thought as he spurted all over her perfect boobs. He felt bad when one stream went astray and hit her lips and cheek, but quickly got over it when he saw how sexy she looked with it dripping down her chin.

Using his cock, he smeared his cum all over her. She looked up at him, grasped his shaft, and put it back in her mouth to clean him off.

He smiled and caressed her cheek with his thumb, murmuring, "You are so fucking sexy."

Ron offered her his hand to help her up. She was buck naked, with red knees and cum-covered tits, in high heels wearing two pearl necklaces. And he was going to be waking up with his hand on her ass tomorrow.

*Yeah, I am definitely one lucky bastard.*

\*\*\*\*

*Brenna*

She was pleased with how their Valentine's evening had progressed. It was better than she had planned. She had been a little worried he wouldn't play along with her 1950s housewife act and instead, think she was crazy for answering the door like she had. Him asking for his slippers was perfect.

She loved how sexy he made her feel. She hadn't felt like that in so long. Actually, maybe ever. Whenever he looked at or touched her, she never doubted how much he desired her. The feeling was mutual.

Cleaning up with a dishtowel, still clad in only her apron and heels, she proceeded to put dinner in the oven.

"Thank you for the roses. They're gorgeous." She gestured to the bouquet of roses on the counter.

Ron had his trousers back on, but no shirt, and glanced briefly at the vase of flowers before returning his gaze to her. She felt a bit self-conscious with how intently he stared at her.

"I'm glad you like them," he said, coming around the side of the island where she was standing. He walked slowly toward her, like he was stalking his prey, and she had a sudden urge to retreat. She made it to the table before he caught up with her.

"What are you doing?" She giggled when he slid his arm around her waist and pulled her bare back against his warm chest.

He pulled the bow holding the apron around her neck then tugged on the one around her waist. "What does it look like I'm doing, *dear*?"

"I have to set the table and make the salad."

He lifted her naked body onto the table, her butt on the edge of slab and gently pressed her backward onto her elbows.

Sitting in a chair, he spread her legs wide like her pussy was a feast set before him, except his only utensils were his hands and mouth.

"No, you don't need to do that right now," he murmured as he stroked the insides of her thighs with the pads of his fingers. Her nipples instantly responded to his touch. He watched her face when he ran his thumb up and down the entire length of her slit. She could tell by how easily it glided that she was already slick.

*How does he manage to make me so wet so fast?*

He smiled, and she wondered if he was thinking the same thing.

His thumb circled her clit, and she let out a moan while arching back and lifting her hips slightly.

"I think I'm going to have to have my Valentine's dessert before dinner," he said as he spread her pussy lips with his hands. She gasped out loud when his tongue explored her folds. He took his time, licking her entire length repeatedly before slipping a finger inside her. She could hear just how excited she was as he slowly finger fucked her.

"Mmm, you taste so sweet," he muttered while continuing to lap her up; the vibrations from his 'mmm' caused her to press her hips against his mouth.

He slid a second finger inside her and sucked her button in between his teeth. She tilted her head back, and he plunged his digits deep inside her, curling them up to find her G spot.

"Oh my God," she gasped.

His mouth gave her clit his full attention at the same time his fingers continued their efforts. Ron flicked his tongue over her sensitive nub, and she felt her body tighten as she whimpered with pleasure. She was close and arched against his mouth. He took the hint and finger banged her at a frantic pace until she cried out, her whole body spasmed as she came.

He stayed between her legs until she pushed him away and pressed her thighs together. She heard his chair move back from the table, and looked up to see him leaning over her with a smile.

"Wow," she said as she exhaled deeply.

"Happy Valentine's Day," he said as he kissed her nose. "I'll be right back."

She lay on the table until she heard the front door open and close, then sat up and hopped off.

She was still naked and wondered if she should put the apron back on or find some clothes when he walked into the kitchen, admiring her with a smile, and asked, "Where's Zona?"

"Cassie took her. She didn't want to be alone on Valentine's Day." Brenna laughed as she moved behind the counter to partially shield her nude body from his view.

Ron chuckled. "I thought there was something going on with Rivas?"

"I thought so too, but apparently not."

He raised his eyebrows but didn't say anything.

Just then, a shiver went down her spine. Ron came around the counter, took her hand, and pulled her against him while he squeezed her butt. His body felt warm against her cool skin, and she got goosebumps when his arms came around her.

"Go put some clothes on, Mrs. Cleaver," he said with a smirk and spun her around to send her off with a swat on her behind.

As she headed toward the stairs, she noticed two pink gift bags overflowing with tissue paper on the table in the entryway. Smiling all the way to her bedroom, she couldn't remember a time when she'd felt so loved.

****

*Ron*

Ron had an epiphany thirty seconds after Brenna left.

*I just told the most beautiful woman in the world to go put some clothes on. What the fuck am I thinking?*

He took the stairs two at a time and found her in her closet, still naked.

"Oh good, I'm still in time."

She started laughing. "In time for what?"

He handed her one of the pink gift bags. "To give you the Valentine's present you got me."

She narrowed her eyes with a bewildered look on her face and pulled the tissue paper out of the bag. The corners of her mouth lifted when she gazed down at the red lace folded neatly at the bottom.

Holding the panties and bustier with garters against her body, she looked in the mirror. "It's beautiful." After admiring it for a minute, she frowned and glanced at him, suspicion creeping into her voice when she asked, "But why is it *your* present? Do you want to try it on?"

He burst out laughing.

"Hell no, I don't want to try it on! It's my present because, well, I get to look at you wearing it."

She seemed relieved when she laughed, "Oh, good," then carefully folded the garments and put them back in the bag.

*That isn't going to work.*

"Try it on."

She shook her head and smiled. "I still need to make the salad and set the table."

"I'll help you with that."

Wrapping her arms around his neck, she pressed her lips against his cheek and murmured, "Later."

Ron felt how cold her skin was when she leaned against him.

*Okay, I get it.*

That probably wasn't an outfit a woman lounged around in on a cool winter night.

Ron rubbed her arms up and down and said quietly, "I'm sorry, darlin', I was thinking with the wrong head. Put something warm on, you're freezing." Then kissed the top of her head before making his way downstairs.

When she walked in the kitchen in a pair of jeans and a red sweater, he decided she could make a potato sack look sexy if she wore it.

She caught him staring at her. "What?" she asked, looking down as if expecting to find a stain on her clothes.

He smiled and shook his head. "Nothing. You're just breathtaking."

Her pursed lips conveyed that she thought it was a line, but she didn't argue, instead she simply smiled and said, "Thank you."

*That's my girl.*

She was learning to take his compliments.

He made the salad while she set the table in the formal dining room. He was going to offer to help her with that but then realized she was way better at it than he was. He guessed she'd hosted a lot more dinner parties than he ever had.

That got him thinking, would they ever host a party together? What would her friends think of him? What would his friends think of her? Besides wanting to fuck her.

Which they better get over quick because he was not above knocking someone out.

Ask Ray Reitmeier.

After dinner, they sat on the patio by the glowing embers in the fire pit. She had brought a blanket out and put it over them as she cozied up to him, wine glass in her hand.

He had a snifter of cognac and swirled the liquid while staring at the fire.

"What are you thinking about?" she softly asked.

"I was just thinking about when the best time to give you your last present would be."

Her body wiggled as she sat up on her knees. Just like a little kid, sweets and presents excited her.

"Well I vote now!"

He smiled and got up to go in the house with her following suit, except she turned towards her office when he passed through the kitchen to retrieve the pink bag on the entry table. She came out with a pyramid of square packages in navy blue gift-wrap held together by ribbons. A card was taped to the biggest package.

"Let's sit on the couch," she suggested, barely able to contain her excitement.

She handed him his presents and clapped her hands when he handed her the gift bag he'd brought in the room with him.

"You first!" she exclaimed.

Ron smiled and opened the envelope with his name on it. It was a sexy card with sappy sentiments—very similar to the one he'd bought her, except her handwritten note inside made him catch his breath.

*Ron,*

*Since I met you, my life has been infinitely brighter. You have brought me more happiness and joy than I even knew possible, and I thank God every day for bringing you into my life.*

*Happy Valentine's Day.*

*Brenna*

He noted she didn't sign it, "Love," something he also had carefully avoided when writing in her card. But if he were honest with himself, he was in love with her, and had been for quite a while. She had done something to him the moment he first laid eyes on her, and he'd only been falling farther ever since.

He didn't tell her that, of course. Things were complicated enough as they tried to figure out how they were going to make things work with his extended absences. Fortunately, there could be an end in sight to that. His trip to Washington meant he was one step closer to his promotion. Earning another star would mean a lot of time in D.C., but he was hopeful she would be willing to go with him, because he could be home in bed with her every night.

Just a little while longer until a decision was final.

He slid the card back into the envelope and reached over to caress her cheek with the back of his knuckles.

"Thank you, darlin'," he whispered softly. "I feel the same way."

Brenna gave an embarrassed smile, then clapped her hands again. "Open your presents!"

He started with the smallest box first. Inside was a dogtag that looked like the real deal. It was engraved: Heart of Brenna Roberts. Please be sure of its safe return.

"You have to wear that with the rest of your tags," she said with a smile.

There wasn't a fuck's chance in a convent that he'd wear anything with her name on it in case he ever got captured, but he loved the sentiment and wasn't going to ruin that.

"I love it, sugar," he said as he leaned over to kiss her. "I will wear it every time."

The next box contained a keyring with the Marine Corps logo that contained multiple keys. He cocked his head at her, not quite understanding.

"Those are the keys to my homes, where you are always welcome. The blue one is for here, the orange one is for Tucson, and the green one is for Sullivan's Island. I tried to match the color of the key to the landscape to help you remember which is which."

*Goddamn.* A key to her San Diego house was huge—but to all three? Not at all what he was expecting.

"Brenna, I—I don't know what to say. I—"

She knocked him down a peg or two. "Don't read too much into it, babe. You're here all the time; it just made sense that you have a key."

He chuckled. "I wasn't reading anything into it. You're right, I am here an awful lot. A key would be handy."

*Except what's the deal with the other keys?*

The last present was John Glen's autobiography.

"Thanks, darlin'." He needed a new book for his library, although he was pretty sure he already had that one.

"Look inside!"

He smiled and opened the first page which was inscribed *"To General Ron Thompson. From one Marine to another, thank you for your service. Semper Fi."* Then had John's signature underneath.

"Wow," was all he could think to say.

She smiled and eagerly asked, "Do you like it?"

"I love it. How did you...?"

She winked and used her best New Yorker accent. "I know a guy."

He'd let her have her secrets. For now.

"It's an amazing gift. Thank you." It became even more treasured after Colonel Glenn died.

The kiss he gave her started out chaste enough, but as usual when it came to her, it quickly heated up and next thing he knew, he was lying on top of her on the couch, pushing his erection against her jeans.

"Sorry," he said with a sheepish smile as he sat up. "You tend to have that effect on me."

"I know. It's so one-sided too," she teased.

Ron picked up the pink gift bag from the table and handed it to her. Her eyes lit up and she theatrically pulled out the envelope first. He hadn't added anything further to the card, other than his signature. He had considered it, but thought the words Hallmark provided were enough. After reading her personal note on his, he wished he had added something after all.

She took her time reading the message in the card, and when she finished, she looked over at him with a serious expression.

"Thank you," she whispered, then kissed his cheek.

"Open your present."

She pulled out the jeweler's box with a dubious smile, then slowly opened the lid with a gasp.

"Ron, it's beautiful," she said as she lifted the bracelet and examined it in the light.

"I thought it was breathtaking, like you," he replied as he took it from her and fastened the clasp around her wrist.

She kept staring at it. The colors glittered under the lights.

"It reminded me of the sea glass you like to collect, so I hoped you'd like it."

"Babe, it's perfect."

Good. It would go great with the red lingerie she opened earlier. She should probably go try that on. He only had so much will power.

She crawled up his body and pushed him back against the couch cushions, her tiny frame sprawled across his. She sucked on his lips, then kissed her way down his neck, across his sternum, and up the other side before back to his mouth.

"Thank you for the best Valentine's Day ever," she murmured against his lips.

Rolling over so she was underneath him again, he growled, "Oh, we're not done yet."

# Chapter Twenty-Eight

*Brenna*

The next morning, she had just dropped to her knees after their playful shower romp when she heard the dreaded ring tone on his phone. With his cock in her hand and her mouth inches from his balls, she glowered at him when he apologetically looked over at his phone on the nightstand.

"Don't you dare," she snarled.

"Darlin', I have to."

He grabbed the towel at his feet that she had just tugged off him and wrapped it back around his waist as he walked over and picked up phone that was ringing insistently.

More like mocking her.

She sighed, sat back on her heels, and watched him retreat to the balcony. She had known the call would be coming; she was honestly surprised it had taken this long. But the fact that he answered it while his dick was in her hand, literally, left her with no doubt where she ranked in his life.

He came back in and offered her his hand to help her to her feet.

"Any chance you could come with me back to my place? I've got to get ready to go, but if I pack fast, I should have a little free time before I have to be on base. Can you get an Uber back so you can ride with me?"

She was pouting at his rejection of her and almost told him no to be spiteful. But then she realized she didn't want him to leave for who-knows-how-long on a bad note, so she swallowed her pride and agreed. She hadn't had to do that since Danny was alive, and it left her with a bitter taste in her mouth.

So she still sulked on the ride to his house.

Running his fingers through his hair in frustration, he sighed when he glanced at her while changing lanes.

"Sugar, you knew I was going to have to go at any time. I don't understand why you're so upset."

She turned and gave him an incredulous look.

"Are you serious? You don't understand why I'm upset? I was *on my knees* about to *suck your cock* and you *took a phone call.* Do you have any idea how undesirable that makes me feel?"

"You know that had nothing to do with how much I desire you. Or how much I care about you."

"Why would I know that?"

Ron remained quiet so she continued. "What if the roles had been reversed? Would you have answered the phone while your head was between my legs?"

She hoped that analogy helped make her point.

The point was moot when he replied wearily, "Yes."

She sat there in stunned silence. That was not the answer she expected.

They pulled into his garage, and it took every fiber of her being to get out of the truck when he came round to her side and held out his hand to help her down.

He closed the door and pinned her against the black steel of the truck, leaning his palms flat on either side of her and moving his face inches from hers.

"This is part of my job, Brenna. People's lives depend on me answering the phone."

Honestly, she thought he was being a little melodramatic. The fact that she came to his house with him seemed to prove that.

"You have time now, what would the difference have been if you'd waited until we finished and called them back?"

"Because I don't know how much time I have until after I answer the phone, darlin'."

*Oh.*

She hadn't thought about that.

She looked away and tried to create some distance between her mouth and his.

"Can you at least tell me where you're going? Do you know how long you'll be gone this time?"

With a frown, he shook his head slowly and stood up taller, taking the weight off his palms.

"I can't. I'm sorry. I don't know how long this time."

Brenna avoided his stare as tears stung her eyes. She felt vulnerable and didn't like it one bit. Bad memories of how secretive Danny always had been came flooding back to her, but she knew better than to verbalize the comparison out loud to him.

"I have an hour before I have to leave," he said as he brushed the hair on her forehead with his fingertips. "I'd really rather not waste it arguing, with you mad at me."

He was right, of course. The threat of him not returning, the possibility that this could be the last time she saw him, and they spent it in a tiff was in the forefront of her mind. She couldn't let him leave with her angry. She needed to pull it together.

She offered an apologetic smile. "I don't want to spend it like that either. Let's get you packed so we can make out before you go."

He leaned down and kissed her softly before murmuring, "Good idea."

# Chapter Twenty-Nine

*Ron*

He leaned against the headrest and looked out over the plane's wing as the jet made its descent into Miramar. He'd only been gone a little over two weeks, and he'd been able to talk to Brenna a few days ago, but truth be told, he hadn't felt like it.

She had been happy to hear from him and chattered gleefully until she realized he wasn't saying much. He didn't have the energy to tell her one of his squads had been hit by an IED, so he told her he was just tired when she asked what was wrong. He got the feeling she didn't buy it.

They'd left things shakier than he would have preferred when he last departed, and he didn't want to add any more stress to their relationship, so he omitted the IED blast that killed two of his men and injured three others. He knew telling her would only make her worry more.

It had been an exhausting mission and his men's casualties did not help. As much as he wanted to crawl into her bed tonight and wrap his arms around her tight, he wasn't mentally prepared to interact with her, other than to hold her. He wasn't in the mood to interact with anyone, frankly.

Ron thought the higher up the chain of command he got, the easier it would be to bear the losses. Turned out, the only thing it meant was more pain as his responsibility increased.

He'd already been through one debrief in Washington, he just wanted to get this next one out of the way, but he knew he owed the people on his base more than a half-assed account of what happened to their brothers, so he took a deep breath and put his game face on.

****

*Brenna*

She knew something was wrong the minute she heard his voice when he called her a few days ago. He blamed it on being tired but she knew it was more than that. Since he wouldn't tell her what was going on, and he didn't really say much, she'd felt extra responsible to keep their conversation going and cheerful. She'd ended up feeling like a blabbering idiot.

The news story the next day of troops from Camp Pendleton being killed and injured explained a lot. Why hadn't he just told her what he was upset about? Did he think she wouldn't understand?

She cared about Ron. A lot. But she'd been here before; only knowing one side of a man, not sharing his life completely... It was not something she was interested in doing again.

Yet, based on how much she'd missed him these last two weeks, she conceded there was no way she wasn't going to at least try like hell for him to let her into his life.

Brenna knew Ron was arriving in San Diego this afternoon. She wasn't sure how to play things. Did she seek him out, letting him know how much she cared for him and that he could tell her anything? Or did she let him come to her? And if she waited, what did she do if he didn't come to her?

She opted to back off and see what he decided to do next.

She didn't like his choice very much.

\*\*\*\*

Ron texted Brenna the night he arrived in San Diego to tell her he was tired and just wanted to go home to bed. She wished he would ask her to join him so she could comfort him and let him know she was there to listen if he needed to talk. Also selfishly, she needed to feel his body next to hers. She'd missed him so much; it stung he didn't need or want her.

He had an excuse not to see her the next day too. On the third day when he begged off, she simply replied: **No worries. I'm headed to Sullivan's Island in the morning. Maybe I'll see you when I get back. If not, please be safe**.

He didn't respond, and she wasn't surprised.

She was done with this shit. She understood he was hurting but shutting her out wasn't going to fix that.

Unfortunately, when she called Cassie to ask if she could stay with Zona, she learned that her sister was headed out the door to a conference. Luke wasn't answering his phone.

Now what?

The last time she'd boarded Zona in a kennel, the pup was skittish for a week, and Brenna vowed she wouldn't do that again, so unless she could talk Kyle into watching her dog, it looked like she wasn't really going anywhere.

Kyle Montgomery had been Danny's teammate and best man at their wedding. He was also her daughter's godfather and had really stepped up when Danny died. Whenever there was an event in Danielle's life that her father would have attended, Kyle was there, every time. Graduation, Honors Night, her volleyball games, Parents' Nights, meeting her prom dates—anything important, he showed up for. She loved him for that. So did Danielle.

He knew Brenna was dating someone, but she had been purposefully vague the last time they spoke. She knew if she called him, and he did her this favor, she'd feel obligated to tell him more. Unable to decide if she was up for that, she opted not to think about it anymore and figure it out in the morning.

She looked around the kitchen and suddenly felt like she was going to crawl out of her skin if she stayed there for one more minute.

Tucson was only a six-hour drive... and she could take Zona with her.

Problem solved.

Brenna raced up the stairs to pack a bag. When she had a suitcase on her bed to start filling, she remembered she needed to charge her phone, which was still on the kitchen counter. She ran back down to the kitchen, grabbed the phone off the island, and headed back upstairs at full speed. By this time, Zona had become excited at all the running around taking place without her so she decided to race Brenna to the top, knocking her owner out of the way to get there first. Brenna tumbled backward, unable to catch herself as she fell down the flight of stairs and landed two steps from the bottom.

She came to, not knowing how long she'd been unconscious. The cracked screen on her phone showed her the time, so she knew it couldn't have been long. She had a hard time getting up, and when she moved to push her body up, she felt the most excruciating pain she'd ever felt in her life shoot through her shoulder.

She lay there for a second before she leaned over the stairs and vomited.

*This is not good.*

The pain was almost unbearable and with clenched teeth, she tried to figure out what to do next. 911 was the smartest option, but she knew that would somehow lead to her picture being in the *Out and About* section tomorrow. Cassie was gone by now, Danielle was four hundred miles away, so that left her with two options, Kyle or Ron.

She refused to be the damsel in distress again for Ron.

Scrolling through her phone as best she could with the broken screen, she found Kyle's contact information and hit 'call'.

He answered on the third ring. "Hey, this is a nice surprise!"

When she heard his voice, she knew he would help her so her survival mode dissipated, and that's when she really began to feel the pain. Brenna managed to get out what happened and Kyle said, "I'm on my way," before hanging up.

Her shoulder hurt so bad that she was crying. God, she had to be the most pathetic site in San Diego. She was sure her makeup had smeared down her face, her shoulder was dangling, a pile of barf was next to her, and the way her head was had started to hurt, she probably had a few good knots on it.

*Fuck, did I lock the front door?*

She was going to have make it over to the entryway to let Kyle in if she had. Brenna thought about all the times she laid in bed wondering if she'd remembered to lock the door. For the first time ever, she hoped she hadn't.

Zona kissed her face with a whine.

"It's okay, girl," she said with her head resting against the wall. She started to feel tired, which Brenna knew was bad.

The doorbell rang, and she was surprised at how quickly Kyle had gotten there. Had she fallen asleep and lost track of time? When Zona started to go berserk at the sound, she became irritated.

*Seriously, Kyle? You're fucking ringing the bell like you expect me to answer the door?*

She could see the entry from where she was lying and hoped he'd have enough sense to look in and realize she couldn't get up. Well, not without crawling through puke.

"Come in," she begged.

*Please be unlocked.*

She heard him try the door.

*Nope, locked.*

*Fuck.*

Maybe he could break a window.

She laid there with her eyes closed, not moving a muscle.

*Hopefully he can figure a way in. Kyle's a smart guy.*

*Maybe just a little sleep while he does.*

When she heard the front door unlock, she willed her eyes to open, but they wouldn't cooperate. A voice called out, "Darlin', oh my God, what the hell happened?"

Kyle never called her darlin'. Maybe she was dreaming.

Damn her shoulder hurt. So did her head.

*Was someone really here?*

She felt arms come under her and gently scoop her up.

*You're fucking hurting me!*

She screamed at herself to open her eyes and say something!

There were now two voices. She knew she was lying in a backseat once she figured out it was a seatbelt digging into her side. Someone stroked her hair. She leaned over and threw up again.

"Sorry about that." She wasn't sure if she had actually said it or just thought it. It seemed as if everything hurt, and she felt the tears stream down, wetting the hair by her ear. She was leaning against something. Or someone?

The deep vibrations of the voice were familiar.

So was the scent.

*Danny?*

*Wait, no, it can't be Danny.*

*Can it?*

# Chapter Thirty

*Ron*

He paced the length of the waiting room, unable to sit still. Kyle was on his phone talking to Danielle; he had the girl's number. Ron didn't. He couldn't help but overhear their conversation when he stopped five feet from where Kyle sat.

"No, sweetheart, I don't think you need to come."

Pause.

*So he's close enough to have her number and call her sweetheart.*

"No, Dani—"

Another pause.

His voice got stern. "Listen to me. I'm here with her. Her friend, Ron, is here with her. We've got it covered."

*Friend? I'm her fucking friend?*

"Yes, he's right here."

He looked over at Ron and held out his phone. "She wants to talk to you."

*Goddamn right she does. She knows I'm not her mother's 'friend.'*

"Hey, kiddo."

He could tell she was crying.

"Ron, you have to tell me the truth. Is she going to be okay? Uncle Kyle says I don't need to come, but I just feel like I should be there."

*Uncle Kyle?*

"Dani, I don't have a good answer for you right now. They haven't let us see her, so we don't know what's going on yet. Why don't you hang tight until we know more?"

"Will you call me the second you know anything?"

"I don't have your number, honey."

"Give me yours and I'll text you so you have it."

He rattled off his number and felt his phone buzzing in his pocket three seconds later. How did she manage to do that while still talking to him? He shook his head.

*Kids and technology.*

"Okay, I'll let you know the second we get an update. Here's your uncle back." He handed the phone back to Kyle just as the doctor appeared in the waiting area.

Kyle saw him too and told Danielle he had to go. They both approached the doctor at the same time.

"How is she?" Ron asked with an urgent tone.

"Well, she's in a lot of pain at the moment. We put her shoulder back in place but couldn't give her any pain medication because we're evaluating her for a concussion. I'd say based on the vomiting and incoherent speech, chances are pretty good she has at least a mild one."

*Fuck me. Putting her shoulder back in place without pain meds? She has got to be in agony.*

Kyle asked, "Can we see her?"

The doctor shook his head. "Not yet. She's undergoing a CT scan right now. As soon as she's done, I'll send the nurse to get you."

They each offered their thanks and sat down in the uncomfortable, green vinyl chairs.

Ron hadn't been able to figure out what Kyle was doing at the beach house. He had just picked Brenna up from the stairs when the man rushed through the door, like he already knew she had fallen.

"Did you know she was hurt before you got there?"

Kyle was texting on his phone but stopped and looked over at Ron. "Yeah, that's why I was there. She called me after Zona knocked her down the stairs."

*She called Kyle for help.*

*Kyle.*

*Not me.*

"Do you have keys to her house?"

"No." Kyle shot him a look that seemed to say, *Why the fuck would you ask me such a question?*

"The door was locked when I got there. That's why I was asking."

Kyle chuckled. "So how did you get in?"

Ron hoped he didn't sound as smug as he felt when he answered. "I have a key."

He wasn't sure how he expected Kyle to react, but a simple nod of the head and a smile was definitely not it.

"Are you Brenna's brother? Danielle called you Uncle Kyle."

Kyle chuckled again. "Nope, definitely not her brother."

*What the fuck is that supposed to mean?*

"Danny's brother?"

The other man's expression took on one of sadness. "No. Danny was my best friend. We played ball together."

That's where Ron recognized him. Kyle Montgomery. He and Danny were the dynamic duo of the Padres in their glory days.

"Shortstop, right?"

"Yeah," Kyle nodded and looked down at his buzzing phone. "Christ, my goddaughter is as relentless as her old man was." Putting the phone to his ear with a smile, he said, "Sweetheart, we still don't know anything. She's getting a CAT scan as we speak."

Kyle closed his eyes and pinched the bridge of his nose as he listened to Danielle on the other end.

With a sigh, he said, "Danielle. You're a grown woman, and you can do what you want, but I feel confident telling you that your mother would not want you to come."

The former shortstop furrowed his brow at what Brenna's daughter said on the other end.

"I know her better than you think."

*Oh really? Please explain what that means.*

"Dee, I'm not going to argue with you about this. Do what you want, but when your mom is pissed off that you're here, don't say I didn't warn you."

She said something, and Kyle's eyes flew to Ron. "Yeah, he's right here."

Pause.

"Probably because we don't know anything yet."

Pause.

"I just told you why."

Another pause and Kyle sounded exasperated when he said, "I have no idea."

Kyle put his hand over the phone's microphone. "She wants to know when you're going to call her. She won't listen to me."

*She is her mother's daughter.*

Ron pulled out his phone and fired off a text to her: *Waiting to hear the CT results before calling. Listen to your uncle.*

The Marine got up and walked over to the vending machine. He brought back two cups of coffee and handed one to Kyle, who was finally off the phone.

"Thanks." The blond-haired man took the Styrofoam cup from him. He blew on the hot liquid before taking a sip. "I appreciate you having my back with Dee."

Ron shrugged. "I think you're right. Brenna wouldn't want her to come all this way."

Kyle sighed. "Dee is not only beautiful like her mother, she's as damn stubborn, too. The Roberts women know how to dig their heels in. They have been the source of many headaches these last few years." He laughed quietly, "And they've made me happier than I knew was possible. *Both* of them."

*Whoa, buddy. What are you getting at?*

A nurse stood in the waiting room calling, "Brenna Roberts?"

"Goddammit," he heard Kyle mutter.

Ron cocked his head, not understanding why Kyle was upset.

"The whole goddamn place doesn't need to know she's here and who is waiting for her. Be prepared to have your picture in tomorrow's gossip section, along with a terrific story about how she's in a love triangle with us and collapsed from the stress of it all. And that's if we're lucky."

"And if we're unlucky?" Ron asked as they moved towards the waiting nurse.

"One of us pushed her down the stairs."

That oughta be good for his promotion.

"Great," Ron said sarcastically. Walking by Kyle to follow the nurse, he added with a smirk, "I hope it's you who pushed her."

# Chapter Thirty-One

*Ron*

Brenna did have a concussion and was going to be released, with the stipulation that she couldn't be alone and had to be woken up every three hours.

Kyle looked at Ron and hesitated for just a second, before stating, "She can stay at my place."

Brenna nodded her head, grabbed Kyle's hand, and looked up at him with a meager smile.

*Yeah, fuck that.*

"No. I'll take her home so she can sleep in her bed, and she doesn't have to worry about Zona," Ron said with authority. The tone in his voice suggested it would be unwise to argue with him, and yet, Kyle did anyway.

"It's really okay. I can spend the night at her place, I forgot about Zona. You probably have to work in the morning. I'm retired, I can make sure to wake her every three hours like the doctor said, and be with her all day, no problem."

Ron shook his head. "No, I don't have to work tomorrow, and I will be taking her home." With a smartass grin, he added, "Besides, your car is going to smell like puke."

Kyle dished it back. "At least I have a car here."

"I do, too. And a driver."

Kyle raised his eyebrows. "Oh?"

Ron shrugged his shoulders. "Perks of the job that I rarely take advantage of."

True to his word, there was a car waiting to drive Ron and Brenna back to the beach house.

Ron helped maneuver Brenna with her sling into the backseat. It bothered him that she did not nestle in next to him, even though he put his arm along the headrests, indicating she should.

*No, that doesn't work.*

He slid over next to her and put his arm around her, careful of her shoulder. He was painfully aware they hadn't spoken while she was coherent, other than her responding when he asked if she was feeling better. The doctors had finally been able to give her some pain medication so she indicated she was.

He kissed her temple and he pulled her closer to him.

"You okay, darlin'?"

She shook her head *no* as tears began to fall.

"Are you in pain?"

Again, she shook her head *no*. That's what he thought.

"Are you upset with me?"

She nodded. "What were you doing at my house?"

"You said you were going to Sullivan's Island in the morning. I needed to see you to talk you into staying. Or taking me with you."

"But why? You haven't wanted to see me since you got back."

He lowered his voice, cognizant of the driver possibly overhearing him. "Things have been chaotic, Bren."

She seemed to understand he didn't want to talk about it there and didn't say anything more. But the tears continued to stream down her face until they pulled up to her house.

He carefully walked her in the front door and helped her up the stairs into her room. Once there, he spun her around to face him.

"It was a rough mission. I lost two Marines, and had three others who were wounded pretty badly, and I have been processing it. It's not that I didn't want to see you, I just knew I wouldn't be very good company."

She sighed then lifted up on her toes to kiss him, stroking his jaw with her good hand as she did.

"I wouldn't have cared how good your company was, I just wanted to be with you," she whispered. "I missed you."

"I missed you too. I'm sorry I was such an ass."

"You're here now, so you're forgiven," she said with a smile.

He put his forehead on hers. "Thank you for understanding."

She closed her eyes and nodded.

"We need to get you in bed."

"I think I have puke in my hair," she said with a wrinkled nose.

Ron checked her hair over. "I don't see any."

"I can smell it," she said as she gestured for him to help unbutton her blouse.

He tried to hide his grin when she asked if he would help with her bra.

His arms came around her and pulled her body into his. Her skin was cool to the touch. Rubbing his hands up and down her back, he kissed her temple and undid her bra. He hoped she didn't notice he was getting aroused when he slid it off her and looked at her perfect tits.

He did, however, notice her goosebumps and stiff nipples.

She had already disappeared into the bathroom when Ron realized why she wanted help with her bra.

Knocking on the door, he said loudly so she could hear through the wooden barrier, "Bren, I don't want you showering unless I'm in there to help you."

\*\*\*\*

*Brenna*

She knew she was poking the bear when she turned the shower on, but she was willing to risk it. She not only wanted to get the smell out of her hair, but she also wanted to see how he would react to her defiance. She was intrigued and nervous, but mostly turned on. She had missed him these last couple of weeks, and he was finally here and apologetic. And once again, her hero. He was so damn sexy, and his care and attention to her, combined with his alpha personality, made him irresistible.

Now if only he would let her in his life.

The drugs they'd finally given her at the hospital were outstanding. She knew he thought she was in pain, but she was feeling nothing but fantastic at the moment. And after being held in his arms again, horny.

Brenna thought about locking the door, but then realized that wouldn't be any fun. She tried to keep from giggling at the thought of Ron's expression when he discovered she had deliberately disobeyed his edict on not showering unless he was with her.

He seemed to have appeared out of thin air, and she jumped with a startled gasp when she saw him in the shower entrance.

"What did I say about showering?" he growled.

"You like it when I'm clean?" she replied in mock confusion.

He was naked and behind her in what seemed like one motion; his arms around her waist while he snarled in her ear, "No, sugar. I like it when you're dirty."

That made her toes curl.

"But you need to rest, so I'm going to help you wash your hair and then you're going to bed. *To sleep.*"

*We'll see about that.*

She turned to face him and reached down with her good hand to stroke his cock that was flying at half-mast. Grabbing her by the wrist, he turned her away from him to face the shower.

"I mean it, Brenna."

He poured shampoo into his hand and lathered her hair, while she pushed her ass back against him and wiggled.

"Evil temptress," he muttered and gave her a swat on the butt with his sudsy hand.

She let out something that sounded like a mix between a moan, a shriek, and a whimper.

Ron continued washing her hair, and she reached behind her to try to fondle his cock again. She was met with another smack on her ass, but she had been expecting it this time, so she didn't make a sound.

The sting on her wet skin felt oddly erotic.

He turned her back around to face him as he rinsed her hair. She sighed like she'd given up and leaned her head against his chest.

"Good girl," he whispered as he ran his fingers through her hair, making sure all the shampoo was rinsed.

*Hardly.*

Brenna softly kissed his neck, pushing her tits against his chest as she did, her stiff nipples caressing his skin. She reached behind his neck and pulled his face toward her.

He only hesitated a second before his lips met hers. She loved kissing him. He was amazing at it; how he coaxed her tongue to tangle with his, the pressure of his mouth, the intensity... all of it. It felt like they were in sync—every time.

Except this time.

She grabbed a handful of his wet hair to intensify things, and he pulled away, breathing heavily.

"Damn you," he sputtered and shut off the water.

Grabbing a towel, he coarsely ran it over himself before wrapping it around his waist and tending to her. With a much lighter approach than he'd just used on his body, he dried Brenna from head to toe, all the while refusing to look at her face.

His rejection stung, but the fact that he seemed mad at her pissed her off.

He held open her robe, indicating she should slip it on, but she ignored the gesture and glared at him as she walked her naked body past him on her way to the bedroom. She continued glaring when she sat on her bed but refused to get under the covers. She was chilly and really wanted to snuggle under the blankets, but she wasn't going to give him the satisfaction. She wanted him uncomfortable at having to look at her naked.

Ron walked over to the bed. The way he reached down, she thought he was going to caress her, but instead produced a tee-shirt to put over her head before helping her into her sling again. He still hadn't looked at her face.

*What the hell?*

If she hadn't been so offended and pissed, and frankly, her pride wounded, she would have asked why he was upset with her. But right now, he could fuck off.

"Do you need anything?"

He barely had the words out when she cut him off with a "Nope," and laid down, rolling onto her uninjured side, which fortunately, meant her back to him.

She felt him hesitate, then the covers were tucked around her, and she heard him move away.

A tear streamed down her cheek.

Then another.

She needed to sniffle but there wasn't a chance in hell she was going to let him know she was crying.

*Why was he being like this?*

"If you start hurting and need your pills, I'll be right over there on the chaise." His voice was distant.

She frowned and rolled onto her back to face him. "You're staying?"

"Of course I'm staying. You can't be alone."

"So why are you sleeping over there?" It was the closest she'd come to asking why he was upset with her.

He came back to her bed with a sigh and sat down next to her. Finally, he looked her in the eye and touched her nose with his fingertip. "Because you need to rest, and I'm not sure I could keep my hands off you if we were in the same bed. I'm not going to be the guy who fucks his girlfriend while she has a concussion."

*Oh, that's what his problem is.*

She started to protest, but he cut her off. "I'll wake you up in three hours like the doctor ordered."

Brenna decided to try again and caressed his thigh with her index finger. "I really do feel better. It's okay. You don't have to sleep on the lounger."

He pretended not to hear her and grabbed a pillow from the bed before pulling a blanket from a closet shelf and slipping on his boxers.

She was pretty sure he'd gotten hotter since she last saw him. The V at his waist seemed more defined, and his chest and arms more muscular. Or maybe it was because she hit her head. Or she was horny. Regardless, he was sexy as hell.

"Goodnight darlin'," he said as he kissed her on the cheek, then shut the light off.

It was a moonless night, so the room was pitch black, and she heard him curse when he ran into something on his way to the lounger by the balcony doors.

"Are you all right?" she asked in the darkness.

"Fine," he grumbled.

*That made one of them.*

It was torture, knowing he was merely feet away from her but she couldn't touch him. How could he expect her to sleep? She had missed him so much, and her anger and hurt had lessened when he revealed he came to her house to talk her into staying, or at least taking him with her to Sullivan's Island. She understood, sort of, why he hadn't reached out to her until tonight.

Brenna tossed and turned. The painkillers were still working wonders, but what she really wanted was to feel his cock against her ass and his arms around her. The fact that she could hear him moving around was not helping.

She let out a big sigh and heard his voice in the darkness. "Are you in pain?"

*Yes, my body is aching for you to touch me.*

"No, I just can't seem to get comfortable," she said softly.

"I can get you some pillows to prop your arm, that might help."

She decided to play a little dirty.

"It might be because I'm not wearing underwear. I'm kind of chilly, feeling the cool sheets on my body with nothing in between."

The silence hung in the air.

Finally, he asked, "Do you want me to help you put panties on?"

"No, I kind of like how it feels. My nipples are poking through my T-shirt though."

She knew she'd just given him a nice visual and suppressed a giggle

Once again, she was met with silence.

Breaking the quiet, she rustled around in bed and let out a tiny moan. Tracing her tits over her shirt, she murmured, "Mmm, goodnight Ron."

He didn't respond so she held her breath while listening to hear if his breathing indicated he'd fallen asleep. She didn't hear anything, so she let out another small moan as her fingertips brushed her belly.

There wasn't a sound in the room when she moaned softly again. She heard Ron say, "Oh fuck this," and his covers being thrown off.

She couldn't see him but sensed his body weight on the mattress before feeling his arms come around her waist. His lips found hers and she wrapped her unhurt arm around his neck while running her fingers through his hair.

The kiss started out urgent, but as she molded her body to his, he slowed the pace. Their tongues touched and retreated, and he sucked her lips. Her mouth eagerly returned the exploration, and soon his kisses became demanding again. She lifted her back off the mattress trying to get her body closer to his. She could feel his erection against her waist.

Oh, how she'd missed that cock!

His mouth broke away from hers in order to explore her neck, and she pulled his head closer to her, still pressing against his body.

Brenna needed to feel him inside her. Now.

"Please," she whispered.

Ron pulled his head away from her neck. Her eyes had adjusted to the darkness and she could see he was smirking when he replied, "Please what?"

"Please make love to me. I've missed you so much, I can't stand it anymore. I want you so badly."

He propped himself up on one elbow while he removed his underwear with his opposite hand. When she felt his warm, smooth cock against her body, she let out a long groan and pressed against him with her eyes closed. She was wet with anticipation as he aligned his cock with her pussy.

Only he didn't enter her.

Her eyes flew open, and she found him staring at her.

When his eyes locked on hers, he thrust his cock into her welcoming entrance. He felt fantastic as his thick shaft inched himself inside her, letting her adjust to his girth as he did.

When his entire length was deep in her pussy, he held himself still. Brushing her hair behind her ear, while continuing to watch her face, he whispered, "You should be resting."

"I don't want to," she said with a smile and moved her hips. She wanted him to fuck her. Sleep could come later.

He moved with her, but his eyes never left hers. "I have no will power when it comes to you."

Right now, she was glad. She felt close to him and that was all that mattered at the moment.

"You feel so good," Brenna whimpered when he plunged into her deep.

Lifting her hips in unison with his, they were in perfect time with each other. He stroked her hair away from her forehead before kissing her again.

It was a slow, passionate kiss. The kind that would have made her panties melt, if she were wearing any. There was a lot being said without words being exchanged. Things she was too scared to say out loud.

*I love you.*

*I need you.*

*I'm lost without you.*

*Please let me into your life.*

As he made love to her, it was if his body was responding to her unspoken words.

He loved her.

He needed her.

He was sorry for hurting her.

He couldn't let her in.

Brenna pushed the last thought out of her head and concentrated on the other three. He never promised her anything or led her to believe something differently. She had no right to expect more.

But she wanted more. She loved him and wanted to be able to love all of him. To know him, not just what he let her see.

This was complicated. More complicated than she thought this would be when they first started messing around at Ava and Travis' reception.

Dammit, he felt so fucking good. He held her close while insisting her body respond to his touch, whispering sweet nothings in her ear. Soon any thoughts not pertaining to what he was doing to her, flitted away from her mind.

How did he manage to make her feel like the most desirable woman on earth?

She felt her orgasm mounting, while he rubbed her clit in circles, murmuring, "That's it darlin', come all over my cock."

*Oh fuck.*

Her stomach clenched and she thrust her hips against him, gasping and crying out. "Yes! Oh God, yes! Oh, that's so good."

Ron continued making love to her, increasing his pace when she began to come. He gripped her hips tighter, thrusting into her fast and deep, and soon she heard his guttural moan as he reached his own climax.

He immediately kissed her, holding her face in his hands while he finished inside her. In that moment, Brenna felt more connected to him than she ever had to anyone, and was filled with sorrow when she realized that connection was fleeting. He'd return to only sharing bits and pieces of his life with her soon enough.

How was she going to get through to him?

She had no idea, she just knew she had to. He had become too important to her not to.

# Chapter Thirty-Two

*Ron*

He set an alarm and woke Brenna up every three hours, just like he'd promised the hospital staff he would. The last thing he had planned on doing last night was making love to her, but she made it pretty difficult to say no.

At first, he was pissed at himself for even entertaining the idea. He should be able to control himself better, but he was a lost cause when it came to her.

He knew her feelings were hurt that he'd avoided her upon returning to the States. He didn't know how to explain that it had nothing to do with her or how he felt about her. He just needed time to process things and grieve the losses one of his squads took. He didn't know how to do that around her, so he chose not to be, or really, even communicate with her. He knew now that was a mistake, but as he analyzed the last few days, he wasn't necessarily sure he'd do anything differently.

Maybe he'd have called her. Or at least texted her more than he had.

Her telling him she was leaving to go to South Carolina lit a fire under him to pull his head out of his ass. Thank God it had, because he wasn't sure he'd even had known she had fallen down the stairs otherwise.

Then there was the matter of Kyle Montgomery. She called Kyle instead of him when she needed help. That was troubling.

"*I know her better than you think.*" That's what the man had said to Danielle. And what the fuck was with the laugh when he told Ron, "*Definitely not her brother.*"

It was funny; he wasn't jealous of Danny, the man she'd been married to for sixteen years, but he sure as fuck was jealous of Danny's best friend.

He slid his hand around her naked waist and spooned into her backside.

*Yeah well, guess who's in her bed, Kyle? Definitely not her "friend."*

Ron was still pissed that was how Kyle had referred to him when the shortstop was talking to Brenna's daughter.

She began to stir and Ron immediately felt guilty that his jealousy had caused him to possessively hold her in her sleep. Between their lovemaking session and having to be woken up every three hours, she had not gotten a lot of much-needed rest. He would see to it that she stayed in bed today. Alone. No matter how hard she tried to get him to join her again.

He knew he was full of shit. There was no way he could resist her if she beckoned him. She proved that the night before.

The next alarm to wake her wasn't for another twenty minutes; he was going to bring her breakfast in bed.

Slipping out from under the covers, he pulled his boxers on and took Zona out before going to work in the kitchen. He made her usual morning meal of yogurt, granola, and fruit sliced on top for the two of them and put it on a tray with glasses of water and juice before heading back to her room. Zona followed but seemed especially careful on the stairs around him, like she'd learned her lesson.

*She is smart.* High strung, yes, but once the puppy stage wore off she was gonna be one helluva good dog.

Ron and Zona quietly entered the bedroom, Ron shut the alarm off before it had a chance to ring, and then he gently shook Brenna. It took her a second to open her eyes, but when she did, a big smile spread across her face when she looked up at him.

"I can't think of a better way to start my day than waking up in bed with you." She sighed.

"I was thinking the same thing."

They sat looking at each other, grinning like idiots, until Ron set the tray next to her on the bed.

"Let's get your sling adjusted and get you fed. I brought your usual."

She grabbed his hand and kissed it. "That was so thoughtful of you. I can't believe you did this."

Ron loved her appreciation of the gesture. "Do you feel like eating?"

"I am pretty hungry. I kind of lost what I ate yesterday on the stairs."

"And in Kyle's car," he said with a smirk.

Brenna groaned. "Oh God. I was hoping that was just a dream. I'm going to owe him big time."

*Owe him what, exactly?*

"I'm sure he understands. You weren't exactly lucid when we got here."

She nodded her head. "I was pretty scared. I've never experienced anything like that."

"You scared me, too."

He wanted to ask why she called Kyle instead of him but didn't think it was the appropriate time. No need to pounce on her when she'd just woken up.

She smiled at him the entire time they ate breakfast. That was not only great for his ego, but it was contagious. He couldn't help but smile back. Brenna made him so fucking happy. He finally felt at ease again. Her effect on him was unmistakable.

When they finished, Ron gathered their dirty dishes and put them on the tray, and Brenna grabbed her robe as if she was going to follow him downstairs.

"Back in bed, young lady. Doctor's orders."

Brenna frowned. "The doctor didn't say I couldn't get out of bed."

"Okay then, *my* orders."

She marched up to him, stood on her tiptoes, wrapped her uninjured arm around his neck, and lifted her face inches from his. She was pretty bold for being as tiny as she was. "You may be the boss of a lot of Marines, Ron Thompson, but you are not the boss of me."

He didn't budge.

Lifting his brows, he shot her a look that suggested, *wanna bet?*

"I cleaned up your vomit, so today, I *am* the boss of you. Get your perfect ass back in that bed before I spank it and then put it back myself."

Ron couldn't decide if her wide eyes were defiance or intrigue. Either way, she said with a huff, "Can I at least go to the bathroom?"

With a smirk, he replied, "You may."

Brenna gave a mock curtsy and said, "Thank you, milord."

She had headed into her bathroom when he shouted after her, "But no showering unless I'm there to help you. I mean it this time."

He didn't wait for her response and returned to the kitchen to clean up breakfast, chuckling to himself when he heard the shower start as he finished loading the dishwasher. She'd had a concussion and dislocated shoulder less than twenty-four hours ago, and she was still feisty as hell.

He fucking loved that about her.

\*\*\*\*

*Brenna*

True to his word, Ron made her stay in bed and rest all day. Brenna found it rather easy to comply—she truly was exhausted, plus the pain medication made her sleepy. A couple of times she woke to find him lying next to her with his hand on her hip. A contented smile would form on her lips, and she'd sigh with happiness before falling right back into a peaceful slumber.

By the time the evening came, she was wide awake. Ron was too and asked her to go with him to his house so he could change his clothes and get something to wear for the next day.

He boosted her into his truck and opened the rear door for Zona to hop in. Her dog was always happy to go for a ride.

The familiarity of his place when they walked in from the garage was comforting, and the smell brought back memories of the times they'd stayed there before his last mission. They'd had a lot of fun together. She wanted more than fun, though.

She knew he made her happy, and she thought she could make him happy. If only he'd let her in.

That was something they were going to need to discuss. Soon, before she fell even further in love with him and was past the point of no return. She wasn't asking him to divulge state secrets, but good grief, she needed more from him. So much more.

She got up from the couch to look at the books in his den while he changed his clothes. Next to his desk, she saw the dog bed he had bought Zona, exactly where it had been the last time they were there. Thinking about that little gesture of him buying the bed had meant a lot to her. It felt like he was welcoming her and her dog into his home.

Something on Ron's desk caught her eye. It was a birthday card. She felt nosy looking at it, but curiosity got the better of her and she picked it up to read the sentiments inside. It was from his mom.

*How sweet. He keeps a card from his mom on his desk.*

She'd never noticed it before the other times she'd been in his den. She looked where the card had been lying and discovered a small stack of birthday cards. The next one was from someone named Sarah who he had obviously been involved with, and it was clear she was not over him based on what she wrote, ending with her wanting to make him dinner and help him "celebrate."

*Does she not know he's dating me?* She must not, otherwise why would she send him a card like that? Why hadn't he told her?

The next one was from his Aunt Phyllis, and it had a date with her message—March 1st of this year.

March 1st was two fucking days ago.

He'd had a birthday and hadn't celebrated with her.

Who had he celebrated it with? Sarah?

Not only had Brenna not celebrated it with him, she hadn't even known about it.

But Sarah did, apparently.

Her head was reeling, and she felt like she was going to throw up. She'd been down this road before; she was so familiar with it she should be a tour guide. There was no way in hell she was doing it again. She made a promise to herself when she filed for divorce; never again would she be anybody's second choice.

She needed a drink and she didn't give a shit she wasn't supposed to mix alcohol with her pain meds.

After tossing back a whiskey, she put the glass in the dishwasher so Ron wouldn't be the wiser and saw a wine glass in the rack.

*Since when does Ron drink wine?*

Then she saw the lipstick prints.

*What.*

*The.*

*Fuck.*

It was all she could to keep from sinking to the floor and collapsing in a bawling heap. How could he do this to her? This hurt almost as bad as the first time she found lipstick on Danny's collar. Talk about cliché.

She was trying to make sense of it all when Ron came hurrying into the kitchen dressed in his fatigues with the phone to his ear and his military duffle in the other hand. Zona was right next to him, looking at him like he was the one who'd created the recipe for dog treats.

*He's not as great as you think, Zona.*

"Yeah, if you can meet us there, that would be great," he said into the phone as he switched ears with it.

Pause.

"Okay, yeah. About twenty minutes. See you then."

He hung up and gave her the look she'd already become all too familiar with.

Sighing he said, "Darlin', I gotta go. Kyle is going to stay with you tonight."

She didn't say a word as she walked out the front door. She couldn't. If she spoke, she knew she would break down. Right now, her anger was keeping her functioning. The time for curling up in a ball would come later.

All she could think while she sat in the front seat of his truck watching out the window was what a fool she had been.

Again.

Was it that all men were cheaters, or just the ones she was attracted to?

She had to admit, this one blindsided her. With Danny, she would always get a feeling that something wasn't quite right, and he would eventually get lazy and not cover his tracks, and her suspicions would be confirmed.

Other than Ron being gone for long periods of time, there had been nothing suspicious up until the last few days.

No wonder he wouldn't let her in his life, he didn't want her there. Not permanently anyway. Not enough to let her know it was his goddamn birthday. He obviously had someone else to help him celebrate that. Someone who wore dark red lipstick.

*Semper fi, my ass, you son-of-a-bitch.*

So what had Brenna been to him? Was she the side piece that no one knew about? She guessed that would explain some things—like why she'd never met his family or any of his friends. Why he was so secretive about his work. Why he didn't let her know much about him. If Luke hadn't confirmed his identity, she'd even be questioning that.

She was silent the entire ride to her house, hopping out of the truck before he'd even put it in park. Kyle was already there, waiting on the bench by the front door. Brenna knew he could tell she was upset when she walked by him, keys to her house in hand.

She opened the door to let Kyle through, and he paused to tilt her chin up to look at him.

"Are you okay?"

She shook her head slightly and cast her eyes toward Ron coming up the walk with Zona, who galloped toward them the minute she recognized Danielle's godfather.

He drew in a sharp breath and squeezed her hand.

"I'll just be in the other room if you need me," he whispered in her ear before disappearing inside with Zona.

Brenna stood in the doorway as Ron approached. He looked confused.

"Darlin', I'm—"

She shook her head to stop him from continuing. "I can't do this anymore," she whispered, tears welling in her eyes.

His jaw clenched like she'd just struck him.

"Just a few more months. Hang in there with me."

He thought she was upset that he was leaving again. She shook her head again.

"Can we talk about this when I get back?" He reached out to push her hair behind her ear.

Brenna jerked away from his touch. "I don't think there's anything left to say."

"There's plenty left to say," he growled.

"Like what? Like the real reason you couldn't come see me when you got back was because you were too busy fucking Sarah on your birthday?"

The look of surprise on his face provided her with momentary satisfaction.

He stared at her for a second while composing himself before responding, "That's not at all what happened."

She snorted in disbelief.

"Brenna, you need to listen to me. I did not fuck Sarah."

"But she was with you on your birthday."

He looked down and quietly said, "Let me explain."

His confirmation hit her like a punch to the stomach. "There's nothing to explain." She shrugged her shoulders in defeat. "You were with someone else on your birthday. I'm not important enough to spend it with you, and, to top it all off, you made up some bullshit excuse about why you couldn't see me."

He closed his eyes and shook his head slightly, like she was trying his patience. "You're not even close."

"Don't fucking insult me like I'm an idiot," she huffed.

He didn't say anything, just looked down and sighed.

"I don't want to see you anymore," she said quietly.

He jerked his head up to look at her. "Is that what you really want?"

She was surprised at how hurt he sounded when he asked that.

Brenna closed her eyes and nodded her head as the tears streamed down her face.

"Darlin', you've got it all wrong, that's not—"

She jumped at Kyle's voice behind her. "I think you better go," he said sternly to Ron while putting his hand at the small of Brenna's back.

Ron looked at Kyle and then back at Brenna.

"I will call you when I get back. We're going to talk about this," he said before nodding curtly at Kyle and turning on his heel to leave.

Brenna held it together until the front door closed, and then she broke down in sobs while Kyle held her tightly against him.

\*\*\*\*

*Ron*

He was pissed.

Pissed that Kyle swooped in and tried to be the tough guy/savior for Brenna. Fuck that guy.

Pissed that Sarah had shown up unannounced on his birthday—after he'd been drinking and his defenses were down. She'd brought dinner and a cake. When she eluded that her body was the present he was supposed to unwrap, he had been put in a terrible position.

Fucking pissed at himself for standing aside, against his better judgment, and letting Sarah come inside his house in the first place.

He was also pissed at Brenna for having so little faith in him.

But mostly he was fuming at how helpless he felt. He was about to get on a plane and fly umpteen thousand miles away from San Diego for Lord knew how long, when what he needed to be doing was setting things straight with his gorgeous girlfriend. And possibly kicking Kyle's ass in the process.

His goddamn promotion couldn't come soon enough.

# Chapter Thirty-Three

*Brenna*

Kyle sat with her on the couch and let her cry in his arms while he stroked her back. When her breathing stilled, he kissed her hair and pulled away. Wiping her tears away, he asked, "What happened?"

Tears filled her eyes again as she shrugged her shoulders. "It was like Danny all over again."

He squinted his eyes and cocked his head. "What do you mean?"

"Really, Kyle? What the hell do you think I mean?" She didn't mean to snap but couldn't help it. He knew damn well what she was talking about, was he really going to make her say it out loud?

"Bren, I'm not trying to be insensitive. I loved Danny, but he was an idiot. He had no idea how lucky he was to have you for his wife. He totally took you for granted."

Kyle had never said anything like that to her before. Somehow, his acknowledgment that Danny was wrong made her feel validated.

"But, I gotta tell you, Bren. I didn't get that impression with Ron. He seemed to understand exactly how special you are. That's why I'm asking *what do you mean.*"

Brenna snorted in disagreement. "Pffst. So special that he spent his birthday with his ex. A birthday that, by the way, I didn't even know about."

Kyle winced. "Are you sure?"

"Yes I'm sure! He even admitted it outside right before you came out."

"Well now I wish I would have knocked him on his ass. He's not the guy who stood you up a few months ago, is he?"

A gasp escaped her. "How did you know about that? Did Dee say something to you?"

He chuckled. "So *Out and About* got something right for once. Was it him?"

Brenna shook her head. "No, his name was Ray."

"Well, that guy is an idiot too. What's with you and idiots?"

She nodded. "I don't know. I'm just lucky *Out and About* never got wind of Ray assaulting me on New Year's Eve."

"*What*?!" Kyle roared.

"Yep. Ron actually was the one who saved me. He knew something was wrong and came back to my hotel room even though he was supposed to be headed to the base. He said his gut told him to turn around, and that he always trusted his gut."

He let out a low whistle. "Well, was his gut not working when he spent his birthday with his ex?"

Tears filled Brenna's eyes again and she brought her shoulders toward her ears. "I just don't get it. He always treated me like I was special, the sexiest woman on earth. Then he got back from his last mission and avoided me. Like, barely a text until yesterday. He only showed up because I told him I was going to Sullivan's Island."

"I know he was pretty worried about you after your fall."

"He was?"

Kyle chuckled. "Uh, yeah. He had a hard time letting even the hospital personnel take you from him, and he was pretty pissed when they wouldn't let him go back with you."

"Really?"

"He obviously cares about you. Maybe you should hear what he has to say when he gets back."

"Kyle, I vowed I would never again go through what I went through with Danny."

He sighed. "You know I love you and have always regretted making Danny show you around the stadium when you were doing research for your movie. It was supposed to be me who gave you the tour, but Danny owed me a favor so I cashed it in. If I had known you're so beautiful, inside and out, I would have snatched you up, and you never would have met Danny until we got back from our honeymoon."

She smiled at how sweet he was being. "You know that..." She started to interrupt but he held his hand up.

"Let me finish. It wasn't me you ended up with, it was Danny. He wasn't worthy of you, but I never said anything because he was my best friend. Ron isn't my friend, and I've only met him once, but from what I saw when I did, and from what Dee has told me about how happy he makes you, I have to say he seems to deserve to at least be able to tell his side of the story."

*Shit.* Was Kyle right? Did she just make a huge mistake? What if something happened to Ron before she got a chance to hear him out?

She reached up and touched his cheek. "Why weren't you the one to show me around the park that day?" she asked wistfully.

He grabbed her wrist and kissed it. "It wasn't meant to be. I would have knocked you up that night, and you never would have written *Warning Track*, or anything else because I would have kept you barefoot and pregnant."

Brenna grinned. "You're such an ass. God, I love you. But you're right, if you would have knocked me up, you never would have knocked Evelyn up, and you wouldn't have Zach. And I wouldn't have Danielle."

His eyes grew wide. "I never knocked Evelyn up. Zach isn't my son—he's Alan's."

She rolled her eyes. "You and I both know that's bullshit. I don't care what Zach's birth certificate says; that boy looks exactly like you, and I also know for a fact that you and Evelyn were having a torrid love affair right around the time she got pregnant."

"Oh, you do, do you? And just how do you know this *for a fact?*"

"Because she told me."

That seemed to knock the wind out of his sails.

"Did she tell you Zach is mine?" he whispered.

"No. But you know he is, don't you?"

He closed his eyes and sighed. "I don't know, Bren. I have a lot of regrets about how I handled things."

She shrugged her shoulders. "So fix it. You can still do that, you know, you're not dead."

A slow smile formed as he stared at her while he took in what she just said. "Um, we're dealing with your love life tonight. Not mine."

She leaned in and hugged him with one arm. "We're a pair of pathetic souls, huh?"

He gave a wry smirk. "Well one of us is more pathetic than the other."

"Hey!" she said with an indignant push to his shoulder.

"I didn't say which one of us!" He laughed and held his arms up as if to shield himself from any blows.

Brenna rested her fist on Kyle's chest and leaned against his shoulder.

"What should I do?" she sighed.

"Follow your heart."

She looked up at him with a wicked grin. "You should practice what you preach, ya know."

# Chapter Thirty-Four

*Brenna*

She was nervous. She knew Ron arrived home today; it had been all over the news. The squad he was bringing home had been in an intense firefight, and all his men made it out alive. They were hometown heroes and all of San Diego was excited to welcome them back.

No one could be as excited as she was. She wished she could be there when he got off the plane. She fantasized about the look on his face when she ran toward him, her arms open wide. He would pick her up and twirl her around before kissing her. His beautiful lips on hers with his arms around her tight, both of them ecstatic to be together again.

She envisioned him having the most perfect, reasonable explanation about why he had spent his birthday with Sarah. He'd beg her forgiveness, and they wouldn't be able to keep their hands off each other as they made their way to his house—barely staying dressed before getting inside. Once they made it inside.... She'd let her body do the talking about how sorry she was for doubting him.

If only life was as good as her imagination.

They had only communicated briefly since he went on this mission. After her talk with Kyle the night Ron left, she had sent the Marine a text asking him to be careful. He responded that he would be, and they'd talk when he got home. He sent her another message right after the battle his men were in, letting her know he was safe, and she was thankful he'd thought of her. He sent her one more text letting her know when he'd be home and asked if they could have dinner the night after he arrived.

She was disappointed he hadn't asked her to be at Miramar with the families to welcome the men home. She understood, given how they had left things, but the fact that he hadn't wanted her there let doubt creep into her mind. Their communication had been brief, and she didn't know if it was because what she had said to him the night he left or because that was all he had time for.

Every news station in town was at the base, filming when the Marines stepped onto the tarmac and into the arms of their loved ones. She felt badly for Ron. Although he hadn't been overseas continually as long as this unit had been, he'd experienced his fair portion of hell with them. The thought of him stepping off the plane with no one there to greet him while his Marines were being kissed and hugged by their loved ones made her tear up. Everyone should be greeted with love when they returned. Especially after what he had been through.

Watching it on TV made her wish she had gone, even if he hadn't asked her to. She almost walked out the door twice to head to the base, but uncertainty edged its way in each time. He hadn't asked her to be there, and she didn't want to overstep. They'd been apart longer than actually together, and their status as a couple was questionable. What if there was something going on with Sarah? Maybe that was what he had to explain?

Thinking about what Kyle, and later Cassie, had said, she vehemently shook her head, trying to make the doubts go away.

She smiled when she imagined his face when he saw her again. He had such a way of making her feel desired. God, she couldn't wait to see him. While she wasn't new to being separated from her lover, she did it with Danny every year once spring training started—she was new to being separated with little contact. Truth be told, she was disappointed that Ron wanted to wait until tomorrow to see her. That he was *able to* wait.

She anxiously scrutinized the news coverage, hoping to catch a glimpse of him. Her heart skipped a beat when she saw him walking in the background of the footage. She'd recognize that swagger anywhere. *God he was handsome!* Then she saw what looked like a younger version of Ron, walk up and embrace him for a long time, well, long for a guy hug, and then they pulled apart, laughing while patting each others' backs.

Brenna smiled at the tenderness of the exchange.

Next, she saw what she assumed were his parents do the same. While she was glad there had been someone to greet him after all, she also felt a twinge of hurt that she hadn't been invited to be there.

Out of nowhere, a tan, long-haired brunette in a sky-blue top and white shorts jumped in his arms, wrapping her long legs around his waist and her arms around neck, before proceeding to plant kisses everywhere on his face. Brenna recognized that shade of lipstick.

The camera panned away as his hands came under her ass.

Brenna sat stunned looking at the television for a few minutes. She didn't know if she wanted to be sick, cry, or break something.

Maybe it wasn't Ron, just someone who looked like him?

Fortunately, she had been recording the coverage so she was able to rewind and pause. That was most definitely General Thompson. Unfortunately, she had the ability to play it over and over, which she did.

She sent a text to Cassie: **Can you come over? Please?**

**Cassie: On my way.**

She loved that about her sister. Cass never asked why, she was just always there whenever Brenna needed her.

When Cassie arrived, Brenna had cried her makeup off and was sitting on the couch under a throw.

"What's going on, Bren?"

Brenna didn't say a word, just hit 'play' on the DVR to start the news coverage. Cassie watched the first few seconds confused, then said, "Is that Ron?"

She kept watching until the camera cut away from him.

Brenna shut the TV off. "So, there's that."

Cassie seemed almost more stunned than Brenna.

"I'm so sorry, Bren."

Brenna pursed her lips and sighed. She was all cried out. "Yeah, me too."

"I can't believe I tried to convince you that there had to be a good explanation about his birthday. God, I feel like such an asshole."

"You're not an asshole. We all wanted to believe there had to be more to the story."

Her little sister shook her head. "I would have bet money on it. I'm—I'm shocked, frankly. He didn't seem the type."

"I'm so fucking stupid," Brenna whispered. "Did I want this fairytale so badly that I overlooked the signs, *again*? Why the fuck haven't I learned yet?"

"Learned what exactly? It's not your fault. He had us all fooled. How could you have known?"

Her sister was right; there was no way she could have known. He didn't give any of the tell-tale signs: no disappearing for hours at a time, no phone calls in the middle of the night, no showering the second he got home. When he was with her, she felt like the most important person in the world, like there was nowhere else he'd rather be than with her.

"I didn't even have an inkling there was someone else. With Danny, I always felt a pit in my stomach that something was wrong. But since I wanted to keep up the façade as badly as Danny did, I never did anything about it."

"You did, eventually."

Brenna gave a half smile. "Funny how getting ready to turn forty makes you realize you no longer give a damn what other people think. Of course, Lisa Weber letting me know she was sleeping with my husband didn't really leave me a choice to keep my head in the sand."

"Ugh, don't say that bitch's name out loud again." Cassie made a mock-spitting motion to the ground, as if cursing Danny's last mistress' name. "Seriously, she is one ugly hag. Why the fuck he cheated with someone who looks like a witch is beyond me."

Brenna painfully remembered her sister cyber stalking Lisa to find out what Danny's lover looked like after she had contacted Brenna. Cassie couldn't get over how unattractive she thought the woman was.

"Well, at least Ron's got better taste," Brenna attempted to joke.

Cassie rolled her eyes. "Please, she looks like a slut."

Brenna knew her sister was just trying to make her feel better. The woman with her legs wrapped around Ron was quite attractive and didn't look like a slut.

On second thought, the fact that she had her legs wrapped around Brenna's boyfriend *did* make her look like a tramp.

Brenna's pride wouldn't let her agree with Cassie out loud.

"I'm sure she has a lovely personality," was as low as she would sink.

They sat in silence before Cassie jumped up from the couch and headed to the kitchen. "Let's have a drink."

After three glasses of wine, Brenna started opening up.

"You know, I used to be upset about how much of my life I'd wasted with Danny. I thought the universe was trying to make amends by sending me Ron. I kept telling myself I'd stayed with Danny instead of moving on, so when Ron was ready to find me, I was available for him. I can't believe I fell for his *Always Faithful* bullshit. I *wanted* to fall for it. He made me feel so damn special."

Cassie gave her a sympathetic hug.

Brenna took another sip of wine before declaring, "That's it. I am swearing off men!"

Unfortunately, Ron had made her realize again how wonderful sex could be. That part of her had sort of withered away while she was with her husband. Maybe she'd take one of those unsolicited dick pic offers up if she got horny, but that was it. Just a hook-up, nothing more.

Except in the back of her mind, she knew damn well she could never do that. But she was pissed and hurt right now, dammit! So, if she told herself that's what she was going to do, that's what she was going to do. She was gonna start swiping left, or was it right?

# Chapter Thirty-Five

*Ron*

He was glad to be back in the States and was pleased his family had been able to make it for his return. He'd thought about asking Brenna to be there—had planned on it, until his kid brother, Greg, emailed that he was going to be home, and their mom and dad wanted him to take them to the base to be there when Ron got off the plane. Ron wasn't ready to put Brenna through the *meet the parents* show yet.

Then Sarah jumped him, literally—he definitely hadn't expected that and was not happy about it. He made that fact quite clear when he set her down and practically shoved her away from him. She'd reached out to Ron's parents to see if they were going to Miramar to greet Ron, and of course, they invited her to join them. His mom loved Sarah and viewed her as the best hope at getting grandchildren. Little did his mother know that was never going to happen.

Ron was annoyed at Sarah's presumptuousness. No, it was more than presumptuousness, it was fucking underhanded how she went about it. Calling his mom for an invitation? Especially after he had asked her to leave on his birthday when she came on to him. She seemed to think she could change his mind by getting his mom on her side.

It wasn't happenin'. Yeah, he'd been a gentleman and didn't embarrass her in front of his family, but they were going to have a *Come to Jesus* session because what she did was unacceptable. They were over; the sooner she came to terms with that, the better.

He listened to Sarah prattle on all through dinner and dessert. She was easy on the eyes, not so much on the ears. His parents didn't seem to notice, although his brother shot Ron a few looks that indicated he did.

Fuck, he missed Brenna.

He had asked her out for dinner tomorrow night so he could explain that nothing happened with Sarah. He still didn't have a good excuse why he hadn't told her about his birthday, other than he hadn't really thought much about it, even on the actual day. He had just wanted to be alone when he got home last time.

He felt the complete opposite today. If he wasn't so unsure that she was going to understand and forgive him, he'd go crawl into bed with her tonight so he could wake up with her in his arms. He didn't want to waste a minute of his leave without her and wanted to be in bed with her all day. And, of course, all night, too. Actually, the whole weekend sounded pretty damn perfect. He couldn't wait to hold her, smell her, taste her, and yes, fuck her six ways to Sunday. If she still wanted him.

**** 

They all stood in the parking lot of the restaurant after dinner. Ron promised he'd be at his parents for Sunday brunch. He considered asking Brenna to join him; he needed to introduce her to his family. His brother, Greg, suggested they play golf in a few weeks when he was back in town.

"I'm going to be home more though, so plan on getting schooled on the course a lot," Greg slapped Ron on the back and squeezed his shoulder, pulling him away from everyone.

"Oh yeah? Why is that? You dating someone?" Ron teased.

His brother just grinned.

"Holy shit! You are. What's her name?"

"Frankie; she's a single mom. I haven't told Mom, so don't say anything yet, but I want you to meet her. Maybe we could have dinner."

Now maybe his mother would get off his back if Greg could give her ready-made grandchildren.

"That sounds great, I can't wait. There's someone I want you to meet too," Ron said quietly.

Greg looked at Sarah. "Oh?"

Ron shook his head in disgust. "I'm not sure whose idea that was," he gestured toward Sarah, "but it was a bad one."

"Sorry. It definitely wasn't mine."

They walked back toward where his parents and Sarah were still talking, and the group gravitated toward Greg's car. Everyone got in but Sarah and Ron. Ron shot her a look that suggested she should get in his brother's car. He started to reach for the door handle to open the door for her, when she said with a smile, "Can you give me a ride back to the base so

I can pick up my car? It's really out of your brother's way, but you'll drive right by."

His mother had rolled her window down, otherwise he might have said what he was thinking. Through gritted teeth and a fake smile, he managed, "Sure."

Greg shrugged his shoulders in a helpless gesture, and his family drove off, leaving him standing alone with Sarah. Without a word, he turned and strode toward his vehicle, while she scurried to keep up with him. He wasn't going to open her door for her, he wasn't feeling particularly chivalrous, but it was too ingrained in him, and he tugged on the handle, gesturing for her to get in. At least he didn't boost her up.

Ron was annoyed as he hopped in the cab. He didn't like being manipulated, and that's exactly what Sarah was doing. He went to fire up the engine when she grabbed him at the sleeve and said, "Can we talk for a second?"

*Only a second because I'm not in the fucking mood for this shit.*

"Ron, when I learned you were over there in that gunfight, I'd never been so scared. I thought, *what if I never got the chance to hold him again and tell him how I feel?* I know you said on your birthday that we weren't right for each other, but I'm still in love with you. I want you back in my life. I don't care about having a family. I just want you, any way I can get that. We were so good together; I know we can be again."

Although he hadn't been exactly heartbroken when she left over a year ago, he had cared about her. Had she said all this to him just four months ago, he would have considered having her back in his life—and his bed. But then he met Brenna, and everything changed.

He stopped Sarah from running her hand up and down his arm and placed it back in her lap.

They were going to have that *Come to Jesus* talk, but he needed to be more gentle than he had originally planned on.

"We can't, Sarah. We both know how it would end again. I'm not what you're looking for. You need a man who can marry you and give you a family. I can't do that."

"I don't care about any of that, Ron! I just care about you, about us."

He shook his head. "We can't."

"Yes, yes we can! We were such a great couple! I know I can make you happy!"

How was he going to let her down easy? He finally decided to just be honest.

"I'm seeing someone else. And I'm in love with her."

The brunette girl jerked her head as if he'd physically slapped her. Fuck, he did not like being in this position.

*Hey family, come back!*

With tears in her eyes, she managed to croak out, "You—you love her?"

Shit, he probably should be telling Brenna this before telling Sarah.

He tried to look as kind as he could when he replied. "I do. I'm crazy about her."

****

Ron sent Brenna a text that evening letting her know he'd arrived safely back in San Diego.

No response.

He tried again.

**Ron: I'll pick you up at six tomorrow was his next text to her.**

**Brenna: I can't make it.**

That wasn't going to work. Ignoring her, he fired back.

**Ron: I'll see you tomorrow.**

She was going to listen to him. He wasn't letting her go that easy.

He loved her, dammit.

# Chapter Thirty-Six

*Ron*

He showed up at the beach house at a quarter to six, roses in hand. He dressed as though they were still going to dinner, dark grey slacks and a sage green button-down shirt, although he wasn't banking on them really going out.

Zona was at the window of the entry with her excited bark but no one came to the door. He rang the bell again and thought about using his key, when Cassie appeared with a frown.

"She's not here," was all the younger sister said when she yanked open the door and didn't even try to hold Zona back from charging at him full speed.

With an "oomph" when the dog knocked into him, Ron asked when she'd be home.

"No idea." She responded like she was bored.

*Ah, Brenna's people definitely love and look out for her.*

Right now, they thought Ron was public enemy number one.

"Cassie, are we going to do this again? You know how much I care about your sister. I need to talk to her; tell me where she is."

"*Care about her?*" Cassie roared. "Is that how they do it in the Marine Corps? Show people they care by seeing other people?"

He didn't want to get into it with Brenna's Mini-Me. He owed Brenna an explanation about his birthday, not her younger version.

"Cassie, tell me where she is." He used his best general voice, the one that most people recognized meant business. He should have known it wasn't going to work on the younger Sullivan sister.

"Go to hell," she sneered before attempting to slam the door, forgetting Zona was still outside with him.

He put his foot on the threshold to keep it from closing and stepped inside with the pup.

"You've got a lot of nerve..." she started again until Brenna's voice came from the hall.

"It's okay, Cass," she said quietly as she appeared barefoot, in light blue jeans and a baby pink cashmere sweater, hugging her arms around her middle.

Cassie obviously didn't know what to do. She looked between Ron and Brenna, grimacing at Ron the entire time.

"Are you sure?"

Brenna nodded her head. "I'll be fine."

When Cassie hesitated, Brenna gave a weak smile and offered her reassurance. "I promise."

Cassie scowled one last time at Ron, then replied, "I'll be on the patio when you need me."

*When* Brenna needed her. That wasn't promising; like Cassie knew something Ron didn't.

Ron offered the flowers to Brenna, who reluctantly accepted them and turned toward the kitchen, where she set them down on the counter without putting them in water.

He stood in the doorway, watching her with his hands in his pockets. Her pink sweater looked fuzzy and soft, and he wanted to run his hands up and down her back.

She didn't offer him anything to drink, which was unlike her, nor did she say anything.

He thought, based on the texts they'd exchanged since the last time they were together, that she would be more receptive to hearing him out. Like she understood nothing happened with Sarah, and things were more innocent than they originally appeared. He was obviously wrong. It seemed like she'd taken the time during their separation to grow angrier with him.

Gesturing toward the couch in the family room, he asked, "Can we sit down?"

Brenna shrugged but made her way to the couch, where she sat with a leg tucked under her so a knee was sticking out, as if creating another barrier between them. He took the hint and sat a foot away from her.

With his elbows on his knees and hands steepled between his legs, he let out a long exhale before blurting out, "Nothing happened with Sarah."

She looked at him for what felt like an eternity before finally nodding her head once. "But you were with her on your birthday."

"She came over uninvited."

"But she was with you. She was, not me. On your birthday."

He didn't have a good response other than, "Yes."

"Just like she was with you yesterday when you got off the plane."

"How did you—?"

She shook her head. "It doesn't matter."

"Nothing happened. She came with my parents. I didn't even know she was coming."

She took a deep breath but didn't respond.

"You have to believe me, Bren."

With a shrug of the shoulders, she said, "I do."

He heaved a sigh of relief. Relief that was short-lived.

"We had a wonderful love affair, Ron, but it has run its course. It's just too hard. You were right, and I'm sorry I didn't listen when you warned me I would be unhappy."

*Why is she using the past tense?*

"Darlin', Sarah doesn't mean anything to me. *You* are who is important to me."

"And yet, it was Sarah who has met your parents. It was her who spent your birthday with you. It was her that was there yesterday with your family and the other families when you got off the plane."

"Brenna, I didn't want her there. I—"

She cut him off as tears filled her eyes. "It doesn't matter. I started seeing someone else while you were away. I'm sorry."

He felt like someone had taken a baseball bat to his stomach.

"Who?" he growled.

"It doesn't matter."

"*Who*?!"

"Kyle."

He knew it. The way Kyle had stood with his hand at the small of her back, how protective he was, the things he said that hinted there was more to their relationship than friendship... Ron had provided Kyle with the perfect opportunity to be there for her. Kyle was no fool, he took it.

He sat silent for a moment before standing up. "Well, I hope everything works out for you," he said before heading toward the door.

"Ron, wait!"

He turned around on his heel and looked at where she had gotten to her feet.

She didn't say anything else, just stood with her bottom lip quivering. It took every ounce of his strength not to take her in his arms and kiss her trembling mouth. But it was no longer his mouth to kiss.

He offered a small smile. "If you ever need anything, you know I'll be there." He then turned around and left.

He had to get out of there before he did or said something he shouldn't. She was Kyle's now, not his. And unlike Kyle, Ron respected that. Regardless if it hurt like hell.

If he hurried, he could still make his dinner reservation.

# Chapter Thirty-Seven

*Brenna*

It'd been six weeks since she'd seen Ron. She thought about him every day and prayed he was safe, and, of course, wondered if he was with Sarah, or dating someone new altogether.

She had hardly left the house since she lied to him and said she was with Kyle. Each time she relived that night and came to the part of the hurt on his face, it filled her with remorse and left her questioning if she had done the right thing. She shouldn't have ended things with a lie.

It did motivate her to finish the screenplay she had started while he was overseas though. She wasn't surprised how easily it flowed out of her; it was inspired by her and Ron's love story, except the characters got the happily ever after ending she and Ron had missed out on.

Brenna's agent forwarded the rough draft to the studios, even before it went to the editors—a move that surprised Brenna, considering how long it'd been since she'd submitted anything. That was promising. Then came the phone call she had been both dreading and praying for; she had a meeting scheduled tomorrow with the studio executives.

She obviously had been praying someone would be interested so her work was validated, but also because, for some reason, the screenplay becoming a movie somehow confirmed to her that their relationship had been real. She had allowed herself to grieve losing him, but in doing so recognized just how wonderful her time with him had been, regardless of how brief it was.

She dreaded it because it brought the fact they were over front and center, and how shitty their story really ended. They didn't get their happy ending.

Nevertheless, she wouldn't trade what they'd had together, even if it meant she wouldn't have the pain. The hurt had lessened, exchanged for regret and wonder about *what might have been* had their circumstances been different. Then there was the loneliness.

She was hopeful her Prince Charming was out there. Ron had made her see there was room in her life, and her bed, if she ever did find him. Maybe he'd also have a crooked nose but, she doubted anyone's smile would ever compare to her Marine's.

Brenna would always consider Ron *her* Marine. Although he probably never really was hers to begin with, he sure had made her feel like she was his. Even if it wasn't real, she cherished the memory of it, regardless if it was bittersweet.

The meeting with the studio execs was in Los Angeles, so Luke was coming by that night and taking Zona home with him. Brenna wished things would have worked out between him and Cassie, but given Cassie's track record, maybe it was better this way.

Luke arrived right on time. Brenna was half-hoping her sister would be with him. He walked through the door alone and she had to agree with Cassie's assessment the first time she saw the SWAT sergeant, he *was* sex on a stick. Not only was he sexy as hell, but he was one of the good guys.

"Hey! Thanks for coming all this way to get Zona. I really appreciate it."

"No problem. It's my day off. It was nice to go for a drive."

"No Rex with you?"

Luke shook his head. "I don't trust him in the Jeep with Zona. I'm worried he's going to show off for her and jump out."

That brought a smile to Brenna's lips.

"No date with you?"

The pained look he gave made her immediately regret asking the tongue-in-cheek question.

"Haven't found one that I trust not to jump out of the Jeep either."

"Hypothetically, if you did find one that you thought wouldn't jump out, but then she did, would you chase after her?"

He gave a rueful smile. "If I thought she was the one, you bet your ass I would."

"I wonder what that would feel like in real life," she mused aloud while staring into space, as if picturing it. She never had had someone chase her, although she'd written plenty of heroine's stories where it happened, so she could imagine it.

Luke brought her back to reality. "Hey, congratulations on your screenplay."

"Thanks, it was a long time coming," she said with a modest smile.

"What took so long?"

"I'd lost my inspiration, but luckily, Ron helped me find it. At least I got my happily ever after on paper."

He gave a quizzical look.

"It's semi-autobiographical. Except I got to write the ending with Ron that I wanted, not the ending I actually got."

"Well, if it helps, I saw him yesterday at a fundraising planning meeting for the Wounded Warrior Project, and he looked like shit."

She remembered the WWP was a charity that was near and dear to Ron's heart.

"He looked bad? Why do you say that?"

"It was as if he'd aged ten years since the last time I saw him. I know he's stressed about his upcoming promotion and making sure this event is successful, but I think there might be more to it than that."

She feigned ignorance to what he was alluding to. "Oh? Like what?"

He shot her a look. "I think it has to do with a certain writer who lives in a beach house."

She didn't want to ask. It was too high-schoolish.

But she did anyway.

"Did he ask about me?"

Luke grinned. "As a matter of fact, he did. I told him you were going to LA tomorrow to meet about your screenplay. I hope that's okay?"

"It's fine, it's not a secret. What did he say?"

"Honestly, he seemed surprised, but at the same time, proud of you. He said to tell you congratulations, he knew you could do it."

Brenna remembered how excited he had been when she told him she had started writing again. He even took her out to dinner to celebrate. It warmed her heart to hear that he was proud of her.

"Aw, tell him thanks for me next time you see him."

"Or you could tell him yourself," Luke said quietly. "He went out of his way to make sure I knew he wasn't dating anyone."

She shook her head. "It wasn't meant to be."

"But what if it is?"

With a sigh, she conceded, "Too much has happened. Things that can't be undone."

"I don't believe that. It's obvious you two care about each other. Don't give up. You owe it to yourselves to give it a shot."

Why did she get the feeling he was talking about more than her and Ron's relationship?

Sexy, a badass, and compassionate. Her sister really should pursue him; this guy was the trifecta.

Kind of like she thought she had with Ron.

*Apples and oranges, Brenna. Apples and oranges.*

271

"Well, I have learned to never say never, but I'm not optimistic." But if she was honest with herself, a part of her was. At the very least she was hopeful that maybe someday their paths would cross again. If they did, who knows what could happen?

****

*Ron*

The courier at Ron's front door stood impatiently, practically shoving the clipboard in the general's face to sign and prove the package had been delivered so he could leave.

Ron took the small white box with bows and ribbons in the Marine Corps signature colors of gold and scarlet back inside and sat down at the kitchen table to open it. Inside was a sealed envelope with a return address of one of the big Hollywood studios, and on the very top was a postcard sized piece of ivory cardstock with Brenna's handwriting.

*Dear Ron,*

*I wanted you to be the first to know—it looks like my manuscript is going to make it to the big screen.*

*Thank you for helping me find my mojo again.*

*I am grateful beyond words. (Ironic, huh?)*

*With much affection,*

*Brenna*

He was so fucking proud of her. He knew what a big deal even starting her screenplay had been for her, but finishing it and selling it just proved how amazingly talented she is. When Luke had told him earlier this week about her meeting in LA, he had desperately wanted to reach out to her, he just didn't know how he'd be received.

So he did nothing. Like a chicken shit.

Inside the sealed envelope was a check from the studio made out to the Wounded Warrior Project with the memo line that read *On behalf of Brenna Roberts (advance).* It had a lot of zeros.

He knew she made a lot of money, but he had no idea it was that much. And this was just an advance. Not to mention she had been out of the game for over a decade.

Her generosity was overwhelming and left him speechless. Why would she do such a thing? Was she trying to tell him something? How did he feel about that?

After she told him she was with Kyle, he hadn't allowed himself to think about her anymore. Well, he *tried* not to allow himself to think about her. When he was wide awake in the middle of the night, he would admit that his heart was broken. That had never happened to him before and frankly, it sucked.

He wondered if they had just met six months later, when he wasn't constantly going overseas, would things have gone differently? What they had was special, she could try to deny it all she wanted, but he knew in his heart that she felt it too. How could she have just thrown it all away?

*Because she didn't trust you.*

*Because Kyle was there for her, and you weren't.*

Part of him just wanted her to be happy, and if that was with Kyle, then so be it. But part of him was pissed that she gave up on them so easily. Well, hurt and pissed.

And part of him just wanted to hold her tight little body next to his again. He could almost feel her silky skin underneath his fingertips and her soft lips on his. Closing his eyes, he could envision how her nipples obediently responded to his touch or the way her tiny hands looked when she gripped his cock. And her taste.

*Fuck.*

Now he was sad and horny. Not to mention confused about what this package meant.

Should he call her and thank her? Send her a text? Drop by her house?

His promotion ceremony had been scheduled for later in the summer and he had been debating if he should invite her. Maybe this was a sign he should ask her?

He opted for a text.

**Ron: Just received your package. I am so proud of you. I am the one who is grateful beyond words. Your generosity is humbling.**

He was surprised when she responded almost immediately.

**Brenna: It was truly my pleasure. I'm honored to be able to contribute to such a wonderful cause.**

He hesitated for only a second before replying. After all, what did he have to lose?

**Ron: Can I take you to lunch and thank you in person?**

Lunch seemed harmless enough. It wasn't like it was a date, and he was moving in on Kyle's territory. It was just an innocent way to thank her for her kindness.

*Oh, who the fuck am I trying to kid?* He was purposefully leaving it open-ended enough that he could pass it off as innocent if she wasn't interested, but could easily escalate it if she was available. He wanted to look into her beautiful blue eyes and find out if her reaching out to him meant more than just her contributing to a noble cause. Like maybe Kyle was out of the picture, and Ron had another shot.

It took her a long time to respond. So long, that he thought she wasn't going to. When his phone dinged indicating he had a text message, he was almost afraid to look.

**Brenna: Drove to Tucson to bring Dee home for the summer. Maybe when I get back?**

He'd take it.

**Ron: Of course. Let me know when you're in town.**

**Brenna: Should only be a few more days. We're packing up her apartment and will be caravanning to SD as soon possible. It's hot here already!** ☺

It took great willpower not to ask who "we" included. Brenna and Danielle? Or did Kyle fit into that equation? Ron knew if he was still with Brenna, he definitely wouldn't let her drive alone. And what was with the smiley face?

Christ, he felt like he was sixteen again and analyzing everything Kristine Casmar said to him on the school bus.

Two nights later his phone rang. He was still on base so he almost ignored it, but then remembered Brenna might be home and calling him to schedule lunch.

His heart leapt into his throat when he looked down and saw it really was her calling him. His heart dropped into his stomach when he heard the terror in her voice when he answered.

# Chapter Thirty-Eight

*Brenna*

She helped Danielle move the last piece of furniture into one of the stalls of her three-car garage. They were storing Dee's larger things at Brenna's Tucson house until fall when her daughter was back in school. Brenna knew they wouldn't be spending any time in Tucson this summer; triple digit heat wasn't appealing to either of them. Between Brenna's and Dee's cars, they managed to fit all of Danielle's smaller things. Brenna had driven the six hours instead of flying; partly because she knew they'd need both cars for all of her daughter's belongings and partly because the drive would give her time to think.

She was about to embark on the crazy LA scene again. It was not her thing, but she knew she'd have to make the rounds to make sure her screenplay was cast properly, and the director stayed true to the story. She'd learned some things along the way and maintaining creative control was now part of every contract she signed.

The little snippet of information that Luke provided about Ron being proud of her and not dating anyone had also occupied a lot of her thoughts. She missed the hell out of him. Maybe Luke was right. Two people shouldn't give up if they truly cared for each other.

And therein lied the problem. Did Ron's definition of 'truly care for' match hers? Because last time she checked, seeing other people wasn't part of her meaning.

Then again, neither was lying. But she wouldn't have lied if he hadn't have cheated.

Besides, for all she knew, he could be lying about not seeing anyone.

She hoped he understood the check she sent was because of him. She would be forever grateful to him for giving her that part of her life back. There wasn't a doubt in her mind that he was the one who inspired her to start writing again. Donating her advance to the WWP seemed like an appropriate way to thank him.

The text he sent thanking her made her heart skip a beat. She knew she should have played it cool, yet she couldn't help texting back right away. When he asked her to lunch, she paused, but in the end she couldn't resist the idea of seeing him again. It was just lunch—that was safe, right?

She wished they could have kept their text conversation going. Their past exchanges used to always make her laugh. He didn't respond to her last message so that ended that.

Still, they were going to have lunch!

That alone spurred her on to push Danielle to finish packing so they could get back to San Diego.

Finally, they started their journey to California. The middle part of the trip was always the worst. It was desolate, then mountainous with lots of twists and turns. It was in the desolate part that Brenna watched in horror as the semi veered into Danielle's lane, sideswiping her daughter's car, and sending the little hatchback spinning before it veered into the desert median and flipped end over end.

There was no time to panic. She needed to get to her daughter. It was almost like she wasn't in her body as she pulled over and ran to the destroyed car. Dee was covered in blood and going in and out of consciousness. Brenna leaned in the broken driver's side window.

"Danielle, honey, stay with me."

People got out of their cars; some offered to help, several were on their phones with 911. Brenna thought God must have been watching out for her daughter, because one of the people who offered to help was a nurse. Her name was Pam, but Brenna wanted to call her an angel.

With the help of good Samaritans, they managed to get Danielle out of the car and onto a blanket someone had offered. Pam immediately began treating her the best she could, relaying to someone on the phone with the 911 operator about Dee's condition, and that she needed to be airlifted.

They kept talking to Dee, trying to keep her conscious and calm so she didn't go into shock. The person on the phone with emergency services broke the news to the group that the Phoenix helivac was unavailable, and neither San Diego nor Tucson would send one, stating it was too far.

A police officer arrived, but no paramedics. After fifteen minutes, they got the news from the officer that the ambulance had broken down. Maybe God wasn't with them after all. The feeling of helplessness was almost unbearable.

The cop offered to put Dee in his car. Pam didn't recommend transporting her like that but it might be their only hope.

Pam stayed close to Danielle but was on the phone with the hospital where she worked. Brenna could hear the desperation in the nurse's voice and knew things were getting dire.

"She's losing a lot of blood. We need to get her there, like five minutes ago." There was a pause before Pam snapped. "You don't have another goddamn helicopter available?"

Brenna knew someone who might. She was sure it was going to break every rule and she didn't know if Ron would go for it, but she had to try; her daughter's life depended on it.

*Please let me have a cell signal.*

He answered on the second ring and somehow she managed to convey what had happened, and that her daughter was losing a lot of blood with no helicopter available to airlift her.

Ron told her not to use her phone until he got back to her and hung up abruptly.

She suddenly got a sense that everything was going to be okay. Her Marine was going to make sure of that.

Brenna returned to Danielle and held her hand. "Hold on, honey, help is coming."

The nurse looked at her inquisitively. Brenna offered a comforting smile. "There might be a helicopter coming."

"How? Neither Yuma nor Blythe have one, and Phoenix's is in service elsewhere."

Before Brenna could answer, her phone rang. It was Ron's number, but it wasn't Ron on the other end. Someone fired questions about Danielle's condition, and Brenna handed the phone off to Pam. After an exchange that did nothing to offer Brenna hope, Pam handed her back the phone. This time Ron was talking to her.

"Bren, don't use the phone for at least fifteen minutes. They're going to track its signal to get to you, and if you make or take a call, it will be lost."

"Thank—"

He cut her off. "They're on their way." Then the line went dead.

It was the most excruciating forty minutes of her life, but she tried to remain upbeat for her daughter. Brenna heard the chopper before she saw it. Medics jumped out and immediately started working on Dee while two uniformed Marines approached Brenna.

One introduced them both as being from the base in Phoenix. She caught neither of their names.

"Ms. Roberts, I've been instructed to accompany you and your daughter back to Phoenix," then gestured to the other man also in tan camouflage. "He will stay on scene to work with law enforcement and get your car back to Phoenix. General Thompson will meet you at the hospital."

She knew then that Ron had to have called in major favors. How could she ever thank him enough? The truth was, there was no way.

They were airborne before Brenna realized she didn't know Pam's last name, or any of the other people who had stopped to help. More people than she could never thank enough in this lifetime.

There was another helicopter at the helipad when they landed on the hospital's roof.

*Why couldn't they have sent that one to help them?*

Hospital personnel had just whisked Danielle away when Brenna noticed Ron in his fatigues standing off to the side. She now understood where the other chopper came from. The Marine who had been with her immediately saluted Ron.

Ron acknowledged the salute then shook the man's hand.

"Thank you for your assistance, Captain. I really appreciate your help."

The captain smiled with a wink. "It was a successful training mission, sir."

Ron took the man's hand a second time as they made their way toward the door. "Thank you again. I'm in your debt."

The other man nodded and said, "I'm glad we could help," then saluted before heading toward the door.

Brenna stopped the captain from leaving and hugged him tight.

"Thank you for everything," she whispered against his chest.

The uniformed man went stiff as if the hug made him uncomfortable. "My pleasure, ma'am."

She released him, and he quickly exited the rooftop.

With tears in her eyes, she hugged Ron next. When his arms came around her, she finally released all the fear and anxiety she'd been holding in. Sagging against him, she began to shake as she silently sobbed, muttering "Thank you," over and over.

He ran his hands over her back and smoothed her hair before kissing her temple. That was something he'd often done when they had been together. The familiarity of his smell and touch was soothing, as was just being in his strong arms, knowing he had her family's back. That knowledge provided tremendous comfort.

"She's going to be okay," he murmured into her hair blonde mane.

Strangely, she believed him.

He tugged her toward the door and said softly, "Let's get downstairs and see how she's doing."

\*\*\*\*

*Ron*

*Holy fuck, what a night.*

Ron was glad Brenna called him when she needed help, and that he was able to provide it. In the short time he'd gotten to know Danielle, he'd grown to care about her. He couldn't imagine how devastated Brenna would be if she lost her, especially in a car accident. He knew that was how Danny had died.

Luckily, the man in charge of the Phoenix base was someone he went through basic with, and they had risen up the ranks at the same rate. He owed his friend, and Ron had no doubt that once he got promoted, he'd be paying that debt in the future.

The paperwork justifying the flight was written as a training operation. He guessed in a way it was, except they were using a real-life scenario. Ron would have to make an appearance in person at the Phoenix base while he was there, since that was the reason he used for taking a helicopter to Arizona. He'd be sure to arrive bearing gifts. There were a lot of men and women who took part in tonight's rescue.

Now, he needed to turn his attention to the gorgeous blonde at his side. He was with her as the doctor explained Danielle's condition, and that she was going to need surgery. Remembering Kyle's concern for her privacy the last time she was at the hospital, Ron made sure they waited in a secluded area.

The wait was agonizing. But it was wonderful to spend time alone with Brenna. He felt useful, and she let him know just how much she appreciated him.

And yes, he couldn't help but notice how fucking hot she was—even after everything she'd been through that night. He was a guy after all, and he'd had those toned legs of hers wrapped around him more than once. Nobody could fault him.

He ran his fingers through her hair while she slept with her head in his lap. The relaxing motion caused him to drift off as well.

Chaos and excited voices woke him.

Cassie and Kyle had arrived.

Brenna lifted her head, and it seemed to take her a minute to register where she was. Slowly rising to her feet, she got up and hugged her sister before turning her attention to Kyle. To the man's credit, he looked pretty distraught.

"How is she?" he cautiously asked.

"She finally got into surgery. She lost a lot of blood, but they're optimistic she's going to be okay once she's stabilized. Right now, we're just waiting for the next bit of news."

Kyle was visibly relieved, melting into a chair as he let out a breath. He grabbed Brenna's hands and scanned her face.

"How are you holding up? Cassie said you saw the whole thing."

The memory seemed to stir up some feelings for Brenna, because her bottom lip quivered, and she appeared unable to speak.

Kyle leapt to his feet and pulled her in close to him, kissing her hair while murmuring soothing words.

That was Ron's cue.

He touched Brenna on the shoulder.

"Hey, I'm going to get going. Keep me posted on how she's doing, okay?"

"What? You're leaving? Now?"

He nodded his head just as the doctor made his appearance.

She looked at the doctor, then back at Ron and asked, "Can you wait a few minutes?"

"Sure."

Brenna and Cassie went over to speak to the doctor while Ron and Kyle hung back. They were still able to hear what was being said: Danielle's surgery went better than expected, she was in recovery, and they'd be able to see her soon.

Brenna closed her eyes as if silently offering up a prayer of thanks.

The doctor said a nurse would be out shortly to take them to the recovery room.

Kyle hugged her and kept his arm around her shoulder while she talked to Ron.

"Will you at least stay so you can see her? I know Dee's going to want to thank you herself."

He looked at how she leaned against Kyle. Ron was an idiot to think she needed him here with her. She only needed him until Kyle got there.

"No, I have to go to the Phoenix base and then head back to San Diego."

"You have to go tonight?" she complained. "Can't you stay until tomorrow?"

Just then, the admitting clerk came in the room and pulled Brenna aside to ask some insurance related questions. With her attention focused on the woman with the clipboard, Ron made his way toward the door.

Kyle looked at him and shook his head with a disgusted look on his face.

"You're a fucking idiot. You realize that, right?"

Ron cocked his head but didn't say anything.

*Why the fuck are you insulting me? I'm trying to be respectful of your relationship, asshole.*

"She needs you here, and you're just going to leave?"

Ron defended his actions. "I'm just going to be in the way. She's got you and Cassie with her now."

Kyle looked at Ron like he'd grown two heads. "Yeah, but she wants *you*."

Shouldn't Kyle be pissed off about that? Ron knew if the roles were reversed, he sure as hell would be.

Brenna came to where the two men were standing and took Ron's hands in hers. Searching his face, she whispered, "Please stay."

He hesitated.

"Please."

He never had been able to tell her no. It didn't look like tonight was going to be any different. He glanced at Kyle, who didn't appear threatened at the prospect of him staying.

"Okay," he said with a small smile.

Her face lit up, and she wrapped her arms around his waist to hug him close to her. He briefly closed his eyes and breathed in her scent.

A nurse came into the room to let them know they could see Danielle. Brenna grabbed his hands again and gave them a quick squeeze before releasing them to go with the nurse.

Kyle patted Ron on the back as they followed suit.

"Maybe you're not as dumb as I thought," he said as he gripped Ron's shoulder with a grin.

Ron felt like he was definitely missing something.

# Chapter Thirty-Nine

*Ron*

He winced when he first looked at Danielle. He'd seen men who'd been injured during combat that looked better than the poor girl did. Her face was swollen and bruised, almost to the point that she was unrecognizable. She was connected to so many tubes and wires that he couldn't count them all, and the breathing tube down her throat made it impossible for her to talk.

They locked eyes and she gestured for him to come to her bedside. He touched her hand and she weakly grasped his fingers in her fist. With her other hand, it looked like she was trying to blow him a kiss.

"She's saying *thank you*," Brenna said from the other side of the bed.

Ron must have appeared confused because Brenna made the same motion as her daughter.

"That is the sign for *thank you*. She's saying *thank you* in sign language."

He smiled and took the hand she had said thank you with and kissed it.

"No need to thank me, honey. Just concentrate on getting better."

He looked over at Brenna, who had teared up watching the exchange between him and Danielle. She made the *thank you* sign again as she mouthed the words at him.

Ron wanted to tell her he'd do anything for her. That he loved her and wanted to make her happy every damn day. That she shouldn't have given up on them so easily; she belonged with him, not Kyle. But considering Kyle was standing right next to him that might not be a good idea.

Instead, he opted for a wink and a smile.

Glancing at Cassie, he knew she had caught the exchange between Brenna and him by the look on her face, but she didn't seem angry. It was like the younger sister was confused more than anything.

"I booked rooms at the hotel just up the road. Ron, can you take Brenna and make sure she gets some rest?"

*Me? Shouldn't Kyle be the one taking her?*

Brenna started to protest leaving her daughter, but Cassie shut her down. "Kyle and I will take shifts being with DeeDee tonight. You are exhausted, and you're not going to be any good to anyone if you don't take the time to rest."

Brenna glanced nervously at Ron.

"Kyle, why don't you take her, and I'll stay here with Cassie," he suggested. He didn't want to make her uncomfortable or Kyle jealous.

"No, she needs someone to make sure she gets some sleep. I think you're the only one she'd actually listen to right now," the other man replied.

Ron and Brenna exchanged looks. He knew she was thinking the same thing he was—he was supposed to make sure she got some sleep when he brought her home from the hospital after she'd fallen down the stairs. There was no listening on her part that night, only seducing. Now that he thought about it, that was the last time they'd made love.

"That didn't work out very well the last time he was supposed to be making sure I got some rest," Brenna teased with a smirk.

Kyle shook his head. "I don't want to know."

*What the fuck? That's it? He doesn't want to know? He should be throttling me.*

Maybe the helicopter rescue had bought Ron a little grace.

But it shouldn't have bought him that much grace. If she was still with him, there was a snowball's chance in hell that he would encourage another man to take her to a hotel room alone. Especially one that had the history with her that Ron did.

Frankly, Ron wasn't so sure he trusted himself alone in a hotel with her, Kyle sure as fuck shouldn't.

She needed to rest, perhaps Kyle didn't trust himself to let her do that and thought Ron would be able to. After all, Ron was a stand-up guy.

*Remember that when you're alone in a hotel room with her.*

It seemed all but settled when Cassie handed him a hotel key card. "Room 336. I'm in 329, Kyle is in 333. I couldn't get us all together, but we're close. I didn't think it really mattered, since we'll probably be there at different times anyway."

*Why weren't Brenna and Kyle sharing a room? Have they broken up? They're not acting like there's any bad feelings between them.*

Of course, he and Brenna weren't exactly acting like there were bad feelings between them either.

Cassie made a shooing gesture with both hands.

"Scoot. Come back in the morning to relieve us. Bren, I brought you clean clothes; they're in your room. Sorry, Ron, I don't have anything for you, you're on your own." She added with a smirk, "Wash your underwear in the sink."

He returned the smirk. It was almost as if Cassie was giving him her blessing. He was definitely warming up to the idea of being alone with Brenna at the hotel. He had never had the chance to explain what happened with Sarah.

"I've got my duffle bag in the chopper. Let me go grab it and call my pilot to let him know what's going on."

"What the fuck is going on?" He muttered aloud as he punched the elevator button for the roof. There were a lot of scenarios about how tonight was going to play out running through his head—everything from the G-rated version to the X-rated one.

After getting his bag out of the helicopter, Ron called his pilot to let him know he could return to San Diego tonight without him, or he could wait and go in the morning, possibly still without him. Ron wasn't surprised that the man opted to leave tonight.

Brenna had just gotten off the elevator when he approached from the doors leading to the roof.

"They moved her into her own room. I didn't want you to think we'd bailed on you."

He chuckled. "I think I'd be able to figure out that at least Danielle wasn't going anywhere tonight."

She pushed the *down* button. They sat in silence waiting for the car to return until she attempted to make small talk.

"I've been assured by the doctors that she looks a lot worse than she really is."

Ron nodded his head. "Thank God for that, because she looks pretty damn awful."

"They've got her on a lot of pain medication, so hopefully she's not in any pain."

The elevator doors opened.

"Morphine can do wonders," he grinned.

They picked up other passengers as they made their descent to the lobby, so the silence between them wasn't uncomfortable. When they reached the ground floor, he stopped by the receptionist desk. She didn't ask him what he was doing; she seemed emotionally spent.

He waved her car keys when he walked towards her.

"That was incredible that you did that for me. One less thing I had to worry about. Thank you so much."

He nodded. "My pleasure."

"Do you mind driving? I think I might be a little skittish tonight on the road."

Reaching for her hand, he sympathized. "That's understandable."

She didn't pull away, so he entwined their fingers together while they walked through the parking lot, only letting go to open her car door. He put his bag in the backseat before coming round to the driver's side door.

He told himself he was just offering her comfort, she'd been through a terrible ordeal. He knew deep down it was a lie, yet he didn't care.

Once they were on the road for the short drive to the hotel, he found her hand again, and brought her fingertips to his lips. He knew he was playing with fire but couldn't help himself.

She smiled and closed her eyes, but didn't let go

# Chapter Forty

*Brenna*

True to her word, Cassie had brought a bag with a few days' worth of clean clothes. Brenna was grateful because in her haste to get home to have lunch with Ron, she had neglected to do laundry in Tucson and had been going home with a bag of dirty clothes.

She took a shower, letting the water symbolically wash away the horrible events of the night. After drying off, she found her seafoam green chemise in the tweed weekend bag sitting on the counter. She had grabbed her toiletries bag from the trunk—she definitely needed her lotion after spending a few days in the desert.

Opening the bathroom door as she rubbed lotion onto her arms, she smiled at Ron, who was sitting in a chair watching TV.

"Bathroom's all yours."

He stared at her with a strange, but tender, look on his face, and she couldn't help but blurt out, "What?"

Ron continued looking at her as he stood and stalked toward her. "I love that nightie on you."

She felt the color rise in her cheeks. The chemise was a little revealing, but she hadn't even thought to be self-conscious in front of him. She realized, maybe she should have.

"It's my favorite. Very comfortable to sleep in." Brenna crossed her arms in front of her and eyed the king-size bed.

It seemed her uneasiness stopped him in his tracks, but he didn't take his eyes off her. It was as if he was contemplating something.

"Would you mind if I borrowed your car to go to the Target up the road? It appears there isn't any deodorant in my bag."

*Would I mind if he borrowed my car? Seriously? Mind?*

"Ron, I would *give* you my car. And even then, it wouldn't be anywhere near enough to thank you for what you did for Danielle." Tears threatened to spill onto her cheeks. "I could try for the rest of my life, but there is no way I could ever repay you. Or, for that matter, anyone who helped tonight. Any way I can think of to say *thank you* seems so trivial compared to what everyone did."

"You in that teddy is all the thanks I need."

Despite the urge to look away, she didn't. There was no mistaking the look he gave her, it made her belly clench. She bit her bottom lip then finally glanced down.

*Holy wet panties, batman. Is it hot in here?*

"Well, I'm glad you like it," was all she could think to say as she smoothed away invisible wrinkles on the fabric.

He stepped in closer and ran his fingertips up and down her arms. Looking down at her, his face inches from hers, he murmured, "I definitely do."

Her breath caught. She was sure he could see her chest heaving under the silky fabric.

She took a step back, trying to break the spell he'd just put her under. "Um, would you mind bringing back some bottled water? I forgot my water bottle in San Diego."

He smirked and picked up the car keys off the desk. "Sure. Anything else?"

"Maybe a Twix candy bar?" she asked hopefully.

He shook his head, the smirk still planted on his face. "Haven't lost your sweet tooth, I see."

Brenna smiled brightly. "Thank you."

The door closed behind him, and she scurried about. She needed to be in bed and asleep by the time he returned, or she was going to do something she'd regret.

Or worse, she was going to do something and not regret it.

They couldn't be together again. Too much had transpired between them. She didn't trust him not to cheat, and to top it all off, she'd lied to him. She knew he would not be okay with that. The best she could hope for was his friendship.

But, damn, he was delicious.

*Maybe they could be friends with benefits?*

Yet, as soon as she thought it, she knew she'd never be content with that arrangement.

Tonight was going to be interesting. There was only one bed. Fortunately, it was a king, so they could realistically both sleep in it without worrying about touching each other.

Unless one of them made an effort to.

*No! Go to sleep!*

She needed to be well rested for tomorrow. She had a feeling she had several long days ahead. She wasn't complaining. Her daughter was alive.

Thanks to Ron.

The super sexy Marine who had, once again, saved the day.

# Chapter Forty-One

*Ron*

The hotel room was dark, so he tried to be quiet when he came back in. He took a shower and slipped on his boxer briefs, then slid into bed next to Brenna. He could tell by her breathing that she wasn't asleep. But her eyes were closed, and she put on a helluva performance to try to convince him she was.

"Sleeping people don't usually smile," he teased.

That was all it took to get her to crack, and her mouth gave way to a grin.

"Shhh," she said, bringing her finger to her lips in the universal sign to be quiet, the smile still on her face and her eyes closed.

He couldn't help it, he kissed her.

And that was after he'd given himself a pep talk on the drive that he was not going to make a move. He hadn't really forgotten his deodorant, he just needed to get the hell out of the hotel room, or he was going to take her against the wall. That goddamn teddy she was wearing was like catnip to a cat, and he was a lion ready to pounce.

Except he couldn't pounce until he knew what was going on with Kyle. Yet, the more Ron analyzed the man's behavior tonight, the more he was able to convince himself the former shortstop was no longer a factor in her love life.

He'd cooled down, or so he thought, but as he got under the covers, he caught sight of her cleavage and his lips took on a mind of their own—along with his dick that jumped a foot the second she let out a little whimper when his mouth touched hers.

Her lips parted and his tongue sought hers out. She eagerly accepted his exploration of her mouth and their heads tilted in order to deepen the kiss.

"Darlin', I've missed you so much," he whispered when he came up for air and pulled her body tight against his while nuzzling her neck.

She pressed the back of his head to her. "I've missed you, too."

They lay there for a moment, holding each other. Soon, he could feel her shaking, and could tell she was about to cry.

"Hey, none of that. It's okay," he murmured as he pulled away and tucked her hair behind her ear.

She took a deep breath. "You are the most amazing man I've ever met. You're like my Superman, always there to save me. If you hadn't been there tonight, I could have very easily lost my daughter."

A sob escaped her when she said the last part out loud.

"Bren, she's going to be okay. She's young and resilient."

"If you hadn't been there—"

"But I *was* there."

"I know, and I'm so grateful. Thank you. From the bottom of my heart." She sniffled.

He pulled her back against him.

"I'll always be there for you," he said as he kissed her hair and breathed in the familiar scent of her shampoo.

Her body softened and relaxed when he enveloped her in his arms. She'd been through a traumatic ordeal, and here he was, trying to get into her pants. Not to mention he still didn't know what the score with Kyle was.

*What a dick move, Thompson.*

****

*Brenna*

Something was different when she woke on her side in the middle of the night. She felt cozy and warm. Content even? There was a comfortable scent filling her nostrils.

When she tried to move, she realized there was a hand on her stomach holding her against a hard body. The smell was Ron. The wonderful warmth of his chest was pressed against her back.

And his cock was hard against her ass.

She had really missed waking up like this.

Almost on instinct she wiggled against him, ever so subtly. She felt his prick move.

The hand on her belly slid up to cup her boob and pull her even closer to him while he pressed his dick harder against her.

"What about Kyle?" he whispered in her ear.

She shook her head. "We're not together."

She *should* have added, "We were never together," but, she neglected to mention that. Or maybe she didn't want to ruin what was happening. She knew he was going to be mad she had lied to him, but she didn't want to fret about that right now, she could worry about that later.

He rolled her onto her back and looked into her eyes before kissing her softly.

"Everything with Sarah, it was a misunderstanding. You're the one for me, darlin'. You're it."

*Now* would have definitely been the time to explain about Kyle.

Instead, Brenna's response was to run her fingers through his hair and pull him closer to intensify their kiss.

Things went from zero to one hundred in three seconds flat.

Arching her back, she pressed her chest against his; tilting her head to expose her throat when he kissed her neck with urgency. One of his hands came under her and pulled her tighter to him. She could feel his erection perfectly aligned where it belonged. The only barrier between them was the thin fabric of undergarments they were still wearing. His other hand worked to liberate her boobs from her teddy.

Once her breasts were exposed, he put both hands to work caressing them. Pinching one nipple and stretching it, then kneading her round orb roughly, he dipped his head to suck on the other rosy peak. She clung to his shoulders and ground her hips into his.

Brenna traced her hand from behind his neck to his bulge and rubbed him over his underwear. She needed that rock hard cock inside her—now. Judging by how frantic he squeezed and sucked her tits, he felt the same. His hand came down and moved her panties to the side, dipping a finger deep in her sex as he did. It was almost as if he was checking to see if she were wet.

Did he really think there was even a question about that? Her panties were no doubt soaked. She wanted him desperately.

Ron pushed her chemise up above her waist and tugged urgently on her panties, getting them just below her butt before he pulled his boxer briefs down. His breathing was as ragged as hers. Brenna bent her knees and finished pulling her undies off. She'd just gotten them to her ankles when she felt his warm, smooth cock rubbing up and down her slit. He tilted his hips and thrust into her.

They both let out a low moan as he filled her. It had been far too long since they'd done this, and he felt perfect.

He began to fuck her with slow, hard strokes. Her body reacted to every thrust.

God, how she'd missed him.

As great as it felt, she needed him deeper inside her. Hooking her arms around her knees, she lifted her legs and spread them wide as an offering to him, and he buried himself inside her pussy, just like she needed. He went balls deep with every thrust, letting out a grunt with each slapping noise their skin made.

She couldn't get enough of him. She felt her pussy quivering while her excitement built.

She thought he must be close to coming because he sat back on his heels, pulled his hard-as-steel rod out of her pussy, and began to rub her clit with it. Brenna lifted her hips, and he plunged back inside her then pulled back out and moved his cock faster over her clit, turning her on more before thrusting inside her.

He did this over and over, each time bringing her closer to her climax.

She reached up to grip his shoulder as he brought her to the edge again, whimpering, "Please," before he thrust back inside her.

Every muscle in her body became taut. The next time he massaged her nub with his cock covered in her nectar, she curved her back and reached her summit, crying out when he plunged back into her again. Everything that had been wound tight unraveled until her body felt like it was made of jelly.

Ron moved into her with a steady rhythm until she felt his release. He collapsed on top of her and held her while his breathing evened out and his hot cum dripped down her thighs. When he tried to kiss her neck, she pulled away and held his face between her hands.

They stared into each other's eyes for a long time.

"You and me, Bren."

"Tell me about Sarah."

He didn't flinch. "You have to know nothing ever happened with Sarah. There hasn't been anyone else since you came into my life on New Year's Eve."

"Why would I *know* that? From where I was sitting, it looked quite obvious you were with her. Spending your birthday with her. Having her there to greet you when you returned with your squad. I can't say I blame you—she's beautiful, and you two have a history."

She could see his anger rising.

"I don't like being accused of things that go against my nature," he growled. "Yes, she and I have a history, and that's exactly what it is, history. No present, no future."

The way Ron told her there was no present or future with Sarah, Brenna knew.

She *knew*.

He hadn't lied to her; he'd been nothing but wonderful. Lying wasn't his style.

It was hers, apparently.

She dreaded telling him the truth about Kyle. She could only imagine how angry he was going to be at her for not being honest tonight when she had the chance.

As if to reaffirm that her dread was warranted, he took her chin in his hand and tilted her head up to look at him.

"I told you the night we first met, *I don't play games, and I mean everything I say*. That hasn't changed."

Would he understand she had been trying to protect herself, that was why she had lied? Or would he be even angrier that she thought she had to protect herself from him in the first place?

He was a man of integrity; how could she have doubted that?

Brenna had been so wrapped in the sins Danny had committed, she hadn't let herself trust Ron. She'd remembered being so eager to believe Danny's lies in the beginning and came away looking like a fool. She hadn't wanted to allow herself to risk that with Ron.

So she lied to him about Kyle, and didn't fix it when the opportunity presented itself earlier.

She did know one thing.

She needed to talk to Kyle to get him to go along with her story or she was so fucked. And not in a good way.

# Chapter Forty-Two

*Ron*

He fell back asleep after their impromptu lovemaking session with his arm around her naked waist.

Earlier, when he'd come back from the store, Ron had been content just holding her. They'd shared a kiss, and while it made him aroused, it had also left him hopeful. When he woke to her rubbing her ass against his hard cock, he didn't need any convincing to escalate things and fuck her. Knowing Kyle was out of the picture was a bonus. He hated to admit it, but there was a real possibility he wouldn't have been able to stop himself even if that hadn't been the case.

That troubled him.

But she and Kyle were over, so it was a moot point.

Sort of.

That she and Kyle had been together in the first place was a sore spot, but one he'd have to get over.

He had Brenna back in his arms and in his bed, at least for tonight. They still had things to talk about. He needed to explain about Sarah so there wasn't a doubt in her mind nothing happened; she could trust him. They also needed to discuss her seeking comfort from Kyle, but he respected her for being honest once she crossed that line. There was also the matter of her not doing okay when he went overseas, but that would be coming to an end once he was promoted. Well, it would at least lessen; enough that he thought it would be manageable.

Provided his promotion still came through.

Hopefully this helicopter rescue didn't come back to haunt him. Not that it ever could, even if it cost him a rise in rank. He did the right thing and would do it again.

The sun peeked through the sides of the blackout curtains, and he reached over, intending to gently rub Brenna's hip and wake her.

The bed next to him was empty.

The note on the desk explained that she couldn't sleep and went to the hospital, and for him to call for a ride when he woke up.

He caught a cab to the hospital. Hopefully Danielle was still doing okay, and Brenna wasn't making herself sick with worry. He had so many plans for the future now that he could allow himself to picture her in. He'd wanted to tell her last night that she was his present and future, but thought better of it. Now he wished he'd had while they had been alone.

He found Cassie and Danielle sleeping in Danielle's room, so he went to look for Brenna. Maybe she was in the small waiting area on the hospital floor that held a TV and computer. He approached the door and smiled when he heard her voice, but stopped cold when he heard what sounded like an argument. It took him a second to realize it was Kyle she was having the heated exchange with.

Kyle's voice was angry. "You did what?! What the fuck, Brenna. I can't believe you'd do that. That's something I'd expect Danny to have pulled, not you."

Ron heard repentance in Brenna's voice. "I'm sorry! I was upset, and I wasn't thinking. It made sense while it was happening. I screwed up, okay? I get it."

"Screwed up? *Screwed up?* This isn't like you bought the wrong brand of bottled water or paid a bill late. You fucking lied to Ron and used me in the process. I don't even know what to say to you right now."

The remorse in her voice had given way to desperation. "Look, I get that you're upset. I do. I don't even have a good excuse, other than I was vulnerable, and I didn't know what else to do. I'm so sorry, Kyle. It was wrong, and I know it. Just tell me what I need to do for you to forgive me, and I'll do it."

Kyle let out a long sigh, his voice gentler, almost as if he was chuckling. "What the hell were you thinking?"

"I was thinking you love me and would understand, and Ron would never be the wiser. Bad judgment I know, and if I could take it back, I would."

"You're going to have to tell him the truth about us."

"I know, I just—"

*No way. No fucking way. They were still together? How can Kyle be so calm?*

Ron came around the corner and didn't even bother disguising he'd overheard their conversation.

Brenna jumped when he walked in. Her eyes widened and she looked like a deer caught in the headlights. Dressed in jeans and a tee shirt with her hair pulled up in a high ponytail and minimal makeup, she could be Cassie's younger sister.

Shaking his head, he muttered with disgust, "I can't believe you."

"I'm so sorry," she eked out in a whisper.

Ron looked at her as if she repulsed him and smirked. "Sorry for what?"

She looked down then walked toward the window without answering. Grabbing her by the elbow, he swung her around to face him.

"Sorry for what?" he repeated.

She looked at the buttons on his shirt when she answered, "For lying to you about Kyle."

"Lying about what exactly?" He was going to make her say it out loud.

A little sob escaped when she replied, "About being together."

Ron was floored. He wouldn't have believed it had he not heard it with his own two ears. What was he supposed to do now? Yell? Commiserate with Kyle? Punch something?

He needed to keep his cool.

As empty of any emotion as he could muster, he flatly told her, "You are something else. You sure had me fooled. No wonder you didn't believe me when I told you nothing happened with Sarah. It has to be hard to trust someone when you're not trustworthy yourself."

There was nothing left to do but walk away. It wasn't like he was going to make her choose. He didn't want anything more to do with her.

Ron felt guilty as he told Kyle, "I had no idea, man. She said you were over. I would have never—" He stopped short of finishing his thought. He'd just admitted to himself that morning he very well may have still slept with her had he known. What this woman had turned him into sickened him.

Kyle seemed to be at a loss for words. He wasn't nearly as pissed off as Ron thought he should be. Was Kyle considering forgiving her? Apparently Ron wasn't the only one she'd done a number on.

He glared at Brenna as he told the man, "She's all yours," then turned on his heel and walked out the door.

He heard her protest, "It's not what you think!" and had half a mind to go back and give Kyle all the dirty details of last night just in case Kyle thought about giving her a second chance. The man had been just as much a sucker as Ron had been, yet apparently he still needed to learn the hard way, so Ron kept walking.

He couldn't remember ever feeling this betrayed before. It hurt like hell.

# Chapter Forty-Three

*Brenna*

She had been so worried he would be mad at her for lying about being with Kyle, she hadn't considered he thought she was lying last night about Kyle and her no longer being together.

That she had cheated on Kyle with him.

She wanted to go after him and explain everything, but she knew he was too angry to listen to anything she had to say. She needed to get back to Danielle and send Cassie and Kyle to the hotel to sleep. She'd try texting Ron after she gave him time to cool off.

Over the next five days, she sent text after text from Dee's hospital room, begging him to call her with no response.

She dialed his number and her call immediately went to voicemail. He had blocked her.

There was nothing more she could do from Phoenix, although she considered sending him flowers, but knew they'd end up on his secretary's desk or in the shredder.

She also had to make amends with Kyle. He was pissed at being dragged into her drama, but when he saw how heartbroken she was, it didn't take much time for him to forgive her.

One more reason she loved him.

Of course, the *Out and About* section, as well as the actual news portion of the paper got wind of Dee's accident.

Since she was now an adult, she was considered fair game for the press. The gossip rags had a field day with their speculations. Thank God her daughter didn't have access to any of it. The paparazzi staked out the hospital though, so Brenna's days of her hair piled on top of her head in a messy bun and yoga pants were over.

They actually published a really nice photo of her and Kyle taking a break in the garden area of the hospital. They had been reliving old times of when Danny was alive, and they were both laughing. It was a genuine moment that she hated the press for sharing with the world, but she loved the picture nonetheless. She wondered if Ron had seen it.

She was grateful she'd been too worried about her daughter to mourn the loss of Ron, but soon Danielle recovered enough to be released from the hospital, and they flew to San Diego. Brenna hired a service to drive her car back for her.

She needed to see Ron and make him listen to her. Make him understand. He had said she was it for him. That had to mean something, right? He couldn't just be done with her without a second thought.

Could he?

Maybe he could; he hadn't tried getting in touch with her again. She'd carried that fear around since the day he walked out but hadn't allowed herself time to dwell on it. Now that her daughter was on the mend, and they were home in San Diego, he was all she could think about.

Still, she couldn't find the nerve to go to his house and knock on the door. The fear of him slamming it in her face was too real.

They'd been back in California a week when Brenna asked Cassie for advice. She'd confided in her sister at the hospital about everything that had transpired the night of Danielle's accident and the morning after. The intimate things he'd said, as well as his reaction when he was angry and thought she'd cheated on Kyle with him.

"What am I going to do?" she lamented while they were drinking wine on her patio.

"I don't know? Maybe give him more time to cool down and try again in a few weeks?" Cassie offered.

"What if he finds someone new?"

Cassie frowned. "Then I guess he finds someone new, and you two weren't meant to be."

"Maybe he's back with Sarah."

"Brenna, you can't keep doing this to yourself. If he finds someone new, if he's back with Sarah, if he decides to never forgive you—those are all his decisions. If he chooses any of those, then that right there should tell you something. Ron is a good guy, I don't deny that. He's very noble. But you deserve someone who is going to fight for you."

"Do I? Do I really? Look what I've done."

"You tried to protect yourself from getting hurt. Yeah, maybe you went about it the wrong way, but anyone who knows your history can't blame you for what you did."

Brenna nodded. "That's true."

Then doubt crept back in. "But didn't I owe it to him to give him the benefit of the doubt?"

Cassie snorted. "Like he has for you?"

She sighed. "You're right. But what if he's waiting for me to fight for him? What if, when we're in our nineties, we find each other and discover we were both waiting on the other?"

Her younger sister rolled her eyes. "Write for Hollywood much?"

Brenna glared at her then softened her gaze when Cassie leaned over and squeezed her hand.

"Bren, it's not like you haven't tried reaching out to him to explain things. Maybe you just need to let it go for a while, get on with your life. If you want to try again in the future, you'll know when the time is right. But perhaps your Prince Charming is still out there. Have you considered that?"

"I have, briefly. Like all this happened for reasons I still don't understand. But every time I think about, it seems everything that happened was to bring *Ron and me* together."

Cassie shrugged. "I know you love him and God knows, I'm no relationship expert, look at my track record, but there are plenty of fish in the sea, and you, my beautiful sister, are quite a catch."

Brenna gave a half smile. "Maybe I've been going after the wrong bait. Good looking men with nice bodies don't seem to be working for me."

"I think you need a young stud, or an older, distinguished gentleman, for a rebound fling."

With a long sigh, Brenna countered, "Maybe I need to join a convent."

Cassie winked. "Nah, you wouldn't look good in a habit."

"Spend my days drunk?"

"Too many empty calories."

Brenna pretended to snarl at her sister. "Will you just let me be miserable in peace?"

Cassie stood and picked up their empty wine glasses. "No-can-do, gorgeous," then headed into the house.

Maybe Cassie was right; she should get on with her life. That would mean she'd have to admit Ron wasn't coming for her. Was she ready to admit that?

The realization was like cold water in her face. What choice did she have?

\*\*\*\*

*Ron*

*You'd think I would be over her by now.*

It'd already been a month, but every time Ron thought about Brenna, he still got angry. Not only angry with her, but angry with himself. He slept with her when she was with someone else, and that was just not something he did. The worst part was whenever he played it back in his mind, he found himself trying to justify it.

Kyle practically threw them together.

Cassie, too.

Brenna told him she and Kyle were not together.

How could she have put him in that position? Ron was not the kind of guy who cheated or helped someone else cheat. Semper Fi wasn't just a slogan to him, it was how he lived his life.

And that's what stuck in his craw; when he replayed the morning after they were together, he remembered admitting to himself that even if he had known she was with Kyle, he probably would have still slept with her.

She had a done a number on him. He'd fallen for her poor widow who'd been cheated on bullshit; hook, line, and sinker. She must have seen him coming from a mile away.

Fuck her.

And yet, she haunted his dreams. When he slept, she was still the woman he loved. The one that made his cock hard with one look, and his heart sing with just a touch or word. He'd wake up smiling, then reality would creep in, and he was mad all over again.

He needed her out of his system, one way or another.

# Chapter Forty-Four

*Brenna*

Cassie arrived, uninvited, at the beach house for breakfast one Friday morning at the end of June.

"I am a basket case," she said as she paced around the kitchen island.

"What's wrong?" Danielle asked, pouring her and her aunt a bowl of cereal.

Grabbing the milk from the fridge, Cassie sighed.

"Work wants me to go to the Heroes Calendar judging."

Danielle responded, "Oh! That sounds like fun!"

Scowling, Cassie replied, "Luke's one of the contestants."

Brenna listened from her barstool, drinking her tea. She had lived in San Diego long enough to know that, aside from their annual ball, the biggest money maker for the Wounded Warrior Project was the *Heroes of San Diego* calendar and all the events that went along with it. Tomorrow night's affair was going to be a big bash of sexual energy; a vote for the men who would be featured in the calendar followed by an auction for dates with them.

She knew Luke was on the calendar fundraising committee and he was single; it made sense that he participated, given he was partially responsible for its success.

Brenna giggled. "So?"

"So, we haven't talked in over a month! I'm going to have to watch all these women throw themselves at a guy I may or may not be hung up on!"

Cassie was right, there were going to be women who would be willing to pay top dollar for a date with Mr. Sex-on-a-Stick.

"So you should bid on him! I think I'd go just to watch that." she snickered.

Cassie grabbed her arm. "Oh, yes! Please go with me!"

Brenna hesitated so Cassie started giving her an obviously rehearsed sales pitch.

"I've got an extra ticket, it'll be fun. Hot, shirtless guys who save the world, alcohol, more hot guys, what more could you ask for?"

Cassie turned to Danielle. "Sorry, Dee, it's twenty one and older."

Her daughter finished chewing her cereal before responding. "That's quite all right. The last thing I need burned into my brain is seeing my mom and aunt ogling oiled up, half-naked men."

Turning back to Brenna, Cassie continued. "Maybe there will be someone up for auction who strikes your fancy."

"Maybe," Brenna said, trying to put on her best poker face.

There was only one hot, shirtless hero who struck her fancy, even if she had finally admitted they really were over.

****

Brenna and Cassie arrived early enough to get a seat near the stage. The place reminded Brenna of strip clubs she'd seen in movies, minus any poles. It was dark, and the stage was set higher up from the tables.

In order for the audience to have sufficient information on who to choose for the calendar, the contestants were expected to come out and do their best to win the crowd's vote. She was quite certain women were going to be going wild when the yummy looking first responders and military men graced the stage, shirtless and strutting their stuff.

The auction would be somewhat different. There was a program that detailed the men who had volunteered to be bid on—their vitals, and what they were bringing to the table as far as the date was concerned. You could tell the men who were players based on their date packages. They offered wine, dinner, dancing, and included extras like *a midnight picnic on the beach*, or some were even more blatant with suggestions like, *dinner…. and breakfast*. The men who seemed to be less one-night-standish proposed going to lunch, followed by mild, non-romantic things like, playing tennis, or seeing a play, or a tour of where they worked. One even offered a helicopter ride.

That's when her heart stopped.

General Ron Thompson was Bachelor Number Eleven, and he was giving a tour of the base, followed by a gourmet lunch, and a helicopter ride as his date package.

"Oh my God, Cass. Ron is in the auction."

Her sister leaned over and looked to where Brenna was pointing in the program.

"Huh, imagine that," Cassie replied nonchalantly and sat back up straight.

"Cassandra Jo Sullivan, did you know about this when you invited me?"

Her sister didn't answer the question, instead pointed out with a smirk, "Well, if you paid good money to go on a date with him, he'd have to talk to you, wouldn't he?"

Cassie may be on to something.

"I see your wheels turning, don't deny that you're thinking about it!" Cassie teased.

Brenna shrugged. "We'll see. Who knows, maybe someone else will spark my interest instead. I mean, Craig Baxter is willing to give a full body massage."

She held up the program and pointed to a picture of the very attractive SWAT Captain Baxter.

"That's the spirit!"

They both knew Brenna was full of shit, but she appreciated her sister letting her have the moment to at least pretend to play it cool.

She didn't care the cost, she was getting that date with Ron.

Now, she needed a drink. *There's no courage like liquid courage.*

After they had their cocktails in hand, Brenna continued looking at the program.

"Aw, how sweet. Luke's date is walking shelter dogs, a deli lunch, and a tour of the SWAT station."

Cassie rolled her eyes, then looked around at the ladies starting to fill up the room.

"Yeah, chicks are gonna eat that shit up. Once these bitches get a look at him... ugh."

Brenna remembered that feeling of having women clamoring for her man's attention. She was curious to see how Luke, and Ron, handled that tonight.

They had ordered another round just when Luke and a gorgeous blond man appeared at their table.

"Ladies, so glad you came out tonight!"

Brenna smiled at Luke and answered, since Cassie seemed to be having trouble speaking. "We wouldn't have missed it! Such a great cause. Won't you gentlemen join us?"

They sat down and Luke made introductions. "Cass, Bren, this is my friend, Ryan Kennedy. Ryan, this is Brenna Roberts and her sister, Cassandra Sullivan."

Brenna detected a slight frown on Luke's face when Ryan gave a flirtatious smile and brought Cassie's hand to his lips.

"It's *very* nice to meet you." He cocked his head when he looked at Brenna and offered his hand. "Ms. Roberts, a pleasure."

The men disappeared to the bar and when they came back, Brenna noticed a definite change in Ryan's attitude toward Cassie; he had toned it down considerably. They made small talk, and the girls learned that Ryan, a fire captain on the fundraising committee, was Number Eight in the calendar competition and Number Ten for the auction. He was one of the men providing a romantic date.

When Brenna teased him about that, he replied, "See the girl over there in the red dress?"

He subtly pointed to a stunning brunette with long, wavy hair.

"After six months of dating, she decided three weeks ago that we needed time apart."

"That's rough. I'm sorry."

He shrugged his shoulders, trying to act unaffected, but she could see the hurt in his eyes and gave a sympathetic smile when she offered, "Her loss."

"Maybe you could bid on me," he said to Brenna with a crooked smile.

Cassie interjected, "I think my sister has her sights on the one right after you."

Luke and Ryan exchanged knowing looks, and a slow smile appeared on Ryan's face.

"Oh, *you're* the screenwriter?"

*What the fuck?*

"Yeah, I'm *a* screenwriter. I don't know if I'm *the* screenwriter."

Luke gave a lopsided grin. "No, you're most definitely *the* screenwriter."

She wanted to grill him about what the hell that was supposed to mean, but the music stopped, and the place went dark. A spotlight followed an emcee as he took the stage and greeted the crowd. After the usual pleasantries, the tuxedoed man explained how things were going to work tonight, in case one couldn't follow along with the program. Then he introduced the event's committee members, with the spotlight finding each one as they stood and waved to the crowd. Brenna caught her breath when her sexy-as-hell Marine was illuminated.

He'd obviously been out in the sun, because his tan skin was in stark contrast to the crisp, white button-down shirt that he left untucked from the Levi's he was wearing. Of course, he'd be wearing the pair of jeans she liked best on him.

Damn he was hot. She certainly didn't like the pretty women at his table stroking and pawing his back and arms as if they were congratulating him on a job well done. The way they pushed their tits at him, Brenna knew they wanted to do more than congratulate him. The smile he gave them was his best fake one—she at least took comfort in that. Still, even fake, he had the most gorgeous smile.

"Looks like you might have some competition," Ryan whispered in her ear just as the spotlight shone on him and Luke when they were introduced. They both gave a relaxed wave to the crowd, and Ryan threw his arm around Brenna's shoulder.

"A little jealousy never hurt," he said with a wink.

She smiled and rolled her eyes as she shook her head. "Just who are you trying to make jealous?"

He feigned to be hurt. "Why, General Thompson, of course."

"Not your ex?"

"Well, if she happens to get jealous in the process." He grinned. "That's a bonus."

The man on stage finished the introductions and called for the calendar men to go backstage.

The fire captain motioned to Luke. "That's us."

Luke stood and winked at Cassie.

Brenna saw her whisper something in his ear, and he pulled away with a smile.

"What was that all about?" she asked her sister after the two men had walked away.

Cassie shot her a devilish smile but didn't say anything more.

# Chapter Forty-Five

*Ron*

He saw Brenna with that hose dragger, Ryan Kennedy. He had to be at least ten years her junior. Not that he could fault the man—she was as hot as any woman in here, including ones half her age.

Still. Where was Kyle? What the fuck was she doing with the fire fighter?

*What she used to do with you.*

His gut clenched when he answered his own question. The thought of her lips wrapped around Ryan's, or Kyle's, or anyone else's dick made him see red.

He needed to quash those thoughts. They were over, she could put her lips around any cock she wanted; that was no longer his problem. She seemed to have moved on—again, perhaps it was time he did too.

Maybe some hot woman would bid on him tonight. He knew at least one of the women fawning all over him at his table would. Except, try as he might, he wasn't interested. It appeared a certain screenwriter had ruined him for anyone else. Logically, he knew that it was only a matter of time before he was ready to get back in the saddle, but from where he stood right now, he didn't see it happening anytime soon.

He needed to forget about Brenna once and for all. She was a liar and a cheater, no matter how fucking gorgeous she was. Once his promotion happened, he would be in the country more, and he could devote more time to someone. Now, it was just a matter of finding *the one.*

Who knows, maybe *the one* was here tonight.

Or maybe for the time being he could be happy with *the one... night stand.*

The sexual energy of the place was almost palpable as the calendar contest got underway. He had to admit, Luke's idea of having the judging before the auction was brilliant, since most of the men currently on stage were also donating a date to be sold to the highest bidder. The women were almost in a frenzy wanting more after the guys left the stage. Once the men made their way back with an opportunity to go on a date with them, the purse strings would be loosened.

It was for a fantastic cause, so he didn't feel bad about that in the least.

He stole glances at Brenna, which annoyed him. They were finished, he didn't give a damn what—or who—she was doing. Still, he noticed that she didn't seem as impressed with the shirtless guys as the other females were. Every time he looked at her, she was either looking at her phone, chatting with her sister, or had a polite smile on her face while she looked at the participants on stage. That was vastly different from some of the women around him who were cat calling and practically drooling.

Probably because she already had her calendar boy shored up.

He didn't give a shit. She could play her fucking games with some other poor schmuck.

The emcee announced the auction was about to start and Brenna had the same polite, but disinterested, look on her face. Once Ryan and Luke returned to the table from their calendar display, everyone at their table seemed to be having a fun, spirited conversation. When it came time for Ryan's romantic date to be auctioned, the firefighter stood to take the stage. Ron saw Brenna pat his back and mouth *good luck* just before he left the table.

She gave the opening bid but quickly dropped out once the offers reached five hundred dollars. He smirked. She gave a fuck of a lot more than that to WWP when she sent him a check from her movie studio.

A hot little brunette in a red dress and another equally good-looking redhead were in a bidding war over the blond fire captain. Maybe Ron had been too harsh with his hose dragger assessment. He might not be with Brenna after all, and it seemed like he was raising some decent money for the opportunity to be his date.

Finally, the redhead conceded to the brunette's winning nine-hundred-dollar submission. He watched the man descend the stairs and, per protocol, escort the winner to where she could pay. It seemed the custom was to also spend the rest of the evening with the lady who ponied up the money to go out with the gentleman in the future.

Ron was up next. He hadn't been half-naked on stage earlier so he didn't expect his date would bring in very much money. He'd be impressed with three hundred dollars.

One of the busty brunettes from his table, who had been quite blatant about rubbing her tits against him, started the bidding with two hundred dollars.

*Not bad.* Maybe he'd pull in more than he thought.

The auctioneer couldn't keep up with how fast the smaller increments were being signaled so he increased the bid by fifty dollars instead of twenty-five.

As the dollar amount increased, most of the women dropped out. It was down to just two—the woman from his table who'd started the bidding and...

Sarah.

He sighed internally. He thought she'd understood things weren't going to work out between them.

Both women seemed equally determined, and they had raised the bid to eleven hundred dollars. He was sort of relieved when it appeared the woman from his table was the winner. She was hot, in a slutty way. Maybe it was time he let loose, and she seemed to be perfect to help him do just that.

The auctioneer was saying, "going once," when out of nowhere, he heard a voice say, "Five thousand dollars."

He knew that voice. It came from a goddamn blonde in the front row wearing a baby blue sleeveless dress that made her blonde hair stand out and her eyes look like the ocean in her backyard.

The one who he'd told he didn't want to see again.

There were no more bids after that and the place erupted with applause when the auctioneer announced, "Sold!"

What the fuck was Brenna up to? She wasn't going to fuck with his head again. He'd write her a five-thousand-dollar check to cover her cost, but he was *not* going out with her.

He knew the whole place was watching, so he put on his best smile as the spotlight followed him down the stairs to where Brenna was sitting and offered her his arm. Once the spotlight left them, he yanked her into an empty office before they made it to the cashier.

Her skin felt like silk.

"What the fuck do you think you're doing?" he snarled.

She played dumb as she looked up at him with her big doe eyes. "Buying a tour of the base and a helicopter ride."

He could smell her flowery shampoo. The effect it had on his cock only served to piss him off even more.

"You should have bid on someone else's date. I'm not going out with you. I'll pay your bill."

"Won't that be an interesting headline. *General Refuses Widow's Money for the Wounded Warrior Project.*"

He glared at her. "They're getting paid either way."

She smirked and he wanted to wipe it off her face—with his cock.

"Do you think the press will care about that detail, especially when I go to them insulted and hurt after having made such a nice donation in the past? People will think twice before giving Wounded Warriors any more money, if that's how you treat your donors. And don't you have a big promotion coming up? That probably won't reflect very well on you."

She pretended to grimace on his behalf.

*She is fucking blackmailing me.*

At least she had the decency to take a step back when he loomed over her. Then she licked her fucking lips, something his dick took notice of.

*Goddamn this woman.*

Ron took another menacing step toward her, and she continued to retreat until she was against the wall.

He was livid. But his cock wasn't getting the message. Maybe he could fuck her out of his system.

Trapping her body with his, he brought his face within inches of hers as he pressed against her.

"Is this what you want, Brenna?"

She didn't answer him, but he could see by the way her pupils dilated it was exactly what she wanted.

His lips hovered momentarily before capturing hers, almost gently at first, but when she returned the kiss, he took a deep breath then enveloped her mouth with his.

He ran his hands crudely over her tits and down her sides and hiked up her dress to her waist. He reached between her legs, and found her panties wet, just like he knew he would.

Her hands came up to his chest in a mock attempt to push him away. Grabbing both her wrists, he pinned them over her head with one hand and pushed her underwear aside with the other.

"Is this what you were hoping to get for your five thousand dollars?" he growled in her ear.

He thrust two fingers inside her soaked pussy, and she cried out, pushing her hips against his hand. His mouth was forceful on hers, and he continued to roughly ram his digits inside her, pulling his lips from hers only to hurl more offenses at her.

"Kyle can't get you off so you have to buy a date with me?"

His thumb grazed her clit, and he felt her jump.

"Do you moan my name when he fucks you?"

Panting heavily, she still said nothing while she moved her hips in rhythm with his hand, and he felt her getting wetter.

*Uh uh. She's not coming this way.*

He unbuckled his belt and lowered his pants just enough to get his cock out. With no pleasantries, he pushed himself inside her. Fuck, she was tight.

Like she'd been waiting just for him to fuck her again.

He'd had makeup sex before, but that's not what this was. This was angry sex. He wanted to punish her for everything she'd put him through—every sleepless night, pissed off feeling, pang of guilt and regret, and the fact that even angry, his need for her consumed him. His cock was going to take it all out on her pussy.

He let go of her wrists and tugged her hair, pulling her head back and exposing her neck to feast on while he buried himself inside her. His other hand roughly squeezed and pinched her boob at the same time he punished her with his cock. He wanted her to feel every thrust to her core.

Burrowed into her neck, he realized how much he still craved her smell, her taste, her touch... and it made him want to fuck her even harder.

Thrust after thrust, he drove into her while she whimpered and moaned. Her tits moved with every push.

"Damn you for making me want you," he growled as he slammed into her.

"Damn you for making me love you." Another hard thrust, and she held onto him with all her might.

"And damn you for breaking my heart," he said through gritted teeth, spilling his seed inside her.

He continued to ram into her, and she cried out while she clung to him as she came all over his cock. He used to love how her pussy quivered around him while he was still inside her. He fucking still loved it, but he'd be damned if he was going to admit it, even to himself.

Ron pressed his arm against the wall next to her ear and leaned his forehead onto it as he caught his breath.

She hadn't uttered a word since her blackmail threat.

When he looked down at her, he felt ashamed to see her gazing at him with an expression of hope.

She was not supposed to look at him like that. She was supposed to hate him. This was not a new beginning; this had been an attempt to exorcize his need for her.

It appeared he failed all the way around.

*Fuck, fuck, fuck.*

Tucking himself back in his pants, he averted any more eye contact and grumbled, "Call my secretary and schedule a day to come to the base," then turned and left her leaning against the wall, her skirt still hiked around her waist.

He had to get out of there before he swept her up in his arms and fell for her lies again.

# Chapter Forty-Six

*Brenna*

She touched her bruised lips as she watched Ron walk out the door of the deserted office he'd just pushed her into.

*Are you fucking kidding me?*

Bidding on his date had been a mistake. A huge one. She should have listened when he said they were done. But as usual, she didn't.

She knew she'd made him lose control, and she knew that was something that didn't happen very often to her Marine. But still, she thought he owed her more than a "call my secretary" while he zipped up after their little rough and fast dalliance.

She pushed her skirt down; the effects of Ron's orgasm leaked out of her.

*That bastard fucked me and left.*

It was slowly sinking in, and she became more pissed by the second.

Brenna came out of the office angry. Their conversation was not done, and she definitely wasn't okay with him walking away after what just happened between them.

*And what the hell did he mean I broke his heart? I made him love me?*

She laughed out loud.

*Look in the mirror, prick. You were the one who broke my heart, and I didn't make you do anything.*

Except she was going to make him listen when she gave him a piece of her mind.

She looked around and couldn't find him.

*I'll bet that bastard left.*

Then she spotted him. All cozied up with the woman from his table that Brenna had outbid in the last second.

Talk about a blow to the gut.

She had a decision to make. She'd come out of the office, guns a-blazing, ready to take no prisoners and let him have it, but looking at him with that woman less than five minutes after he'd just been intimate with her made her feel used and cheap.

Taking a deep breath, she turned toward the bathroom to compose herself in private.

After she cleaned up and fixed her hair and makeup while she talked to herself, she knew what she had to do. Hopefully the son-of-a-bitch hadn't left yet with the woman who was going to get her sloppy seconds.

Nope, they were still at the table flirting when she walked out of the restroom.

Brenna approached them without a step of hesitation. Ron seemed startled to see her standing there.

*Really? You're surprised? That just shows how little you really know me, fucker.*

With a sweet smile, she turned to the woman whose chair he had his arm on.

"The committee would like to accept your offer of eleven hundred dollars for a date with him." She jerked her head toward Ron. "I agreed to make up the thirty-nine-hundred-dollar difference of my original bid."

Not pausing for a reply, Brenna then focused her attention to Ron. Looking him up and down, she said with disdain, "Your performance wasn't even worth a tenth of that, but I'm feeling generous." She didn't wait to see his reaction before returning to the brunette.

With a smirk, she told the pretty bitch, "Enjoy. You might want him to shower first though, you know, to get my scent off him," then spun on her heel and headed back to her table.

*Go fuck yourself, Ron Thompson.*

She put one arm around Cassie and the other around Luke, and smiled at the new handsome strangers who were sitting at their table.

"Who feels like getting drunk with me?"

Thank God she got a unanimous "me!" from everyone.

"First round's on me," she exclaimed way more merrily than she felt.

They got their shots and Brenna offered up a toast. "To heroes in calendars!"

"To heroes in calendars!" they all repeated as their glasses clinked in the middle. She looked over and saw Ron watching her. With a cold glare she gestured her shot glass toward him, then tossed the Patron back. She kept his stare, while nonchalantly sucking on the lemon slice. Someone approached his table, and he broke away to focus on the person talking to him.

She learned her new tablemates consisted of one Marine captain, Cooper Johnson, who worked at the same base as Ron, and the rest were all SWAT guys who worked with Luke. Craig Baxter, Mr. Full Body Massage himself, was now part of their group since the woman who paid top dollar for a date with him had to go home because she had to work in the morning.

Brenna also discovered while she was getting fucked by Ron, Cassie had bid on Luke's date and got away with paying just five hundred dollars for it. Turned out, Luke winked and blew a kiss to her sister while he was on stage, quashing any other girl's hopes she had a chance with him, so Cass didn't have a lot of competition.

"I wonder if I'll get anything else for my five hundred dollars," Cassie whispered to Brenna.

Luke's smile let them know he'd heard and looked forward to showing her what she was going to get for her winning bid.

They did shot after shot, and eventually the ache in Brenna's heart was dulled, probably because she was no longer thinking, or seeing, straight, which helped her stop looking for Ron. Captain Baxter was getting friendlier by the drink and more than once suggested he help her get home.

Each time, she'd smile and tell him in not so many words, *thanks but no thanks*. He was fucking gorgeous, but she wasn't feeling it. Brenna got the feeling he wasn't told *no* very often.

When last call was announced, she stood, wobbling a little, and declared she was leaving. The SWAT captain rose to walk her out and the rest of the group followed suit. They all stood on the sidewalk out front as they said their goodbyes and waited for cabs and Ubers.

"Why don't we share a cab?" Craig offered one more time.

Brenna laughed. "I'll be okay to get home. My favorite Uber driver is working tonight."

"Are you sure?"

Just then, Ron appeared at her side.

"Well, well, well... if it isn't Superman himself," Brenna sneered then put her index finger to the side of her mouth in a contemplative gesture. "Or should I say, Mr. Fuck and Run? Personally I like just plain ol' asshole; it rolls off the tongue easier."

Holding her elbow, he said, "Let's get you home," in a low voice, like he didn't want to draw unwanted interest to what was transpiring.

*Ha ha, fat chance, fucker.*

She belligerently tugged her elbow out of his grasp and loudly said, "Don't touch me! Don't ever touch me again!"

Ron looked around at the group whose full attention was now on him and Brenna. Craig seemed to have squared his shoulders, then Cassie walked by and patted his back on her way to put her arm around Brenna.

"Honey, let Ron take you home."

"No, Greg is going to take me home!"

The captain corrected her, "Craig."

"Sorry," she threw back over her shoulder.

Cassie used her soothing voice, which never actually soothed Brenna, it usually only pissed her off more. "Craig isn't able to drive, Ron is. Let him drive you home."

Brenna whirled back at Ron, slurring her words as she taunted him.

"Did Sloppy Seconds have a change of heart? Is that why you want to take me home? Pick up where we left off?"

Ron seemed amused. "I just want to make sure you get home safely, and since I know where you live and still have a key to your house, I can easily do that."

Drunk, aggressive Brenna came out swinging.

"Why do you care what happens to me? We're over, remember? You said so yourself. Except you must have forgot that when you fucked me tonight. But boy, it all came back to you once you pulled your pants up and went to be with your new big-boobed girlfriend!"

Ron took a deep breath. She had hoped to embarrass him, but he seemed more annoyed than anything.

When she failed to get the reaction she was hoping for her, she spat out, "And I definitely didn't get my money's worth!"

****

*Ron*

Ron shot Cassie a questioning look and she nodded slightly.

"Okay, drunk girl, time to go."

Ron hoisted Brenna over his shoulder and carried her off while she began having a temper tantrum, kicking and hitting his back and butt with her fists.

*Whack!*

"Did you just spank me?" she shrieked.

*Whack! Whack!*

"You spanked me!"

Ron didn't miss a step while telling her, "If you're going to behave like a child, I'm going to treat you like one."

That seemed to settle her down.

"Put me down."

He ignored her and kept walking.

"You better put me down right now or I'm going to puke all over you."

That got his attention, and he set her on her feet, steadying her until she got her bearings.

Poor, pitiful drunk Brenna decided to make an appearance and tears flowed down her cheeks.

"I don't want to go with you."

"Well, you've had too much to drink, and I need to make sure you get home okay."

"Why do you care if I get home okay?"

With a grin and an amused tone, he replied, "Because I care about you."

He'd admitted that to himself somewhere between coming inside her tonight and watching her get drunk with a table full of guys who were doing their damnedest to take her home, despite her obvious lack of interest.

She stuck her bottom lip out.

"You don't care about me; you used me. You think I'm a cheater. You love Big Boobs now."

He smirked and thought about telling her that nobody's tits would ever compare to hers, but instead urged her to keep walking.

"I don't love her—I love you," he whispered in her ear and put his arm around her shoulders to help steer the stumbling woman to his black F150.

After boosting her into the cab and getting her situated, he came round to the driver's side and started the engine.

Brenna stared at him for a minute before stating matter-of-factly, "I don't like you anymore."

He glanced at her as he drove. "I'm sorry to hear that."

She let out a dramatic sigh, flopping back against the seat.

"Me too. You used to be one of my favorite people."

Placating her, Ron replied, "Well, you're still one of my favorite people."

"No, I'm not. You think I'm a horrible person," she lamented in a way that only a drunk girl can.

Baiting her, he stated, "Why would I think you're a horrible person?"

She didn't answer the question when she responded, "You hate me now."

"I don't hate you, darlin'."

"Yes, you do! I lied to you. You saved my daughter's life, you were always there for me, and I should have trusted you and told you the truth."

She let out a deep breath that made her lips flap as she did.

"Kyle's a great guy, but there's no way I could ever have been with him. I loved you too much. You should have known that."

*What does she mean, I should have known that? Known what, exactly?*

He was enjoying this and wanted to keep her talking.

"You said loved, past tense. Don't you love me anymore?"

She shook her head furiously and made pouty lips. "Nope. I can't."

"You can't? How come?"

"Because you broke my heart into a million little pieces."

"I did?"

"Yep. Maybe even a billion," she slurred.

"How did I do that?"

Belligerent Brenna was back, and she glared at him. "You know how."

"No, I don't. Why don't you tell me?"

343

"You weren't really my Superman after all."

He suppressed a smile. "You thought I was Superman? Like with the cape, and everything?"

She made a face and mimicked him. "No, not with a cape and everything, jerk."

Shrugging her shoulders, she continued, "Just like... Just like someone who would never let me down or hurt me."

He didn't like where this was going, but after how he'd behaved tonight, he deserved it.

"How did I let you down, darlin'?

"You turned out to be just like Danny."

That wasn't the answer he expected; he expected her to be mad about him fucking her tonight, and the way he'd left afterwards. He was having a hard time keeping up with her train of thought, and he did not like the Danny comparison at all.

Ron gripped the steering wheel of his truck a little harder but tried to keep his tone light. "Danny, huh?"

She let out another big sigh. "The only thing I could count on him for was to sleep around."

"But you know I didn't. I told you that was all a big misunderstanding."

"Yeah, well, I told you I only lied because I thought you were a big fat cheater and knew you'd leave me alone if I said I was with Kyle. But noooo... *I* can't be forgiven for that."

He took his eyes off the road and looked at her.

"You didn't tell me you were never with Kyle."

She frowned and seemed to be getting more exasperated with him.

"Yes, I did. At the hospital."

He shook his head. "No, you didn't."

She appeared to ignore that little detail before getting louder. "Oh, that's right! You walked out and wouldn't let me explain. You thought I cheated on Kyle with you and—"

He interrupted. "So you were never with Kyle?"

She was exasperated with him.

"Are you listening? No, I was never with Kyle. You'd know that already if you would have taken my calls."

"I didn't see the point."

*Fuck, she was never with Kyle.*

"Well, the point would have been so you could talk to me, and I could tell you. That would have been the point."

Her facial expression read, *duh!* When you're intoxicated, the answers are so obvious.

"So why was he mad at you at the hospital?"

"Because I wanted him to pretend we had dated. I thought you'd be mad at me for lying about that."

He groaned internally. Yeah, he would have been upset, but not heartbroken like he had been since leaving the hospital.

She narrowed her eyes. "Then you fucked me tonight like I didn't mean anything to you and went off to be with your new girlfriend, Boobs Magee."

Yeah, he'd done that, and he felt shitty about it. He knew he couldn't justify to his very inebriated passenger what made him behave that way. He regretted it, and then watched her get smashed because of him.

He'd thought about ignoring Cassie when she'd approached him at the bar, thinking she was going to continue where Brenna left off in letting him have it, but all she did was hint there might be more to her sister's story, and he would probably be interested in what she had to say. Then off-the-cuff, suggested he drive her home.

"Would it help if I said I was sorry? That I was just sitting with her to make you mad?"

"That wasn't very nice," she pouted. "Does she know you were just using her?"

*Ouch.* That's the thing about drunks. They didn't mince words.

"Well, I don't think it took her long to figure out that I love you and wasn't interested in her."

He felt comfortable throwing around the L word since she probably wouldn't remember a thing tomorrow.

"Pfffft." Brenna flapped her lips again.

"You don't believe me?"

"Nope." She closed her eyes.

"Which part don't you believe? That I love you or that I'm not interested in her?"

She didn't even bother to open her eyes. "I saw the way you were looking at her."

He chuckled. "How was I looking at her?"

"Like you used to look at me. Like you wanted to fuck her, and you'd just got done fucking me!"

"Brenna, I could have taken her home tonight if I'd wanted to. I had no interest. You're the only woman I love and want to take home."

"You don't love me. I'm not *trustworthy*."

She had thrown the word he'd said about her at the hospital back at him.

He opened his mouth to reply, but she kept going.

"I can't even be trusted enough to know your goddamn birthday," she grumbled.

"You know my birthday, darlin'," he teased. "It's March first."

She sat up and opened her eyes to scowl at him. "Well, it wasn't because *you* told me. That's just one of the bazillion things you refused to tell me."

Closing her eyes again, she slumped against the door and muttered, "You only love your stupid job."

That made him laugh out loud.

"Aw, Bren, I love you way more than my job. I love you more than anything."

He really did.

"Pffst," was the only sound she made before she quickly fell asleep.

*Well this has been an enlightening drive.*

He appreciated Cassie for suggesting it.

# Chapter Forty-Seven

*Ron*

He carried a passed out Brenna up the stairs to her bed. Looking down at her sprawled out on the mattress with her hair wild against the pillow, he contemplated putting her teddy on her, but when his cock twitched at the idea, he decided against it. He left her in her dress and pulled the covers up around her. With a kiss to her, he whispered, "Goodnight darlin'," before heading back downstairs.

He sat at the kitchen island and scrubbed his hand against his stubbly chin. He had a dilemma; did he stay here tonight or go home? It seemed like they had a lot of unfinished business they needed to discuss, and it wouldn't be difficult to come up with an excuse why he stayed—in the guest room.

He heard the front door open, and Zona give a welcoming whine to whoever just walked in. Cassie appeared in the kitchen doorway.

*Why is she here?*

His face must have given away his thoughts, because she answered the unspoken question. "I didn't know if she was going to need me after you left."

He winced, thinking about the hurt he'd put Brenna through, and wondered exactly how much Cassie knew.

"How's our girl?" she asked.

"Passed out."

There was an awkward silence, then Ron asked her, "When did you know she lied to me about being with Kyle?"

Brenna's Mini Me looked sheepish. "The night she did."

He tried not to let his face show he was pissed at her about that, but he was certain he wasn't doing a very good job.

Cassie defended herself. "You have to understand that after everything Danny put her through, she just didn't have it in her to do it all over. And frankly, I couldn't watch her do it again."

"I'm nothing like Danny," he replied in an irritated tone.

She didn't acknowledge him, her attention was on what she was doing on her phone. After a few minutes, she handed him the device to view an old video clip from the Internet. It seemed to be filmed in a hotel lobby and was of a reporter interviewing the Padres' manager about their win that afternoon. In the background was Danny Roberts, and the girl he was all over was not Brenna.

"That was just one of many over the course of their marriage."

Ron stared blankly at Cassie who had turned the TV on while he was looking at her phone.

"He was a cheating asshole. What the fuck does that have to do with me?"

She didn't say anything, just hit play. It took him a second to recognize the footage he was watching was taken at Miramar on the day he had returned home with his Marines. He finally saw himself in the background being hugged by his parents, and his jaw clenched at what he knew was coming next. Watching Sarah wrap her legs around his waist and kiss him all over made his stomach turn.

"I was never with her. I didn't even know she was coming. If the camera would have stayed on me for five more seconds, you would have seen me push her away."

"But it wasn't on you for five more seconds."

"She should have known there was more to it," he said in a low voice.

"She should have? Why? Because you've been so upfront with her? After all the shit Danny did to her, but could always explain away, you can't blame her."

No, he couldn't. Not seeing it from this perspective.

"She shouldn't have lied to me."

Cassie shrugged.

"Maybe not. But she did try to explain, and you wouldn't let her. Using your logic, you should have known there was more to it."

Fuck. She was right. He should have.

Zona streaked out of the room like she'd heard something. The door leading to the garage opened and moments later, Danielle appeared in the kitchen with the dog at her side. She had healed up nicely.

The girl looked at Ron wide eyed before breaking out into the biggest smile he'd ever seen. She walked over to him and gave him a bear hug.

"I knew you'd be back," she whispered before releasing him.

Ron didn't have the heart to correct her. Probably because he wanted it to be true. But after everything he'd said and done to her mother, he wasn't sure that was a possibility anymore.

He smiled as he touched her chin. "You look great, kiddo."

"Hope to see you at breakfast in the morning." She grinned and then said goodnight. Zona followed her to her room.

Cassie disappeared momentarily at the same time as Danielle, but returned holding a leather-bound file a few inches thick.

"Here," she said, handing it to him. "Maybe this will give you some insight."

"What is it?"

"It's her screenplay."

He furrowed his brow. "Why would this give me insight?"

"Because it's about you."

*Oh fuck.*

*Why hadn't Brenna said anything?*

In retrospect, he realized there hadn't been much of an opportunity for her to.

"Is it bad? Is that why she gave her advance to the WWP?"

"She did that?" Cassie asked with raised eyebrows.

"Yeah. A pretty sizable one, too. I hope she at least makes some money from it."

Cassie seemed smug when she gestured to their surroundings.

"You didn't think this was from baseball money, did you? Danny was too old when owners started giving out hundreds of millions of dollars to players. Brenna made more than he did, even after she stopped writing. The studios know what her screenplays are capable of. Trust me, there's plenty more where that came from."

"Is it bad?" he repeated, and motioned to the document in his hand.

"Read it yourself and find out." Cassie continued with stage whisper, "Spoiler alert, it definitely does not end well for the bond trader."

They both laughed out loud.

"Good," he said as he thought back to what that fucker did to Brenna, and the slap on the wrist he received for it.

Ron leaned down and kissed Cassie on the cheek.

"Thanks for talking to me tonight. I appreciate your honesty."

He started toward the front door and paused.

"Make sure she has a glass of water and two Ibuprofens on her nightstand for when she wakes up. I have a feeling she's going to be hurting tomorrow."

Cassie scrunched up her nose. "I have a feeling you're right."

He hadn't made it out the door when he heard her call his name. He turned around and saw she had followed him.

"Don't be a stranger."

He winked and waved the screenplay at her. "Depends on if she kills me off."

One side of her mouth raised. "Then we'll see you soon."

*Well, that was a relief.*

He needed to get home and start reading.

# Chapter Forty-Eight

*Brenna*

Her pounding head woke her up, and the light shining in her windows was not helping. She sat up slowly and noticed the water and pain pills on her dresser. Someone was thinking about her.

But who?

A sense of dread filled her as she remembered getting drunk last night and being flirty with the men at her table. Did she bring someone home? That didn't sound like her, but the way she had been behaving last night, anything was possible.

She noticed she was still wearing her dress; that was promising.

How the hell did she get home?

*God, I hope Danielle didn't see me like that.*

The events of the night came back to her in bits and pieces and most seemed to revolve around Ron. She remembered him being surrounded by a table full of women, and how she outbid one of them for a date with him. Then the memory of how he'd fucked her and left without saying anything more came flooding back. She sighed when she recalled telling him off while he was cozied up with the slutty brunette ... things got fuzzy after that.

She seemed to remember being in his truck with him. Is that how she got home? How the fuck did that happen? Did they have sex again?

All those thoughts were not helping her head stop hurting.

She pulled the covers over her head and groaned. Maybe if she slept a little while longer, she'd feel better.

Brenna lay there and knew she wasn't going to fall back asleep, her mind was racing too much, so she got up and threw on some shorts and a T-shirt before heading downstairs to get something to eat. Maybe food would help her feel better.

Cassie was sitting at the kitchen island, a cup of coffee in one hand while she scrolled through her phone with the other.

"Good morning," her little sister said way too cheerfully for how Brenna felt.

Ignoring the friendly greeting as she headed directly to the coffeepot, Brenna grumbled, "Did you bring me home last night?"

Cassie broke out into a smile. "No, Ron did."

"What? How? Why?"

Brenna slid onto the barstool next to Cassie.

Her sister shrugged with a sly smile. "You were drunk, he offered."

"So why are you here? Did you ride with us?"

"No, but I wanted to make sure you were okay. You seemed pretty upset after *he took you to the cashier.*" She put her fingers up as if making quotation marks when she said the last part.

Brenna looked at Cassie suspiciously. "What do you know about that?"

"Sweetie, everyone knows. You kind of announced it on the sidewalk when you were yelling at him."

Brenna laid her head on the countertop and groaned. "Oh, God, shoot me now."

Cassie got up to pour herself more coffee.

"Pretty much everyone else but Ron was drunk, so I doubt they'll remember."

She lifted her head a few inches and asked, "What else did I say?"

"Not much while you were with all of us, but you must have said something while Ron drove you home because he asked me when I knew you lied about dating Kyle."

That caused her to jerk her head up, then wince from the pain. "So he knows about Kyle?"

"Apparently."

Bits and pieces of the night were coming back to her. Cassie interrupted her train of thought.

"I think he really loves you, Bren."

Brenna shook her head with a grimace. "I think he did. I'm not so certain he still does."

"He does," her sister said authoritatively.

"What makes you think that?"

"He cared enough to make sure nobody else took you home last night when you were drunk."

Brenna was unconvinced. "Just because he doesn't want anyone else to have me, doesn't mean he wants me."

"He made sure you had water and painkillers on your nightstand for when you woke up."

A small smile broke out on Brenna's lips. "That was him?"

"Well, technically, it was me, but he asked me to do it."

Brenna sat thinking in silence. Her sister might be right. Something in Brenna's subconscious told her he still loved her.

*Still? How do I know he ever did? He never said it.*

No, she conceded, but neither did she. Yet, they both knew. Deep down, they knew.

"Do you think he'll talk to me?"

With a big smile as she brought the mug to her lips to blow on her coffee, Cassie said, "Only one way to find out."

\*\*\*\*

*Ron*

He sat at his desk with a scotch in his hand and stared at the manuscript he'd just finished reading, as he tried to make sense of it all.

She'd never been with Kyle.

She'd loved him.

According to the leather-bound document in front of him, more than she ever did her husband. More than she had any other man. He smiled wistfully thinking about the ending of her story. That should have been them.

Maybe it still could be.

Taking a long pull from his tall glass of the amber liquid, Ron scowled. She thought he'd let her down, said he wasn't her Superman after all.

*Bullshit.* He was her Superman.

He set his glass down hard.

This wasn't over. Not by a long shot.

Just then his doorbell rang. Did he dare hope it was Brenna at his front door?

It was a beautiful woman standing on his sidewalk. Only the wrong beautiful woman.

"Sarah, why are you here?"

"Nice to see you again too, Ron," she patted his cheek and walked inside, uninvited.

He stood at the door and looked at the summer sun starting to set, then gave a resigned sigh before shutting it and turning to follow her.

"So, is the blonde who bid on you last night the one you're in love with?" Sarah wasn't mincing words that evening.

"Yes." He didn't feel she needed any more details.

"She's Danny Roberts' widow." She said it like she knew something he didn't and was letting him in on the secret.

"I know." Again, he wasn't telling her anything.

"I noticed you didn't spend any more time with her after the auction. As a matter of fact, she seemed to be having a grand old time without you."

He smirked, he wasn't taking the bait. "And yet, I'm still the one who took her home."

That shut her up. For a second.

"And yet, here you are, all alone."

Ron sighed. She really needed to leave. "Why are you here, Sarah?"

"Because I care about you and wanted to make sure you are all right."

"Well, now that you've seen I'm just fine..." The doorbell interrupted him.

*Dammit. Please don't be her.*

It would be just his luck that *now* Brenna was at his door.

He stood at his entryway looking at the beautiful woman on the other side of the threshold. The right one this time.

It wasn't possible that he could be happier to see her, and yet, fuck. He knew how it looked with Sarah being there. The only way to face it was head-on.

With a big smile, he leaned down and kissed her cheek. "Hi!" he said and ushered her inside. "I'm so glad to see you."

Brenna gave a shy smile. "I didn't know if it was okay that I came over uninvited."

"You are always welcome any time." *That includes in my bed.*

He was about to introduce her but knew the exact moment she realized Sarah was there by the look on her face.

She mumbled, "I'm so sorry, I shouldn't have come without calling," and turned for the door.

"Wait!" He grabbed her wrist and pulled her into a hug from behind. "Don't leave like this," he snarled in her ear.

"Let me go!" she seethed.

"Not until you listen to me."

"What is there to say?"

He loosened his grip and spun her around, holding her at the shoulders.

"She just got here. Uninvited. I had no idea she was coming. I was actually hoping it was you when I went to the door."

Sarah made an indignant gasp at his revelation.

"I'm not interested in her. I'm not interested in the other woman bidding on my date last night. I'm not interested in anyone but you, darlin'. I told you before, you're it for me. And even though I haven't behaved like it, I still mean that."

Brenna stared up at him, speechless.

"Don't go. Please," he whispered.

Sarah stormed by them. "Goodbye, Ron. Thanks for everything." Her voice dripped with sarcasm.

He didn't even acknowledge what she said, and the door closed behind her. At least she finally got the hint.

"You're it for me, Bren," he reiterated, sounding almost desperate for her to believe him.

She cupped his jaw and caressed his cheek with her thumb as she searched his eyes.

"I love you. More than you know."

A huge smile spread from ear to ear, as he pulled her against him. "I love you, too. So damn much."

With tears in her eyes, she whispered, "There was never anyone else. I'm so sorry I lied to you. I tried—at the hospital, after Danielle's accident, but then you misunderstood and—"

He remembered that all too well. "I'm sorry, Bren. So sorry..."

They embraced each other for several minutes. Ron closed his eyes and held her tight against him, taking in her smell and how she felt in his arms again. He knew she could feel his hard cock against her stomach. He didn't even try to hide it.

"I've missed you so much," she mumbled against his shirt as she rubbed the length of him over his pants.

Ron grinned. "Is that why you're here?"

She nodded her head then laughed when she corrected herself. "Wait, no! I came to thank you for taking me home last night."

His fingers traced in between her cleavage. "Are you sure that's the only reason you came?"

A little grin escaped her lips. "Well, and to tell you I love you."

He bent down and kissed her softly. When he pulled away, his expression was serious.

"I'm sorry, Brenna. Sorry about everything. About not listening to you, about not believing in us, about the way I— Last night, the way I behaved in the office."

"I think we both made mistakes. I should have known you would never hurt me like that; I should have trusted you. And I should have explained when I had the chance about Kyle—or at least made you listen to me."

Ron chuckled at the idea of her making him do anything. Although, she was probably only one of a few who even stood a chance at that.

She smiled shyly. "As far as last night, in the office. I thought it was sexy, right up until you walked out."

*That was definitely good to know.*

"Oh yeah?" His eyebrows lifted with surprise.

A little bolder than she had just been, she wrapped her arms around his neck and replied, "Yeah."

Their kiss was less chaste this time, and she finally broke away.

"But, there's a lot we still need to talk about."

Seeking her mouth out again with his, Ron murmured against her lips, "Can't it wait until later?" and caressed her sides with his fingertips.

Victory was his when she conceded with a breathless, "Okay, but you have to promise we'll talk."

He lifted the hem of her shirt as he agreed. "I promise."

He was going to take his time and reacquaint himself to her body. All night long.

The moan that escaped her after he unhooked her bra made him smile, and he ran his tongue underneath her tits, causing her nipples to pebble. He was about to take her right one between his teeth when he felt her tug on his shirt.

"Please, I want to feel your skin next to mine."

He was more than happy to oblige. Brenna melted against him, and Ron cupped her ass and lifted her up. With her legs around his waist, they blindly made their way to his bedroom, kissing the whole time. He deposited her on his bed, then crawled on top of her, and they resumed making out. Ron pressed his erection between her legs while she arched against him.

Fuck, he'd missed her.

She pulled him closer to her when he nuzzled into her neck. He didn't think he'd ever get tired of her scent. It was intoxicating.

Then he heard it. The one thing that could ruin this reunion before it got started.

His work phone ringing.

*You have got to be fucking kidding me. The universe had to be playing a cruel joke on them.*

For a split second he considered not answering it, but his sense of duty quickly quashed that idea.

He could feel her heartbreak as he pulled away from her.

God, he hoped he wasn't asking too much of her. He'd almost rather see her with someone else if it meant she'd be happy and loved.

Almost.

Yet there wasn't anyone else on this earth who was capable of loving her like he did.

****

*Brenna*

*No! Oh please, no. Not now!*

Brenna knew what that ringtone meant and wanted to cry. Or break his damn phone.

She knew better than to ask him not to answer it, but there was no mistaking her silent plea with the look she gave him.

"Any other call, darlin'," he said before he pecked her lips and stood to get his phone.

She nodded her head in defeat and watched him walk out of the room. With a sigh, she gathered up her bra and blouse and got dressed, then sat on the bed to wait.

Could she ever learn to accept that she would never be more important to him than his job? She admitted that he put her first the night Ray assaulted her, so perhaps she wasn't exactly being fair when she said she wasn't more important. But that was then. Right now, she wanted to be the most important thing to him. She *needed* to be.

The look on his face and the hurried footsteps when he came back in the room told her all she needed to know. He was leaving. Immediately.

"We didn't have time to talk," she lamented in a soft voice.

He frowned as he headed to the closet. "I know, sugar. I'm sorry."

*I'm not going to cry. I'm not going to cry. I'm not going to cry.*

"Do you know when you'll be back?"

Ron shook his head from the doorway. "But I'll be able to email or Skype this time."

Brenna shrugged her shoulders in resignation and feigned a smile when she followed to watch him pack.

"That's something, at least."

She was doing her best to pretend to keep it together, but judging by the glances he was stealing at her while he collected his things, she must not have been doing a very good job.

Midway through gathering his gear, he pulled her back in his arms and whispered against her hair, "I love you, Brenna. Don't give up on me."

With her head against his chest, she murmured, "Not a chance, Devil Dog."

That made him smirk. "Devil Dog, huh? Where'd you hear that?"

"When I was doing research for my screenplay." She looked up at him as she confessed, "It's about you; well, us really."

He winked at her. "Is that so? No wonder they gave you such a big advance."

After his duffle bag was packed, they stood in his garage as he leaned down and kissed her. "Stay as long as you want. Hell, move in while I'm gone if you feel like it."

Her bottom lip quivered, and a small sob escaped her lips. It wasn't fair. They hadn't had time to talk or even be together again.

*At least he knows I love him.*

"Fuck, darlin', don't do this to me."

She choked out, "I'm sorry."

Ron wiped her tears with his thumbs. "I love you, sugar. I'll be back as soon as I can."

When she gave her best fake smile, he kissed her lips again. "Don't give up on me, Bren."

"I won't," she whispered.

Then he was gone. Who knew for how long this time.

# Chapter Forty-Nine

*Ron*

He felt lighter than he had in a while. The timing of being called out couldn't have been worse, but at least he left her on good terms. Not to mention he was coming back to her. There were so many things he was going to do to her hot little body...

He felt his cock move. *Down, boy. Be patient.*

When he told her she could move in while he was gone, he meant it. Although, he knew the chance of that really happening was zilch. She loved her beach house, and he didn't blame her. It was a great place. Still, after his promotion, he was going to ask her to marry him, so they'd need to get their living situation figured out. She was going to be in his bed, he didn't care where.

It came as a surprise when she hadn't returned his email about setting up a Skype date. Was she having second thoughts?

He started to think so when she didn't respond to two more of his emails.

Maybe they hadn't had enough time to reestablish their bond before he had to go? Maybe she realized being a military spouse wasn't for her? He hadn't had the chance to tell her his extensive traveling was coming to an end soon. He'd be able to be there for her when they went to bed each night. Maybe she did give up on him, in spite of him practically begging her not to.

Dammit. They just couldn't catch a break. Was the universe trying to tell them something? Everything happens for a reason and all that bullshit.

*Fuck that.*

In three days, he was going straight to D.C. and was scheduled to arrive the night before his promotion ceremony. He sent her one last email and asked her to be there. When he still hadn't gotten a response, he arranged for an actual invitation to be hand-delivered to her. He should have done that sooner, dammit. He asked his secretary to include a personal note that he hadn't received a reply to his emails and wanted to be sure she received her invitation. He'd put her name on the approved guest list at the Pentagon. He'd love it if she was there, and if she wasn't, he'd understand.

That was all he could do from the tent he was currently in. Hopefully it was enough.

*****

*Brenna*

She only saw the uniform when she rushed to answer the door, the disappointment that it wasn't *her* Marine must have been obvious on her face because the man chuckled. "Not who you were expecting?"

She did recognize him though. He had sat at her table at the Heroes Calendar Event.

"Cooper? What are you doing here?"

"What would you say if I told you I came to ask for your sister's phone number?"

The smile on his face made it hard for her to know if he was kidding or not.

"I'd say you were in a long line of men who'd love to have it."

Brenna thought she saw a flash of disappointment on the handsome captain's face, but he quickly masked it with his boyish grin. "Good thing that's not why I came then."

She returned his smile. "So how can I help you?"

With white gloves, he presented her with a fancy envelope. "I came to deliver this to you personally."

Her eyes grew wide. "What is it?"

"Well, ma'am, if I had to guess, I'd say it was an invitation to General Thompson's promotion ceremony."

"Really?" She had been hoping Ron would invite her but given how she hadn't heard from him in spite of him saying he'd contact her, she hadn't counted on it.

Should she invite Cooper in and open it in front of him? What was the proper procedure for this kind of thing? Hell if Brenna knew.

"Would you like to come in?"

"Thank you, but I'm afraid I need to get back to the base. Besides, if I came in, I might be tempted to snoop around for your sister's number."

He nodded with a devilish wink, then told her goodbye.

Brenna got the feeling he wasn't really teasing about wanting Cassie's number. Cooper seemed like a good guy, and he was definitely rocking that uniform, but Brenna was rooting for her sister and Luke. She acknowledged, however, that Cooper would be a nice Plan B, should it be necessary.

She opened the envelope to find a beautiful engraved invitation to Ron's promotion, but only briefly glanced at it in favor of the handwritten note that was with it. It was obviously a woman's handwriting.

*Ms. Roberts,*

*General Thompson has asked me to ensure you get this invitation. He is uncertain if you have received his emails requesting you be at his promotion, as he has not received a response from you. He will leave your name to be an approved guest and allowed access to the Pentagon, and it is his hope that he see you there, however, he will understand if you are unable to attend.*

*Sincerely,*

*Patricia McMahon*
*Executive Assistant*

She wondered why she hadn't received any of Ron's emails, but that explained why she hadn't heard from him. She hadn't let her imagination run wild this time; knowing there had to be an explanation why he hadn't reach out when he said he would.

She was learning. Maybe there was hope for her after all. Maybe she could handle being a General's girlfriend.

*Wait, did his assistant's note say the Pentagon?*

Brenna quickly scanned the invitation for all the pertinent information. Yep, the ceremony was taking place at the Pentagon and... it was tomorrow afternoon.

"Oh, for fuck's sake," she said out loud and scrambled for her phone after she turned on her computer.

It was going to take some maneuvering, but she was going to be there to watch him tomorrow, come hell or high water. She needed to show him that even though she didn't love it, she definitely supported his career. But more importantly, she supported him, whatever he was undertaking.

The only flight available was a red eye that would get her there with plenty of time to check-in to her hotel and get ready.

Deciding what to wear was a whole other issue. What did one wear to a promotion ceremony? Obviously not jeans, but how formal? Frankly, she wanted to look sexy for him. Sexy, not slutty, and that wasn't going to be accomplished in a business suit.

She sent a text to her sister: **Help!**

In no time, Cassie was standing in her kitchen.

"You rang?"

"Ron's promotion ceremony is tomorrow—at the Pentagon. What the hell am I supposed to wear? What on earth am I going to get him as a gift? Do you think he'll be offended that Dee can't take off work?" Brenna was talking a mile a minute.

"Breathe." Cassie took a deep breath in, as if illustrating how to do it.

"I can't breathe! I have to catch a flight in five hours, and I have no idea what to pack!"

"Let's go upstairs and pick something out. Good news is I know you have to have something in that huge closet of yours, so we won't need to go shopping."

They rummaged through Brenna's clothes for fifteen minutes. Cassie pulled dresses out while Brenna wrinkled her nose at each selection. Finally, Cassie pulled out a short-sleeved red dress that came just above Brenna's knee. The bodice was fitted with a scoop neck, and the skirt flared with large box pleats and scalloped edges. If she added strappy gold heels and gold jewelry, it would be perfect. The Marine Corps colors.

"Okay, on to the next part of your dilemma. No, I don't think he will be offended that Dee couldn't get time off work. He of all people should understand people having to work. As far as a gift..."

Brenna interrupted. "I already know what I'm getting him."

"You do?"

"Yes, I have a call I need to make and then I think I can finish packing."

Cassie asked, "How long are you staying? Do you need any more help?"

"Can you come by and make sure Danielle isn't overdoing it? Otherwise, I think I'm okay. Thank you, you always manage to save the day."

"So, can I have that blue dress?"

Brenna eyed her suspiciously. "Which blue dress?"

"The sexy backless one. You're going to be a general's wife, not a ball player's, there's no way you'll be wearing that out again."

She started laughing. "First of all, I'm not getting married again, and second of all..." Brenna sighed. "Okay, yeah, I probably won't wear it out again. You can have it."

Cassie squealed and ran into the closet. She had a stack of dresses waiting when Brenna came back after making her phone call about Ron's present.

"You're probably not going to wear any of these again either."

Brenna grinned and shook her head. "You can have them. But only if you promise to wear them."

"Cross my heart."

Then as if worried Brenna was going to change her mind, Cassie scooped up the dresses, kissed her sister on the cheek, and walked toward the door.

"Have a great time! Take lots of pictures. Tell Ron congratulations from me!"

****

Brenna worried she wasn't going to sleep on the plane. Fortunately, she was flying first class, so that helped her get comfortable enough to get some shuteye on the overnight flight. Arriving at Reagan International in D.C. in the early morning hours, she was able to catch a few more hours of rest at her hotel before she had to get ready.

She decided against texting or calling Ron; she wanted to surprise him. After checking her spam folder for his emails, she found several from him and felt horrible that she hadn't received them so she could reply. But it would make her showing up unannounced that much sweeter.

Sliding the red dress over her new sexy bra and panties, Brenna checked how she looked in the mirror. Her lipstick was the perfect shade of red, and she loved the gold Jimmy Choos. Just a spritz of perfume and her jewelry on, then she was ready to go.

After she requested a ride from Uber, she transferred some cash, her ID, the invitation, her lipstick, and her phone into a gold clutch, then made her way down to the lobby to wait for the car to pick her up.

Once in the back seat, she began to get nervous. Her palms were sweaty. She'd never been to the Pentagon before and had no idea what to expect. Unfortunately, her driver wanted to chat, and all she wanted to do was collect her thoughts.

Would Ron be surprised?

Would he be upset that she hadn't responded to his emails?

Would he like the way she looked?

Would he take her back to the hotel and fuck her silly?

Did he have parties that he needed to attend tonight? Would he want to bring her?

Should she act like she was his girlfriend or just a friend?

Brenna wanted to imagine different scenarios of how seeing Ron would go, but the man driving the car would not stop talking to her.

Not.

Stop.

Talking.

When they arrived at the Pentagon, Brenna thanked him and practically leapt out of the car without looking back. That is, until she arrived at the front entrance, and the officer requested her identification and invitation, which was still in her clutch in the Uber car.

She pleaded with the man who stood guard. She was on the list, Ron would vouch for her. He called the room where the ceremony was taking place and no one answered. He said if Ron came to the lobby and escorted her back, he would let her through.

*Great!*

Except.

Her phone was in her clutch.

No problem, the cute, helpful officer said he would call Ron for her.

But she had no idea what Ron's number was. Once a number was programmed into her phone, all she had to do was look for the person's name; there was no sense in wasting valuable brain space memorizing people's phone numbers.

Brenna did her best not to cry and smear her makeup. She had to see Ron's promotion ceremony. *She had to!*

She gave her best, charming smile.

She flirted.

She even begged.

While the man with the badge was sympathetic to her plight and felt bad for her, he wouldn't let her through. As a consolation, he told her she could wait on the bench outside and hopefully see Ron when he came out.

*This wasn't happening.*

Except it was.

She'd come all this way, only to be stopped at the entrance of the Pentagon. So close, and yet...

A tear escaped and ran down her cheek. The officer standing in her way of seeing Ron get promoted offered her a tissue and his heartfelt condolences.

So that was it.

Brenna turned, dejected, to make her way to the bench when she heard her name. Looking around, she didn't see anyone she recognized.

She heard it again, and finally saw Cooper Johnson, the Marine captain who had brought her the invitation, once again in his dress uniform.

"Cooper! What are you doing here?"

He grinned as he approached her. "Same thing you're doing here. Watching my boss get promoted."

"Oh my God, can you please vouch for me? I left my identification in my Uber ride and they won't let me in!"

His boyish grin grew wicked. "It's going to cost you."

With one eyebrow raised, Brenna told him, "Fine. I'll give you Cassie's number. But it will have to wait until I get my purse back from the Uber driver."

Cooper jerked his head toward the team of security officers manning the metal detectors in the lobby.

"Did any of those guys even offer to contact Uber to see if they could get your driver back?"

"No." She hadn't really thought of that.

He shook his head, not really in disgust, more like annoyance, and started typing on his phone. Soon, he was speaking to someone, then covered the mouthpiece to ask her, "Where did you get picked up at?"

She told him the name of her hotel, which he repeated into the receiver. He nodded and talked to the person on the other line, then hung up with a smile.

"Ten minutes."

"I'm sorry?" Brenna didn't understand.

"Your driver will be back here in ten minutes with your purse."

She was beaming when she hugged him. Yeah, he was definitely a solid Plan B for Cassie, should things with Luke not work out.

"I'll wait with you. This place is pretty big, and easy to get lost in if you don't know where you're going."

A very solid Plan B, indeed.

Unfortunately, waiting for the driver to bring her purse back and the long line at security caused them to be late. Brenna was grateful Cooper knew where he was going and was able to slip them in a side door to the auditorium quietly because the ceremony was already underway when they arrived.

She and Cooper discreetly found seats in the back of a sea of officers in their fancy uniforms while Brenna stared in awe at her Marine sitting on the stage. He was so fucking handsome that he took her breath away.

The four star general who oversaw the swearing-in was announced and everyone stood at attention. There was a lot of pomp and circumstance, then the man in charge started talking about Ron's many accomplishments. *Many* accomplishments.

Brenna couldn't be more proud of him.

The general stopped, smiled, and started speaking directly to Ron's family in the front row. He thanked them for their support and care of Ron, then turned to her Marine and asked him who should come up and pin his new rank emblem on his uniform.

Brenna gasped when Ron looked directly at her and made a motion with his index finger that said, 'Come here.' She'd had no idea that he'd even seen her and was definitely not expecting him to want her to put his pin on, although she was honored. He said something to the general, who nodded his head with a smile and announced her name in the microphone.

Making her way down the aisle, she knew all eyes were on her and was, at that moment, grateful for her time in the spotlight, both on the red carpet and as Danny's wife. Otherwise, her knees might have buckled when she reached the stairs.

The look on Ron's face let her know he approved of her attire, and that he was happy she was there. Brenna's eyes were locked on his while she walked across the stage toward him, and she couldn't help it, she cupped his face and gave him a chaste kiss on the lips once she reached his side.

In her hair, he murmured, "You are breathtaking."

Brenna smiled, then whispered, "I'm so proud of you."

At least she thought it was a whisper, until everyone in the audience let out an "aww."

She quickly glanced up at Ron, who leaned in close to her ear and said, "Stage. Acoustics."

*Damn. Oh well, it was true.*

She was proud of him, and she really didn't care if everyone there knew.

The general then turned to speak to Brenna directly. "It's my privilege to meet the woman who won General

Thompson's heart. Not an easy task." The audience let out a low laugh. "It's plain to see the feeling is mutual. He told me personally how your love has carried him through some difficult times, and the entire Corps thanks you for supporting him."

Brenna glanced up to find Ron watching her with a smile. When she caught his eye, he winked and her stomach flipped.

She was honored and a little surprised at the attention being placed on her. But mostly, she was proud. Proud to not only be standing next to this amazing man, but that the whole auditorium knew he loved her.

*He* loved *her*.

That thought would never get old, because damn, she loved him too.

The rest of the ceremony went by in a blur. Brenna basked in her contentment next to the three-star general. *Her* three-star general, she'd pinned the insignia on him herself. Pictures were taken, introductions made. She'd finally met his parents and brother and was looking forward to brunch with just his family the day after tomorrow. There was still the formal dinner they were all to attend that evening.

Ron excused them, citing they needed to return to the hotel "to rest and get ready for the evening's events."

There were knowing looks exchanged between those currently in their company, but Brenna couldn't care less. The idea of him naked and touching her trumped everything else.

As they walked toward the door, he murmured in her ear, "We will be doing anything *but* resting, in case you were wondering."

Suppressing a grin, Brenna replied, "I'd be disappointed otherwise."

He chuckled as he placed his hand at the small of her back. "That's my girl."

Just being near him made her want to snuggle and kiss him but she was cognizant of the public image he needed to maintain. Which was really too bad because she'd love to give him a blowjob while he was wearing that uniform.

Because… damn. She'd never seen him in his dress blues before, and he was downright edible.

Maintaining an appearance of decorum was somewhat difficult for her when he whispered dirty things in her ear, all while he continued to look dignified; like he was talking to her about the weather instead of what he was going to do to her when he got her alone.

"Darlin', I am going to eat your pussy all night long, I'm starving for it," he growled while they walked through the halls of the Pentagon.

He nodded and smiled at people walking by, then continued, "I am going to lick that little clit, and then tongue fuck you until you come all over my face."

He'd grin every time he'd get her to gasp at the filthy things he was saying.

Getting in the hired car offered her no reprieve, since he continued his naughty dialogue via text so the driver wouldn't overhear.

**Ron: Mmm, is your pussy wet for me?**

**Brenna: BEHAVE**

**Ron: Not a chance.**

**Ron: I can't wait to see your lips wrapped around my cock.**

She crossed her legs and rubbed her wet thighs together, and he let out a soft laugh.

"Everything okay, darlin'?

She couldn't help but smile at his cocky grin. He definitely deserved to be cocky, today of all days, and it just upped his sex appeal. There was no way he didn't know how badly she wanted him. If he had any doubt, the lustful look she gave him should have alleviated that.

The sharp intake of his breath assured her the message had been received loud and clear.

# Chapter Fifty

*Ron*

Oh, goddamn. That's my future wife. And she is fucking *hot*.

That was the first thing Ron thought when he watched her walk into the auditorium with Coop. Followed by the realization that, technically, she wasn't his future wife, yet. But he planned on rectifying that this weekend.

He felt confident she'd show up after he had the invitation personally delivered, but when he still hadn't heard from her, and she wasn't there when the ceremony started, he experienced a feeling of panic.

When she came through the doors, he felt an immediate sense of relief and a little tingle between his legs when he got a better look of her in that red dress. Then she leaned forward to take her seat, he caught a glimpse of her cleavage and, well, things moved.

Having her onstage with him made the day complete. The only thing that could make it perfect would be if they were alone and naked, which would be remedied soon.

They grinned at each other like teenagers on a first date the whole ride back to her hotel. Ron suggested they go to her room. Since he planned on ruining her hair and makeup, she'd need her toiletries. Besides, his room was for later that night.

The best way to describe their sexual encounter was *fast and furious*. There was no way he could go slow, she'd been tempting him all afternoon. She looked and smelled amazing, and her little touches had been driving him wild. The minute her hotel room door was closed, they kissed like they were making up for lost time.

He was careful of her dress since he didn't know if she planned on wearing it later. But when he got her out of it and she stood in front of him in her red bra and panties, all he could mutter was, "Fuuuuuck," before he grabbed a handful of her hair and kissed her more.

Pulling away, Brenna purred, "This isn't really fair. You have far more clothes on than me."

One second later, Ron kicked his shoes off and unbuttoned his jacket. She didn't have to tell him twice.

Once he was in only his boxers, she ran her hands over his chest and kissed his neck. If she kept that up, he wasn't going to last long. When she pulled his boxers down and dropped to her knees, he realized there weren't enough baseball stats in the world to help him.

He felt her tongue on his tip, circling and sucking, and he knew he shouldn't look, but he couldn't help it. The visual of her looking up at him, in that red bra with his cock between her red lips, made him even harder, if that were possible, and he let out a long moan.

She smiled and slipped his shaft halfway in her mouth before slurping off, then she went further before withdrawing. She did that repeatedly until she had engulfed his entire cock.

*Don't look, fuck, don't look.*

He looked.

Her red lipstick was smeared and his cock had all but disappeared in her throat, and her eyes locked with his.

"Oh fuck, darlin'," he moaned and closed his eyes, digging his fingers in her hair.

She bobbed her head up and down while stroking him from the base to her mouth.

*Fuck, her mouth feels like heaven.*

"Brenna. Oh goddamn, sugar."

He fisted her hair and tugged her gently off him.

With a pout she asked, "Why did you do that?"

Ron kissed her lips before responding against her lips, "Because you're going to make me come."

"That's a bad thing?"

He chuckled as he caressed her face. "It is when I want to fuck you, darlin'."

The smile on her lips told him that she was okay with that.

Although he loved her in that bra, it was quickly dispatched, and his hands came around to cup her breasts in his hands. Rolling the pebbled tips in his fingers, he leaned down to suck her right nipple.

They were both breathing heavily, and Brenna urgently clawed at his shoulders. He reached down to grab her just below her ass and lift. Instinctively, she wrapped her legs around his waist and her arms around his neck while he carried her to the bed. This was where they'd left off the last time they were together.

Her panties soon went the way of her bra, and he enveloped her body with his.

Grinding her hips against his while he devoured her tits, she begged, "Ron. Please."

He smirked when he looked down at her. "Please what, darling?"

There was desperation in her voice when she gasped, "Please, fuck me." Then as if for good measure, she added, "General."

His cock lined up with her entrance, and with a gentle thrust he was inside her. They both moaned as he filled her pussy balls deep.

"You are so wet, sugar," Ron growled while he plunged fast and hard, bottoming out before pulling back, and driving his cock in again.

He needed to slow down. The chance of him coming before her was as good as a snowball's chance in hell.

Not.

Happening.

He sat back on his knees and rubbed her hard clit in circles with his thumb while he rolled his hips into her.

Brenna moaned and lifted her back off the bed while she thrust forward. Her cries and quick breaths let him know she was close.

He increased the tempo and pressure of both his thumb and his cock.

"Mmm, come for me, sugar."

She panted, "Oh, yes. Oh, Ron. Yes, Yes, *Yes!*"

Her pussy contracted around his cock as her orgasm hit. With gritted teeth, Ron grunted and slammed into her. His balls slapped against her ass while the juices from her orgasm spurred him on and with a guttural cry, he released rope after rope of cum inside her.

Still gasping for breath, he put his arms around her tight and buried his face in her neck.

"You are so fucking sexy," he gasped underneath her earlobe.

Brenna's arms were around him and she gently scratched his back up and down.

"So are you, baby. You're lucky I didn't jump you in front of everyone once I saw you in your uniform," she teased.

"The jumping would have been mutual, darlin'. You almost got felt up on stage in front of dozens of Marines."

She giggled. "I think they might have withheld your star if you had done that."

Ron lifted his head up from her neck. "Are you kidding? They probably would have given me another one. You are fucking gorgeous, and I guarantee I'm not the only one in that room who noticed. I'm quite certain there were more eyes on your ass than on me while you were pinning my star on."

With her hands in his hair, Brenna whispered, "Stop. That's not true."

He knew that wasn't her first time in front of an audience. She knew damn well he was right, but he loved her for her modesty.

Ron kissed her then rolled on his side. "Do you want to nap for a while before getting ready?"

Brenna wiggled her ass and got into the spooning position. "Just for an hour."

He cupped one of her tits in his hand and snarled, "Keep moving like that and you won't be napping."

When she put her hand behind his head and pulled him in for a kiss, he knew she didn't give a damn about his warning.

He nudged her onto all fours.

Round Two was about to start.

# Chapter Fifty-One

*Brenna*

She came out of the bathroom, dressed in one of her standard little black dresses and heels; ready to go to dinner. Ron, back in his dress blues, stood up from the bed the second she appeared and gave a low whistle.

"Goddamn, darlin'. You look beautiful."

How did he always manage to make her feel desired? Cherished even?

She didn't know, but she wasn't complaining.

"General Thompson, you look very sexy yourself."

He leaned down to kiss her below her ear. "Are you ready to go?"

"Ready as I'll ever be! Thank you for including me today in, well, everything."

"I love you, Brenna. There's no one else I'd rather have by my side than you. Thank you for being here. I gotta admit, I was a little nervous that you weren't coming when I didn't hear from you."

"Oh God, baby! I'm so sorry about that. All your emails were in my spam folder. I got your invitation yesterday and was on a flight seven hours later. I wouldn't have missed this for the world. Although, if it weren't for Cooper, I might have."

He raised an eyebrow and she proceeded to tell him the story of how she forgot her purse in the Uber ride, then security wouldn't let her through, and she didn't know his phone number.

"Sounds like you've had quite the adventure. I guess I owe Cooper one for getting my girl to me."

Her toes curled when he called her *his girl*. She loved the idea of being *his* girl.

"Well, I gave him Cassie's phone number."

He chuckled. "Why did you do that?"

"Because that's what he wanted in return for helping me."

That caused him to raise both his brows. "Interesting."

She felt a sense of worry in her chest. "Is there something wrong with him? Should I not have given him her number?"

"No, no. Nothing like that. I just wouldn't have put the two of them together. But now that the idea is out there, I could see them dating."

"Well, I'm still rooting for Luke, but Cooper would be an acceptable alternative."

"He's a good guy. Hell, they both are."

Ron offered Brenna his arm. "Shall we go?"

****

There was a car waiting to take them to Ron's hotel. The dinner reception where Ron was the guest of honor was being held there. Brenna loved seeing him in this light. He was in his element, and it was easy to see how dynamic of a leader he really was.

Brenna knew he had a commanding presence, she just had no idea to the extent. For most of the night, she sat back and observed him in action.

It was sexy as fuck.

Every now and then, he'd catch her watching him and give her a wink and a smile.

Which made her panties a mess.

She enjoyed getting to know his family better and almost squealed with delight when his mother told stories about his youth. Ron had told Brenna when they first met that he'd always been a risk taker; judging by his mother's accounts, he wasn't lying. Fortunately, Ron had excused himself to go speak to someone, otherwise Brenna was sure he would have shut down his mother before she had a chance to get started.

The older woman had a gleam in her eye when she told Brenna that she'd never seen him so happy and alluded that Brenna was the source of that happiness.

"You're still not getting grandbabies, Mother," Ron said with a smirk as he sat down. "But Brenna does have an amazing daughter, Danielle, who I'm sure you'll love."

That ended story time.

Fortunately, dancing started and Ron escorted her out to the dance floor for a traditional waltz.

"Do you realize that we haven't been dancing since the first night we met?" he asked.

"We've been busy," she replied with a smile.

That made him laugh. "You could definitely say that."

He wanted to leave much earlier than she expected. They were having a wonderful time, so she didn't understand why he wanted to cut it short.

"I think it might be considered bad form for me to close the place," was his explanation.

Brenna didn't know a lot about military etiquette, but that made sense.

They said their farewells, and he surprised her by holding her hand on their walk to the elevator. His touch was comforting and assuring. She realized at that moment just how much she'd missed him in her life.

"Please don't disappear on me ever again," she whispered as she hugged his arm when they stepped into the elevator.

He hit the button for his floor then slid his arms around her waist from behind once the doors closed, murmuring in her ear, "You have my word, I won't."

The rest of the ride was in comfortable silence, and he took her hand again once they got off the elevator. There was an enormous grin on his face as they walked down the hall to his suite.

"What?" she asked with a suspicious smile.

"Nothing. I was just thinking I was the most envied man there tonight."

"Well, I should hope so. You were the guest of honor."

He shook his head. "No, it had nothing to do with that. It was because I had you as my date."

Brenna smiled and shook her head at him. "Ever the charmer," she scoffed.

He stopped her in the hall. "When will I get through to you that I don't play games, and I always mean what I say, and what I'm saying to you right now is that you were the most breathtaking woman in that room."

Brenna smiled. She knew better than to argue with him. "Thank you, babe. That's very kind of you to say."

Ron placed his hand at the small of her back to indicate they should start walking again. "Good girl," he whispered in her ear.

A shiver shot through her. She shouldn't love it when he called her that, but damn, she did.

With his keycard out, he paused before inserting it in the slot.

"I need you to know I love you, Brenna. No matter what, and I want to be in your life however I can be."

A small smile formed on her lips. "I love you too, Ron,"

His brows were furrowed. "I mean it. No matter what, you need to know that I'll be satisfied with whatever you want. I love you and that's not going to change."

That made her nervous. Why was he telling her this?

The trepidation replaced her smile. "Okay. I know that. I hope you know that I love you too."

His face relaxed, and he hugged her around the shoulders then kissed her temple. "I know you do, darlin'."

The green light lit up when he inserted the card, and he held the door open, gesturing for her to go first.

She let out a gasp when she walked in. There were candles and roses everywhere, and rose petals adorned the floor like a path leading to the bed, which was also covered in rose petals. A bucket of ice with a bottle of champagne stood next to the bed with two glasses on the nightstand.

This was the ending scene in her screenplay, down to the placement of the candles. The only thing missing was…

Her eyes quickly scanned the foot of the bed.

It was there.

An engagement ring in a blue Tiffany's box.

With tears in her eyes, she whirled around to look at him leaning against the doorjamb.

"How did you know?" she gasped.

He pushed off the wooden frame and slowly walked toward her, never taking his eyes off hers.

Wiping her tears with the pads of his thumbs, he grinned. "Cassie gave me a copy of your screenplay."

Leave it to her sister.

"I can't believe you did all this."

Ron took her hand and brought her knuckles to his mouth, kissing them gently. "I don't know if you've noticed, darlin', but there isn't much I wouldn't do for you."

"I have noticed, and I hope you know how much I appreciate everything—*everything*—you do. For me, my family, and our country. You are an amazing man, and I'm so lucky to have you in my life."

He stood there a moment, just looking at her, before leading her to where the ring was, and just like in her story, he took the diamond from the box and got down on one knee.

"Brenna Roberts, make me the happiest man on earth and say you'll marry me."

She stroked his face with her fingertips and looked into his brown eyes. "I would love to marry you, Ron Thompson."

He seemed relieved when he stood up and slid the ring on her finger. He bent down to kiss her softly, and her arms came around his neck, tugging him closer.

With his forehead resting against hers, he murmured, "I love you, Bren. Forever. No more misunderstandings, no more being proud and not listening—this is it. I want there to be something in our wedding vows about communicating. I almost lost you because I refused to communicate with you. Never again. I never want to be without you again."

Brenna took a deep breath in. "I never want to be without you again either. And you're right, we should say something in our vows about communicating. Think about all the time we missed out on, simply because we didn't talk."

Ron slowly unzipped her dress and kissed her shoulder once her dress slid down.

"I think we should include nonverbal communication too." Moving his hands up her thighs, he said with a smile, "I'll start."

The things he said to her body that night were dirty, naughty, and an incredible preview of her future with Lieutenant General Ron Thompson.

He truly was her Superman. Granted, a dirty Superman, but she wouldn't have him any other way.

# Epilogue

*Ron*

Brenna and Ron drove along the Pacific Coast Highway with the top down in his red Corvette convertible. It had been a promotion gift from Brenna. Well, a promotion and an engagement gift; she surprised him with it waiting for him in his garage when they returned home from D.C. and teased him that the car counted as both.

After he told her she was the only present he'd ever need, he tied her wrists using the gold ribbon of the big bow that was on the windshield, bent her over, and fucked her on the hood.

He didn't say anything when he learned that she'd bought the car from Travis Sterling. Turned out, Ava was pregnant again and insisted on a more mom friendly vehicle, so one of Travis' cars had to go to make room for her new Escalade in the garage. Ron didn't think Brenna knew that he and Ava almost dated and didn't see the point in telling her now.

"Mrs. Thompson, are you hungry?"

Brenna broke out into a broad smile. "Say that again."

"Say what again? Are you hungry?" he teased. He knew what she wanted him to say.

She leaned over and kissed him on the cheek. "No, silly. Mrs. Thompson. Say *Mrs. Thompson* again."

He downshifted as he exited the highway and growled, "*Mrs. Thompson*, you're going to make it hard for me to walk into the restaurant."

She gave him a quizzical look.

"Calling you *Mrs. Thompson* makes my cock rock hard, darlin'."

With a coy smile, she cast her eyes down and whispered, "Oh."

Ron didn't think she had any idea how much she turned him on, but he looked forward to helping her figure it out. He thought by the end of their honeymoon, she would be better informed.

He was damn sure going to continue reminding her.

Years later, when they snuck off at his retirement party so he could feel her up in the coat room, he asked her, "Do you know how much you still turn me on? After all this time."

Reaching down to stroke his hard-on over his uniform pants, she smirked. "I think I have an idea."

Ron slid her dress up her silky thighs while he reached between her legs and pulled her panties to the side. As his finger stroked her wet slit up and down, he murmured in her ear, "Mmm, glad to see the feeling is still mutual."

With mock indignation, she protested, "You didn't figure that out last night?"

The right side of his mouth lifted. "I'm getting old, darlin'. Sometimes I forget things."

Brenna dropped to her knees and undid his belt. "Well, let me remind you, General. I've wanted to suck your cock in your dress blues since the first time I saw you in them."

It was probably a good thing that she waited until he retired to do that.

He looked down at her and caressed her cheek with his thumb. "You are breathtaking."

She smiled shyly before boldly licking the entire length of his shaft. "Thank you," she purred before taking another swipe with her tongue.

"Good girl," he groaned, fisting her hair as she engulfed his entire length.

Holding his cock in her hand, she popped his dick out of her mouth and grinned. "General Thompson, I'm on my knees, sucking your cock in the coat room at *your* retirement party. I'd hardly classify that as being a good girl."

"Mmm, you're right, Mrs. Thompson. You are a bad girl." He couldn't resist adding with a smile, "But you're still breathtaking."

## The End

Get Cassie and Luke's story, *Playing Dirty*, here! https://tesssummersauthor.com/playing-dirty

Can't wait for Cooper's story? *Get Cinderella and the Marine* here!

https://tesssummersauthor.com/cinderella-and-the-marine-1

Ava and Travis's story, *Operation Sex Kitten*, can be found here:

https://tesssummersauthor.com/operation-sex-kitten

Free Book!

## *The Playboy and the SWAT Princess*

BookHip.com/SNGBXD

*She's a badass SWAT rookie, and he's a playboy SWAT captain... who's taming who?*

*Maddie Monroe*

Three things you should not do when you're a rookie, and the only female on the SDPD SWAT Team... 1) Take your hazing personally, 2) Let them see you sweat, and 3) Fall for your captain.

*Especially*, when your captain is the biggest playboy on the entire police force.

I've managed to follow rules one and two with no problem, but the third one I'm having a little more trouble with. Every time he smiles that sinful smile or folds his muscular arms when explaining a new technique or walks through the station full of swagger.... All I can think about is how I'd like to give him my V-card, giftwrapped with a big red bow on it, which is such a bad idea because out of Rules One, Two, and Three, breaking the third one is a sure-fire way to get me kicked off the team and writing parking tickets for the rest of my career.

Apparently my heart—and other body parts—didn't get the memo.

*Craig Baxter*

The first time I noticed Maddie Monroe, she was wet and covered in soapy suds as she washed SWAT's armored truck as part of her hazing ritual. I've been hard for her ever since.

I can't sleep with a subordinate—it would be career suicide, and I've worked too damn hard to get where I am today. Come to think of it, so has she, and she'd probably have a lot more to lose.

So, nope, not messing around with Maddie Monroe. There are plenty of women for me to choose from who don't work for me.

Apparently my heart—and other body parts—didn't get the memo.

Can two hearts—and other body parts—overcome missed memos and find a way to be together without career-ending consequences?

# Dedication

To every single person who helped me navigate the writing business once *Operation Sex Kitten* was published and I didn't have a flipping clue how to get it in reader's hands.

# Acknowledgments

Mr. Summers: Thank you for being such a good sport about the tales I tell out of school about you on social media. You will forever be my real-life superman.

Summers' children—a.k.a. 'Oldest son', "Youngest son', and 'Daughter': You are also amazing sports, and the fact that you're so supportive of your mom as I am off writing smut speaks volumes of how cool you are. Or how fucked up I've made you. Or both. Good thing you're still on your dad's insurance and can go to therapy.

Bad Girls' Club—expanded version: You are the best freaking beta readers I could ever ask for. Thank you for helping me make this book better, even if it meant hurting my feelings in the process. My ego got over it.

Richard, the lead singer from Dead Man Dom: Thanks for an incredible night.

The amazing writing community—fellow authors, bloggers, readers, and industry counterparts: There's not a chance in hell I would've had the guts to self-publish this book without the wisdom and advice that you generously gave to this newbie. "Thanks" seems so inadequate, but I don't know what else to say. I promise to pay it forward.

All my friends on social media: You make me laugh every single day. I'm so glad you're a part of this journey with me. Even you perverts (you know who you are!)

My real-life friends: Thanks for being proud of me and supporting this new career path. MS sucks ass but there have been a lot of silver linings; writing is definitely at the top of the list.

My extended family for buying my books even though you will never read them. It's pretty cool that you do that and I love you for it.

Lastly—thank you to my readers. I'm humbled that you let me share my work with you. Extra special love if you left me a review. I can't even begin to tell you how important they are!

# A Note From Tess

Thank you for reading my sophomore novel. I fell in love with Ron in *Operation Sex Kitten* so it was important that I tell his happily ever after story. I think Brenna was the perfect choice for him. To this day, Ron makes my insides go gooey. I love what a good man he is to his core and how much he adores Brenna.

If you enjoyed this story (and even if you didn't) will you leave me a review wherever you purchased this book? Reviews are so important for authors!

I really do appreciate you reading my work. I know you have so many wonderful authors to choose from, I'm honored you picked up *my* book.

## *Operation* Sex *Kitten*
## San Diego Social Scene, Book 1

Ava Ericson thought she had her life planned out: graduate with her Ph.D., marry Brad Miller when he finished law school, have 2.5 babies... and mediocre sex for the rest of her days. But when Brad dumps her upon learning he's passed the bar, citing new "opportunities" available, she has to rethink her future.

Believing her lack of experience was the reason Brad broke up with her, she launches Operation Sex Kitten (OSK), a plan to become a vixen in bed and get Brad back. Things might go astray when she meets the notorious attorney, Travis Sterling, the bachelor who she is sure can teach her a thing or two in the bedroom. As she enjoys putting OSK theories into practice, she realizes the real 'operation' will be for the two not to fall in love.

Fun and romantic, *Operation Sex Kitten* turns up the heat with explicit scenes while you root for love to conquer all.

Get it here!
https://tesssummersauthor.com/operation-sex-kitten

## *Playing Dirty*
### San Diego Social Scene, Book 3

*Cassie*

I'm a career woman. I wear success like a second skin, and I'm rarely satisfied with anything less than the best. This includes my love life. If you want to date me, you better bring your A game because I don't play with the B team.

The only type of commitment I'm interested in is the one I have with my career. There is no man strong enough to tame me. Bold enough to rattle me. Or confident enough to win my heart. But then again, I have never met a man like Luke Rivas.


*Luke*

Cassie is one feisty, fiery, demanding woman who has enough confidence to intimidate even the bravest of men. She's driven, ambitious, and clearly has no interest in anything more than a casual fling.

But here's the thing. I want her, and once I have her, there will be nothing casual about it.

I will crack through that tough exterior she wears so well and bend her into submission. I'll make her break every one of her own damn rules just for me. And in order to accomplish just that...

I'm willing to play dirty.

Get your copy here:

https://tesssummersauthor.com/playing-dirty

## Cinderella and the Marine

**San Diego Social Scene, Book Four**

One night. No strings attached. What could go wrong?

*Cooper*

I was pretty happy living the carefree life of a successful bachelor. Money to spend, a revolving door of women, no commitment, no relationship troubles—it was perfect. At least, that's what I thought until I held my friends' newborn baby in my arms, and she smiled at me.

That was the moment I realized what life was all about. That was also the moment it occurred to me I needed a baby mama—stat.

So... the hunt is on for the perfect candidate. But first, I might have to have one last fling—you know, go out with a bang. Literally.

*Kate*

Thanks to making a few wrong decisions along the way, I'm now busting my ass waiting tables while putting myself through college. It's not ideal, but I'm determined to stand on my own two feet and take care of my responsibilities the best I can.

But I'm still a woman. I have needs. I just don't have the time for any kind of commitment. Naturally, when a smoldering hot Marine offers me a no-strings-attached one-night stand, I'm all on board.

Turns out... he wants more than I'm willing to give.

# San Diego Social Scene

*Operation Sex Kitten*: (Ava and Travis)
   https://books2read.com/u/3yzyG6?affiliate=off
*The General's Desire*: (Brenna and Ron)
   https://books2read.com/u/m2Mpek?affiliate=off
*Playing Dirty*: (Cassie and Luke)
   https://books2read.com/u/3RNEdj?affiliate=off
*Cinderella and the Marine*: (Cooper and Katie)
   https://books2read.com/u/3LYenM?affiliate=off
*The Heiress and the Mechanic*: (Harper and Ben)
   https://books2read.com/u/bQVEn6?affiliate=off
*Burning Her Resolve*: (Grace and Ryan)
   https://books2read.com/u/bzoEXz?affiliate=off
*This Is It*: (Paige and Grant)
   https://books2read.com/ThisIsIt?affiliate=off

# Agents of Ensenada

*Ignition*: (Kennedy and Dante prequel)

> https://tesssummersauthor.com/ignition-1

*Inferno*: (Kennedy and Dante)

> https://books2read.com/u/bpaYGJ?affiliate=off

*Combustion*: (Reagan and Mason)

> https://books2read.com/u/baaME6?affiliate=off

*Reignited*: (Taren and Jacob)

> https://books2read.com/u/3ya2Jl?affiliate=off

*Flashpoint*: (Sophia and Ramon)

> https://books2read.com/TessSummersFlashpoint?affiliate=off

## Boston's Elite series

*Wicked Hot Silver Fox*
https://tesssummersauthor.com/wicked-hot-silver-fox-1

*Wicked Hot Doctor*
https://tesssummersauthor.com/wicked-hot-doctor-1

*Wicked Hot Medicine*
https://tesssummersauthor.com/wicked-hot-medicine

*Wicked Hot Baby Daddy*
https://tesssummersauthor.com/wicked-hot-baby-daddy

*Wicked Bad Decisions*
https://tesssummersauthor.com/wicked-bad-decisions-1

*Wicked Little Secret*
https://tesssummersauthor.com/wicked-little-secret

# About the Author

Tess Summers is a former businesswoman and teacher who always loved writing but never seemed to have time to sit down and write a short story, let alone a novel. Now battling MS, her life changed dramatically, and she has finally slowed down enough to start writing all the stories she's been wanting to tell, including the fun and sexy ones!

Married over twenty-six years with three grown children, Tess is a former dog foster mom who ended up failing and adopting them instead. She and her husband (and their three dogs) split their time between the desert of Arizona and the lakes of Michigan, so she's always in a climate that's not too hot and not too cold, but just right!

# Contact Me!

Sign up for my newsletter: BookHip.com/SNGBXD
Email: TessSummersAuthor@yahoo.com
Visit my website: www.TessSummersAuthor.com
Facebook: http://facebook.com/TessSummersAuthor
My FB Group: Tess Summers Sizzling Playhouse
TikTok: https://www.tiktok.com/@tesssummersauthor
Instagram: https://www.instagram.com/tesssummers/
Amazon: https://amzn.to/2MHHhdK
BookBub https://www.bookbub.com/profile/tess-summers
Goodreads - https://www.goodreads.com/TessSummers
Twitter: http://twitter.com/@mmmTess

Made in United States
Orlando, FL
14 August 2023

36074449R00252